HOME RULES

PAUL McDERMOTT

Paul McDermott

December 2023

Home Rules

First published in 2023

Cover Design by InRoad

ISBN: 978-1-7395102-9-9

TAUK Publishing

To the World in One City:
"Come on in, Our Kid – it's been too long."

With all my heart, for family and friends
who believed in me and brewed the coffee.

HOME RULES

CHAPTER ONE

"WORK WILL START *today to re-lay Old Hall Street and renovate a number of properties in the area,"* the local radio advised, *"and problems with traffic will be unavoidable. If it's possible for you to find an alternative route, especially during daily commuting times, or use public transport while this essential much-postponed work is carried out..."*

Billy Lynch turned off the radio and reached for his hard hat. "Right, lads, might as well get on with it!" He killed the ember on his cig and put the remainder of it in a battered tobacco tin, which had accompanied him on countless work sites throughout the UK over the years.

His three-man gang took their cue from the gaff and climbed out of the van. By arriving in Old Hall Street before seven-thirty, Billy had 'bagsied a spec' in a layby designed for at least three standard-size cars. Swinging open the rear doors of the Transit, the first item the lads unloaded was a folded trestle table. This was a deliberate ploy. Billy had discovered long ago that unloading and opening up a table as a work area that you might—or might *not*—need always created some extra space behind your vehicle.

Most of the space inside the van was taken up by the inevitable and frustratingly bulky safety barriers, which had to be erected before they could even begin the job they'd come to do. That would take them at least an hour, Billy thought resignedly, but at least it was a chore they wouldn't have to repeat every day. Once the barriers were in place, they could stay out and be moved along the street as each section of the job was completed.

"Ey up, Gaff!"

Nobody was quite certain why Billy Lynch didn't care to be known by the name printed on his National Insurance card and every other legal document he possessed, but he was, without doubt, good at his job, one of the best navvies in Britain, possibly in Europe.

He looked towards the ganger who'd murmured the warning. He, in his turn, nodded towards the junction of Tithebarn Street, about a hundred yards away.

"Tweedledum an' Tweedledumber! Just what I need before we even get started!"

Two portly figures in identical uniforms, rain jacket and flat military cap rounded the corner and could be seen to increase their speed as they approached. At that distance, they could easily have passed for identical twins: they even marched in perfect, if unrehearsed, synchronised step.

Billy gave the barrier he was assembling a final tap and pushed it to one side. He stood with hands on hips but remained tight-lipped, forcing the intruders to declare themselves and state their business. Not that he was in any doubt: every driver in the UK knew *exactly* what a traffic warden looked like.

Billy had developed a way of 'hazing' wardens by slightly de-focusing his eyes, creating the impression that he was looking at a specific individual, ignoring anyone else who happened to be present. It was just a question of who blinked first, and invariably, his victims forgot any numerical advantage they might have had.

Even up close, it was difficult to tell the two apart, but they weren't identical twins. The weaker one reached for a pencil, thereby offering himself as the sacrificial lamb. As he opened his mouth to speak, Billy pre-empted him.

"Got a problem?" Billy had made his point without saying a word. Now he had an opportunity to twist the knife and make it *really* hurt.

"Er…will you be…is this going to be a long job?"

"Oh, is it that hard to find the right words for the question? Well, let's keep the *answer* simple, so's y'can understand it, hey? I mean, I could ask you 'How long's a piece o' string?' but that might be a bit hard!

"Tell you what. I'll show you the contract I signed at the town hall last week, wi' the council leader's countersignature. You can pass the word to the rest o' the flock, and that'll save us *all* time!"

"What d'you mean, 'flock'? Who d'you think—"

"Sorry, mate! Slip o' the tongue. 'Course I meant 'the rest of the *folk* in your office'!"

Of course, Billy had meant no such thing, and they both knew it, but he'd won this particular battle of wits without breaking into a sweat. Whether he'd warned his adversary off or made himself a spiteful and vindictive enemy as a result would become apparent in the next few days.

"Look, mate! We're going to be here for as long as it takes to do the job, and standing here isn't helping us to get started! Yiz've *seen* the paperwork now. If yiz want a copy, they've got top-of-the-range photocopiers over the road at the *Echo,* but I'm not payin' fer them! And you'll find that copies were left with your office last week. I took 'em there meself!"

Without even raising his voice, the gaff had just earned a bonus point. He'd allowed the slightest edge of coarseness to creep into his speech and picked up the pace of his delivery, deliberately seeking to force his intended victim into a defensive position: as always, his tactics worked perfectly.

Tweedledumber, who had taken no part in the battle of wits to date, chose this moment to fish a mobile out of his pocket. He listened to an indistinguishable squawked message—presumably from a central office of some sort—and leaned over to murmur in his colleague's ear.

"We'll be back!"

"I think someone's used that line already!" Billy shouted after the departing wardens. "But so will we, and our papers will *still* be valid for however long the job takes. Why don't you go and do something useful or get a life or something?"

"Hope there's no comeback on that, Gaff. You were a bit hard on 'em!"

"You might be right, Eddie, but he walked right into it! And by the bye, I've asked Andy to come round and pick us all up when we knock off. This van's staying here for as long as we can get away with it. We'll use it as tool store and general office."

By the time all the safety barriers had been assembled and placed along the first section of the street, the morning lemming run had eased off. Most commuters were now where they would remain for the next eight hours or so before repeating the morning's mad scramble but in the opposite direction. There were still a significant number of vehicles crawling a few yards at a time along Old Hall Street, despite the sensible advice issued by the local radio and the temporary narrowing caused by the roadworks.

Once the digging itself started, however, the news seemed to spread immediately by some sort of silent grapevine. Traffic from all points north that frequently used Old Hall Street to avoid a series of sets of traffic lights along The Strand fell to almost zero, and the lads were able to make a good start on breaking through the worn, patchy tarmac top surface of the road from the layby back to the next junction.

On the second day, they were able to excavate down to the service level, a subterranean maze of gas and water mains, criss-crossed by a variety of telephone, cable TV and electricity supply lines that required detailed maps for safe navigation.

This was where Billy demonstrated the very special gift that made him an exceptional leader of any navvy crew. From a single glance at maps which would bewilder most people, including many of those responsible for drawing up the original schematics, Billy could interpret them and trace the precise route of what led where, a forgotten skill that was behind the original job title of navigator, or navvy. On more than one occasion, he had studied a schematic for a few seconds and *known* that something on it had been wrongly recorded. In each and every case, he'd been proved right. This unique ability had, without question, saved many people's faces and significant amounts of cash over the years by ensuring that any disruption of essential services was kept to an unavoidable minimum.

"There's something iffy about this, Norm, but I can't quite figure what it is."

"How's that, Gaffer? I've never seen you stumped by anything!"

"Sez you, Yozzer! But thanks anyway…I think!"

Billy smoothed out the schematics diagram representing the chaotic underground they had to deal with and placed a finger on one corner.

"It's this bit over here—on the corner, past the supermarket. I dropped a cone there last night, and when I climbed down to get it out, I felt the ground shift beneath my feet."

"We're down to the lowest level there, aren't we?" Norman groused. "I don' fancy digging any deeper than we have to. We'll be pushed to get this job done on time as it is, an' I could do with the bonus payment this month!"

"We've cleared the water lines at about four-foot depth. The only other line will be the waste water, but that's at least three foot deeper. The ground should be solid here."

"Is it possible there's been a cave-in of some sort? Subsidence, maybe?"

"If there's something down there—below the water lines—it *could* have been there from an earlier dig," Eddie said. "Bet them Victorians didn't have all the Elfin Safety regs an' paperwork we have to fill in ferra start!"

"You may have a point there, Eddie. Listen, I want you down in the trench—you're a damn' sight lighter than me—and have a poke about in the bit I've taped off, but be careful. We don't want the whole thing collapsing on us!"

***

"Sounds a bit 'oller, Gaffer... There could be some sort of hole or a space here. Seems more at the base o' the trench wall, though. It doesn't feel like it's under my feet. My lump hammer's givin' a bit of a dead sound. I'll try pokin' it with a rod or something..."

"Lemme get a bag o' tools from the van, Ed."

There was an odd pitch to Billy's voice as he spoke, and the words came out in something of a rush, which caught Eddie's attention. Norman and Yozzer sensed it too: the gaffer never got over-excited about the everyday snags they encountered in their work.

"There's a stack of tools in there, Eddie. You should find something you can use. See if you can shove a rod through the walls o' the trench—if they're as fragile as they seem to be, some of the rods at least should be long enough for that."

The tool bag itself might have been a traditional cricketer's holdall in a previous incarnation: at least, that was the approximate size and shape of it, but it certainly hadn't been used for that purpose for some considerable time. Eddie looked at Billy, who shook his head.

"Don't go there! Don't ask me whose tools they are or how I come to have them on hand. Just have a root around, see what you can find."

Eddie selected a wooden mallet and tapped around the section of the trench that had been taped off. He chose a spot a few inches from the base of the wall, picked up a length of hollow tubing, which appeared to have been sharpened at one end, and gave it two or three powerful blows with a lump hammer. He had to snatch at the rod when it began to slide out of his grasp after the final stroke.

"There's certainly some sort of open space here!" Eddie called. The comment was superfluous: he had an attentive audience of three standing so close they couldn't fail to witness what had happened.

"Okay, Eddie, come out of there. We'll take a breather before we go any further!"

This was so unlike the gaffer that it puzzled the gang once more. Norman and Yozzer had been with him over three years. He had a reputation of being a fair boss, and a good man to work with, but at the same time a bit of a slave driver who always met his targets.

"We're still pretty clean. Eddie, if you scrape your boots, I'm sure Costa will let us sit at a pavement table—I'm buying."

Yozzer got his question in first, although it came out sounding more like a statement.

"It's pretty obvious you know something or other you aren't telling us, Gaffer! That's not your style, and it's not the way we've always worked, so come on! What's the score?"

Billy passed around the tall, cardboard coffee cups and opened his battered cig tin. When he ran out of delaying tactics, he sighed deeply and looked around the table.

"My oldest, Maureen, is in her final year at Liverpool University, studying history. When she found out I had the renovation contract for this area, she asked me to keep an eye out for any arty...artef...old stuff anyway! She reckons there's a fair chance we might find things as we dig, and since this is one of the oldest parts of town, she might be able to use 'em for her final...whatsitsname...thesis? Dis-something-or-other? It counts towards her exam results anyway, and it has to include some original work.

"I loaned the toolkit from one of my cousins, but that's another story—you don't need to know *his* line of work. Point is, we might have stumbled across something here, so this is what I suggest..."

Back in the trench, Billy settled himself at one end, armed with a small garden trowel. The rest of the gang formed a line.

"I'll be taking it dead steady while I open up this hole. All youse need to do is clear the loose soil an' rocks so's I've got room to work an' keep Dixie just in case anyone gets nosy 'bout why we're not getting stuck in on the job we're s'posed to be doing. We may have to do a bit of token digging, extend the trench a bit to make it look good, but we have to have somewhere to scatter the dirt we dig out, I guess."

Before lunchtime, the hole in the trench had been widened far enough to make it possible for Eddie to ease his head and shoulders through it.

"I hope there's a decent-size flashlight of some sort in yer cousin's bag o' tricks!" he said as he backed out, "because I can't see a blind thing in here without one!"

"Yeah, that won't be a problem. I'll check the batteries in a minute, but it's probably a good idea to shore this up before we go any further. We don't want it caving in on us!"

"How come you 'just happened' to have a load of planks in the van, Gaffer? Were you planning this?"

"Not really planning, Norm. Hoping, maybe, I'll admit that much. I just didn't think we'd strike lucky on the first day of the job! Now, let's get the side walls secured before they collapse, shall we?

"Okay, Eddie, you're 'it'—you're a lot slimmer than any of us. Here's a flashlight—see if you can spot anything in there."

Eddie was the 'noob' of the team: he'd been with them for just on six months, serving a semi-formal apprenticeship of tea-making and gofer duties for the first few weeks.

Billy passed him a tarpaulin. "That should keep the worst of the crap off your clothes. Just be careful you don't slide off it into the hole."

Eddie eased his shoulders into the shored-up excavation, which was a comfortable, square opening about three feet each way and a mini-tunnel about two feet in length. It ended abruptly in an open space. The flashlight revealed a chamber of some sort: they had broken through at a point which was perhaps five feet above the floor. Slowly, to avoid causing further mini-landslips, Eddie turned the flashlight to inspect the chamber and began a running commentary. Billy had a firm grip on Eddie's belt to give the youngster at least an illusion of safety. He looked back and made a hand signal for Norm to find pencil and paper.

"It looks like a room of some sort, not a natural cave or anything like that. I'd say it's about fifteen, twenty foot each way, maybe thirty foot high."

Eddie's voice was slightly muffled: there wasn't a lot of clear space between his body and the walls of the shaft he was lying in. What he was reporting was easy enough to understand, but Billy wanted more detail.

"Does it look tiled, flagged, decorated? What makes you think it's man-made?"

"The walls are too smooth, too regular. The roof and floor look like someone's used a plumb line to check them."

Billy relayed this to Norman, who jotted it all down word for word.

"Okay, Eddie, tell us what else you can see. Anything in the room—furniture, books, something you can identify?"

"Loads of stuff! But not easy to ID from this range. I'm maybe five foot off the floor. I could wiggle out, turn round and slide in feet first—'ave we gorra rope or summat? If I go *in*, I'm gonna need a bit o' help getting *out* again!"

Yozzer was already heading for the van: he'd been feeling frustrated at not having a specific task other than 'keeping Dixie' and pretending to dig at the furthest end of the trench whenever anyone showed any curiosity about their progress.

"This tow rope's ideal, Gaff! We can run the end through a spike an' plant it in the trench. The ground looks solid enough to hold Eddie's weight."

Eddie humped out of the tunnel and shook off some loose dirt before re-entering feet first. The anchored rope was a bonus, and he touched down on the floor without any problems. The running commentary resumed where it had left off.

"Lots of what I have to assume are small objects dotted around the space…room…chamber…whatever it's supposed to be. Different shapes and sizes but all completely covered by dirt—either fallen from the roof over the years or drifted against them, it's hard to tell! I'll try and give you an accurate count in a few minutes, but I'm not going to risk damaging any of it by pawing at it. If it's all as ancient as this hole looks, it's guaranteed to fall apart if I look at it the wrong way! But there's plenty o' space fer me t' plonk me size twelves. I can squeeze between them, no probs! I'll pace out the length and breadth of the room, get some idea of how big it is. I'll say this much, though. It goes a good way back—it must be right underneath the Costa coffee shop!"

Billy could see the torch beam turn left and right. Eddie's disembodied voice floated up to him: it had a slight echo behind it.

"Back against the wall, just to the left of the tunnel I came through. The room is roughly a rectangle, and I'm standing against one of the long sides. On my left—which direction's that, Gaffer?"

Billy had to think for a moment.

"Old Hall Street runs towards Switch Island, Formby and Southport, so we'll call that north. Carry on, kiddo!"

Eddie had been called far worse names in the past and continued blithely.

"I'm going to heel-and-toe it from end to end. That's got to be more accurate than trying to use full paces anyway, plus I can be certain I won't accidentally damage anything!

"One...two...three..." Eddie's voice faded gradually but remained distinct as he paced out the chamber.

"Thirty-six. Say, thirty-five foot north to south."

"Got that, Eddie. Norm, sketch a rough rectangle. Scribble thirty-five on the long side..." Billy relayed Eddie's comments to the team scribe. "...and I make it about twenty-eight feet across—oh! What's this?!"

"'Ow the bloody 'ell do I know, Eddie? *You* can see it. We can't!"

"Sorry, Gaffer! I was just, y'know, surprised. This is...different. It's like a...a long tube of some sort. It's the only thing on a table in a corner at the, er...north end of the room, like it's something special. Oh—it's not actually a table. It's some kinda stand—reminds me of an ol'-fashioned whatchamacallit, a candle-thingy? I'm bringing it out ferra better look at it. It's not buried in dirt like the other stuff, and it lifts easy from the stand, so I won't be damaging it or disturbing anything else."

In the bright light of day, Eddie's find was laid carefully on a fresh-bought copy of the early edition of the day's *Echo*.

"Careful brushing it down," Yozzer warned. "If all the telly programmes are to be believed, even the dirt can tell the forensics boyos something!"

Billy paused and thought about this. Yozzer had a point.

"Maybe you're right. Perhaps we shouldn't be touching it at all. Perhaps we should be calling on someone who knows how to handle stuff like this. I'll call our Mo, ask her to bring one of her tutors down here."

***

"No, you've done exactly the right thing, Dad. It's best you leave everything as you found it—apart from the one thing you've already brought out. What's done is done, and from the sound of it, you haven't damaged it in any way...whatever it is. If you've a camera with you, a few photos might be useful, but I can be there with Professor Midler in twenty minutes or so."

"It's too dark down there to get anything useful with my mobile phone, but we're right outside the *Echo* offices. I'll ask if one of their pros can do the honours."

"Good idea, but you've got to persuade them *not* to make it a front-page splash. We need time to examine whatever it is you've dug up, authenticate it, identify it—tell them they can have the exclusive tag if we can have a day or two. It sounds as if you've stumbled on a load of stuff that's been lost for who knows how long. We need to keep this under wraps for at least twenty-four hours, and we can't hope to get anything more than a preliminary *guess* at a probable age even for this solitary item in that time. From the photographs you've already sent, there's months of work ahead of us."

Maureen paused a moment and thought rapidly.

"Actually, if you're outside the *Echo*, go in and ask for Kevin Wyatt. Tell him I want to talk to him."

Fortunately, Kevin Wyatt was on duty and in the office. The name Maureen Lynch had him scurrying down to the mezzanine reception area before Billy had had the chance to feel guilty about the clay from the soles of his boots making a mess on the tiled floor.

"Message from Mo? Is she all right? She hasn't been in an accident, or...?"

Billy shook his head, speed-dialled Mo's number and passed over the mobile.

"Nothing like that, lad. Mo's my daughter. She's got something to ask you."

***

"Yes, of course I'll cover it," Kevin assured Maureen, who had come down to the Old Hall Street site with her professor. "This looks like a mega-story! But I'm telling you, my editor's going to have kittens if we sit on it a second longer than necessary!"

John Midler leant forward to add his support. His gravelly, measured delivery had the effect of defusing the potential clash of interests.

"Maureen is one of my best students, and I can only say that she's spot on about the time it will take us to do a full, professional assessment of what's been uncovered. We can, I think, promise you something your readers will appreciate by this time tomorrow, but a full investigation with proper research, provenance, exact dates...that's going to take months!"

"I appreciate what you're saying, Professor—"

"John, please! That title makes me feel as old as the objects I handle every day!"

"Fine! Whenever you call the office, someone will find me. Now, I've taken a total of forty-eight shots of the underground chamber. The editor is going to be over the moon with that, but there's no clue to suggest what any of them are."

"Which means you can't run a story about the objects themselves before we've had a chance to examine them," John pointed out.

"Fair enough," Kevin agreed but with a shrug of resignation, which said quite clearly that as a media pro he wasn't happy about any delays in releasing the story.

"Let's see if I can give you some details of this one item we've got in front of us," John said. "That's the least we can do in the circumstances."

Kevin's face lit up like a young pup thrown a juicy bone. "That would be fantastic! What can you tell me?"

"Let's see what this tells us," John murmured. "But this is too public a place—too many eyes and ears. Billy, I'm not trying to exclude you or the rest of your crew, but..."

Billy glanced at his watch. "We've already lost a couple of hours' work, and we're on a tight enough contract to start with. Yozzer and Norman should be back soon—they went to pick up some more timber to shore up the walls of the access tunnel. Eddie's been pretending to tidy up the trench so passers-by think there's some real work going on, but we really should be cracking on with what we're being *paid* to do!"

"I can offer you the privacy of an office over the road," Kevin said with a nod towards the *Echo* office. Now it was John's turn to react positively.

"That's fantastic! And this item's already wrapped in an *Echo* anyway. How appropriate! Lead on, MacDuff! We'll be right behind you, but for the moment, you have to make sure that *nobody* other than us three gets wind of what's going on."

Even with only three occupants, the office space Kevin led them to felt overcrowded, but the plus points were it was windowless and boasted just the one door. It wasn't just clean: it was sterile, and there were no books, files or magazines evident on shelves or desk.

"The last reporter to use this room left last week. He hasn't been replaced yet."

"I can't imagine anyone cutting someone's throat for the privilege of being the next jock to fly *this* desk. It feels more like a broom cupboard than an office space."

"I chose it *because* it's secure from any eyes other than ours—you'll notice there's no frosted glass in the door panels—and also because it's unlikely to be top of any shortlist the replacement journalist will be offered."

"All I need is the table and power for my little black bag of electronic tools and gizmos..." John assured him. "It's only for this one inspection, anyway, and I don't even know how much I'm going to be able to tell you, but at least I can run a full diagnostic."

The newspaper was unrolled carefully: John nodded for Kevin to turn on the small recorder, which had effectively replaced the traditional steno's notepad. John took three small support stands from his bag of tricks and placed the wooden rod gently upon them. Next, he selected a number of small brushes and began to tease the remaining grime and dirt from the crevices of the surface. As he worked, an engraved pattern emerged. He began a running commentary.

"The object is wooden, 1.016 metres from end to end, cylindrical. It has been shaped by hand. There are no indications of tool marks from a lathe or other mechanical device, and it has a diameter of 102 millimetres throughout, no significant variations. Central balance point. Sounds hollow when tapped..."

He paused and struck it several times with a pencil, a plastic rod and, finally, with the smallest hammer Kevin had ever seen, allowing the timbre of the sounds produced to be recorded on tape.

"Almost all the loose dirt in the engravings, which cover the entire length of the rod or hollow tube, brushes away easily. Weight of the dirt removed is 235 grams, and I am placing it in a sealed sample bag for later analysis. My assistant, Maureen Lynch, will sign and date all today's logged samples."

Slightly taken aback by her 'field promotion' to the dizzy height of assistant, Maureen moved quickly to suit action to word as the professor continued his investigation.

"The tube is a worked piece and is a very dense wood no longer in common use, most likely a variety of oak or teak. It is heavy for its size, weighing 2.4 kilograms. Given that I have already established this is a hollow object, the weight is very surprising. I will ask both of my witnesses to sign a statement confirming this anomaly."

He extracted a battery-driven mini-vacuum from his bag, the type commonly used to valet a car's upholstery. The dirt which remained on the surface of the tube or on the table was carefully removed and added to the sample bag, adding a further five grams of evidence to be studied.

John's eyes gleamed as he put the vacuum cleaner to one side and mopped the sweat off his brow. The enclosed room was starting to turn into an uncomfortable sweat box, but he seemed unfazed.

"This is where it begins to be interesting!" He sounded as if he was about to burst into a music hall song-and-dance routine.

"Now the boring facts and figures are all recorded, we can set our imaginations free and start asking the more interesting questions, such as, 'If it really *is* hollow, how do I open it up to find out what's inside?' or maybe, 'What is inside it—and is it valuable?'

"There's only one way to find out. Let's hope I can do so without having to swing a big hammer and smash it!"

CHAPTER TWO

Maureen Lynch hesitated for the merest fraction of a second before she moved into her mentor's field of vision.

"Sir, I wonder..." She bit her tongue: she might almost be a doctor herself and highly favoured by being granted the title 'assistant', however temporary the term might prove to be, but it was definitely *not* a good career move to query the decisions of gods or university professors.

The expression on John Midler's face was one of surprise rather than anger. As no lightning bolt appeared to be seeking her out for immediate despatch, Maureen hurried onwards before she lost her nerve completely.

"Prof...Sir! Do you think there might be a clue—either to the contents or even how to open the tube—in the pictures and engravings you've revealed? I hate the thought that we might damage this incredible piece of history by not reading, or by not making the attempt, at least, to—"

"To 'read the instructions' is that what you're saying, Maureen?" He shook his head and grinned. "That's exactly why *every* don in the 'dreaming spires' of every uni in the realm should have a full-time student attached to their every move—in order to stop them running out in front of a number-ten bus or something equally stupid!

"You're right, of course. We need to study the engravings first. Quite apart from a possible set of instructions, it's also the most likely place to find a hint of *how long* since it was buried."

John decided that the most logical way of determining the top and bottom of the rod was to examine the orientation of the pictures. After all, he told himself, nobody's going to mar such a beautifully crafted item or spoil it by drawing the figures on its polished surface in an upside-down position.

He held the tube at eye level and resumed his commentary.

"The surface of the tube is decorated with a large number of engravings—exact number to be determined after closer inspection. The engravings appear to consist of a mixture of text and artwork. I can identify a number of runes, which suggests a provisional date between the sixth and the ninth centuries. Contraindication—there are also texts written in what appears to be Latin, classical period. Unlikely to connect this item to the period of Roman occupation of Britain. It is too well preserved. More likely to date from twelfth century onwards, when Latin was used as the *lingua franca* throughout Britain's disparate tribes and clans.

"Logically, the opening we seek is most likely to be at the upper end of the tube. I am therefore concentrating on what I consider the upper end when the tube is held with the pictures being—in heraldic terms—right and proper. A fragment of Latin text reading left to right confirms this to be the direction of flow intended.

"The cross-section of the upper end shows a slight but distinct difference of colour—and possibly of texture. This consists of a narrow outer rim averaging—" he checked with callipers "—four millimetres and a central area. The latter is a darker colour and presents a much smoother texture. First impressions—possibly a plug or seal of wax. Taking a sample to test this theory."

This time, John plucked another specialist tool from his treasure trove. Kevin had never actually seen one at close quarters before, but when John stripped it from a paper sheath with the word 'sterile' printed on it, he was reasonably sure it would prove to be a surgeon's scalpel or something very similar.

"The centred mass is definitely not wood, but it has been disguised to resemble wood. The scalpel slices into it easily, and the sample curls on the blade, demonstrating the malleable quality of a substance with a high wax or resin content. Testing to confirm whether the substance is wax before continuing."

Simple tests involving nothing more complicated than hot water and a naked flame were enough to identify the substance as a form of candle wax. John continued his investigation, sounding more and more confident.

"Attempting to remove the plug. This appears to be completely airtight, suggesting that whatever the tube contains may be fragile and/or sensitive to weather and atmospheric conditions. There is a strong possibility that whatever the tube contains was placed there for protection rather than because of its monetary value."

John heated a steel needle over a Bunsen for a few moments, then inserted it into the centre of the plug. He made no attempt to force it through the wax, letting the heat of the needle do all the work slowly. Kevin felt the resumption of the running commentary was more for his benefit than strictly for the record, but he was grateful all the same to be kept informed.

"As I cannot be sure how deep the plug is, I'm accessing the inner space by melting away a small area. I intend to stop before I am completely through and avoid possible contamination or damage of the contents from hot wax dripping on them."

Maureen was drinking it all in. This was the first opportunity she'd had to observe her mentor's investigative skills at such a close range, and she was fascinated at his precise, soft touch. A thought struck her: before he tackled the plug again, she brushed his sleeve to attract his attention.

"Do you think you could ease the plug out by softening the wax at the edges to break the seal? You said you didn't want to drip wax on whatever is inside."

"Thank you, Maureen, that's an excellent idea! Let's give it a try, shall we?"

Strips of cloth soaked in boiling water were wrapped around the plug and replaced as they cooled. The process was repeated again and again until the plug began to change colour.

"Let's see if we can persuade it to move!" John breathed as he reached once more into his bag. He rooted about for a few moments and withdrew another tool. This one was much easier to identify: an ordinary domestic corkscrew, as used to open any wine bottle.

"Yes, why not? I believe this will do the trick..."

It went easily into the softened plug, assisted by the start hole the steel needle had made.

"That feels secure enough. Hopefully, I won't have to go any deeper..."

He didn't make any attempt to pull the cork immediately. Catching the puzzled look on Kevin's face, he dried his sweating palms with an unused piece of cloth.

"I'm letting the wax harden around the corkscrew," he explained. "That should give us a little bit of extra grip when I attempt to pull it out."

When he grasped the corkscrew and exerted a minimal amount of effort, the plug obliged by rotating a few millimetres clockwise and emerging from the neck of the tube with the faintest of all possible *pops*, a vaguely disappointing anticlimax to what should have been a highly dramatic event. The corkscrew was no more than halfway through the plug, and the plug itself appeared to be intact, with no crack, flakes or flaws in its smooth sides to hint at contamination of the tube's contents.

John studied the plug for several seconds before placing it and the corkscrew to one side and turning his attention to the tube. He shook it gently: the faintest of rattles could be heard.

"After all that, at least it's not empty!"

For a split-second, Maureen thought he was being facetious, but a glance at his eyes told a different story. They were the eyes of a thorough professional, excited by the prospect of something really important about to happen. His apparent flippant attitude was a cover for this excitement, nothing more. Maureen couldn't put a finger on the how or the why of the situation, but she knew without a doubt that she'd interpreted it correctly.

John tilted the tube to make it easier to shine a small, powerful torch inside it and paused once more as the open end passed under his nostrils. He took two long, full breaths and exhaled slowly, then a third double-lungful, which he held for several seconds before letting it out again.

"For the record, tube opened without damage at... Maureen, time and date this later. As suspected, an air- and water-tight environment has protected the contents of the tube since it was sealed. Provenance has yet to be established, but the object is clearly of great age and the contents must therefore be at least as old as the container itself.

"I am now using a flashlight to attempt to identify any objects I can see..."

He offered the tube to Maureen in order to have both hands free. She hadn't been expecting this but, from force of habit, had slipped on a pair of latex gloves as soon as they entered the room, so she was ready to participate.

"I can only make out one object," John commented as he shone the torch inside the tube from several different angles, "although there may be more at the base of the tube. What I see appears to be a document, rolled tightly and fitting not-quite-snug to the inner wall of the container. Until I can retrieve it and touch it, I cannot say for certain if the document is paper, vellum or another material.

"Retrieval precautions. The small space between the document and the inner wall may be entirely due to natural causes, shrinkage caused by desiccation over a long period and similar factors. It could also be pure coincidence, the document just happening to fit comfortably into the container, but in view of the elaborate nature of the designs on the outer surface, I am inclined to discount this possibility.

"It is also possible that the document has been secured—tied with a ribbon of some sort—which would keep it under tension and prevent it from springing outwards to touch the walls. This suggests that the document was considered important enough to need preserving, and if the ribbon is intact, that might make it easier to fish it out."

"What have you got in your swag bag for that, John?" It was the first time Kevin had dared to intrude in the proceedings, though as a pro journalist, he had an endless stream of questions demanding answers.

"Good question. I've long-nose pliers, of course, but I'd never even consider using a metal tool on paper, vellum or anything else so delicate and fragile. When you add in the fact that the object in question is old—ancient, I suspect!—and therefore likely to fall apart as soon as you look at it sideways, that's when the problems of how to handle it really begin!

"The top edge of the roll is maybe three or four inches from the top of the tube," John said thoughtfully, "but the tube itself is too narrow for any of us to get even two fingers inside it and I doubt if that would give us enough of a grip to pull it out, anyway."

"Sir?"

John turned to remind Maureen of his aversion to using the academic title, but she stood her ground and looked him squarely in the eye.

"Would these be of any use?" From the depths of her bag, Maureen had managed to rummage out a pair of chopsticks.

"They might just be *exactly* what we need!"

Maureen's chopsticks together with John's patience and soft hands proved to be a winning combination. Once John had got the hang of basic chopstick techniques, it took him less than ten minutes to tease the document at least two inches closer to the rim before it jammed against the constricting inner walls of the tube.

"It's not so tight it can't be moved," John muttered, "but I don't want to risk damaging it by rubbing against the walls if I try to drag it out."

"Can we try to roll it a bit tighter?" Maureen suggested. "That would ease it away from the walls..."

"Nothing to stop us trying. If I can just tweak it a bit tighter starting from the centre..."

Millimetre by agonising millimetre, John managed to bring the document closer to the rim. His fingers ached from the effort required to manipulate the chopsticks, something he had never attempted to use before.

"Take a breather. My chopstick technique isn't too bad," Maureen offered. John flexed his aching fingers and passed her the primitive but effective tools.

Maureen's slim fingers, coupled with her lifelong love of Chinese food, were all that was needed to complete the job. Once a full inch of the roll had cleared the tube opening, it was possible for John to take a firm grip on the document itself. Kevin and Maureen grasped the tube firmly, giving John something to pull against. In less than five minutes, the roll lay on the table, secured by not one but two thin strips of cloth tied about forty-five centimetres in from each end. The scattered tools were swiftly collected and stuffed back in the bag to leave the table surface completely clear.

Kevin spent a few happy minutes taking a further thousand and one photographs of the find from every conceivable angle: John tipped the tube carefully to see if there was anything else of interest to be found, but nothing fell out of it other than dust and a few unidentifiable scraps, which could have been the remnants of just about anything.

"John, you're the only one here with the skill and the knowledge to handle an ancient document like this."

"Thank you for trusting me, Maureen. Kevin, can we carry on? Have you got all the photos you need at this stage?"

"Fine for now, John. Carry on when you're ready."

"Don't forget to turn the recorder on again. Here we go!

"The two tapes are a coarse-woven material, seven millimetres wide, black—Maureen, please make a note to have the tapes tested for dye. The knots in the tapes are extremely tight, and the tapes have also dried over the years. In my professional opinion, it will not be possible to *untie* the tapes, and I have decided to *cut* them instead. The tapes themselves do not appear to have any intrinsic value or historical significance, but they will, of course, be preserved along with all the other evidence collected."

The tapes were added to the small pile of detritus poured out of the tube, weighed, bagged and set aside. Now for the moment of truth: John took a deep breath and began to unroll the ancient scroll. He used the tips of his fingers only, holding it as far as possible by the extreme corners alone. Maureen discovered that one of the cupboards in the room was filled with cups and saucers: tacitly, she showed them to John, who nodded his agreement. She began to place crockery at the very edge of the document to prevent it from rolling back as John worked his way along the table. The table was just wide enough to allow the document to be smoothed out to its fullest extent: looking at it, Maureen was fairly sure the document would also fit comfortably as far as length was concerned.

John was back in his bag of tricks and appeared to be searching for a specific tool of some sort. With a grunt of satisfaction, he found what he was looking for.

"This will help us see the text no matter how small it's penned!"

'This' was a clear pane of glass or Perspex, which for the recording, the professor described as roughly twice the size of a standard A4 page—Kevin could have told them this was called A3 in the trade, but nobody asked him—and about two centimetres thick, a perfect magnifying optic which doubled as an effective paperweight.

It proved to be an ideal size for the close-written lines of perfectly formed manuscript. Maureen's first thought as she peered over John's shoulder was of how long it must have taken the scribe to complete this beautiful work of art. *Scribes,* she corrected herself. No one person could possibly have sat and written a document of this length in one continuous spell. It had certainly involved a number of scribes and taken months to complete—a true labour of love.

"What can you tell us, John?"

John had been hunched low over the document, despite the magnification of the thick pane.

"I can tell you that the language is Latin," he said, "and although it isn't my special field, I think I can say that it has the feel of the Classical period before the Holy Roman Empire began to disintegrate—and with it, the purest silver tongue understood throughout the civilised world. That dates it between late sixth century and perhaps the ninth, maybe a little later. In a document of this nature, I'd bet my life on a date being recorded somewhere, and several signatures. It's clearly an official document of some sort. Let's see..."

He stiffened and stepped away from the table, as if he'd just touched a high-voltage terminal. He was clearly shocked by something he hadn't anticipated. He held out his hands, palms upwards: Maureen and Kevin saw he was trembling, but they were unable to guess if this was due to fear or excitement.

"Maureen, from what I remember of your last essay, your Latin is more than adequate. I want you to look at the first few lines of the manuscript. Even an approximate translation will suffice—I just need a second opinion. I don't want to put any thoughts into your head by telling you what I believe I've just read."

Maureen wasn't quite sure what she was being warned about, but it was obvious John was in no fit state to say more at that particular moment, so she took a deep breath—literally *and* metaphorically—and took her mentor's place at the table. Kevin offered John a bottle of water, which he gulped greedily.

Maureen had always been in love with the Latin tongue, its resonance, its clarity and, above all, the sound of it spoken aloud: 'declaimed', in her opinion, was a much better word. Even so, the first words she read shocked her like a douche of ice-cold water dunked over her head.

"*Ego Iohannes, Dei gratia Rex Anglie...*"

She stopped at the end of the line and locked her gaze on the Professor. She could feel the pulse pounding in her temples as an enormous jolt of adrenaline sent her blood pressure off the charts.

"Sir, this is..." Her mouth was so dry, she was unable to speak. Silently, she signalled to Kevin for a bottle of water.

"I think we agree on the words," John said. "The translation isn't the point at issue here. But as a courtesy to Kevin—who hasn't seen it yet—I'd appreciate your translation?"

Sufficiently recovered by now, Maureen was happy to oblige.

"I, John, by the Grace of God, King of the Britons—"

John Midler raised his hand before Maureen went any further. His gaze had been purposefully directed at Kevin, looking for a reaction. He wasn't disappointed: the young photographer's face was a study in amazement, incredulity and more. Maureen had read often enough of people being so startled, or terrified, that their eyes were said to be 'popping out of their sockets', but this was the first time she'd witnessed a situation which was even close to having such a dramatic effect on someone in real life.

"I believe that line alone dates this document to within a fairly limited period of time."

"Seventeen years. 1199 to 1216," Maureen said automatically. That was her favourite period of English history: all the significant dates were filed and readily accessed in her conscious memory.

"I rather think we'll find a certain date in 1215 will be recorded somewhere in this...remarkable document," John said, picking his words now with great care. "About the middle of June, perhaps?"

"There has always been some dispute about the exact date," Maureen responded, "but most authorities have come to accept the fifteenth of June as the most likely date and Runnymede as the place where Magna Carta was signed...or to give its full title," she added, with a touch of humour in her voice, "*The Great Charter of the Liberties of England, and of the Liberties of the Forest.*"

"But that leaves us with another problem when it comes to authenticating the manuscript we have before us," John said.

Kevin looked totally lost, but Maureen knew exactly what John was referring to and explained.

"There are only four known copies of Magna Carta in existence, and they're all accounted for in various libraries and museums. We're faced with the task of establishing full provenance of a previously unknown *fifth* copy!"

"And we don't even know—yet!—whether it *is* a true and faithful copy in every respect of the document, both the wording of it and the signatories," John added.

"How about the copies which already exist?" Kevin asked. "Are they all exact duplicates?" It was a fair question and an astute one, coming from a non-specialist.

John nodded his approval. "With Maureen's permission, I think I can answer that?"

Maureen blinked and ceded place to the university's senior historian.

"There are minor variations in the four known versions that have been found and verified. There are spelling variations—not all the monks were conscientious in their spellings, and not all had what you'd call a legible fist in their writings. But the variations are minor, certainly nothing that could be used to raise any legal challenge to the specific intent of each of the sixty-three clauses in the charter itself."

"Sixty-three clauses? I never realised!"

"It's longer than people think, Kevin. Just short of five thousand words—about ten pages of an A4-size document, single-spaced—though the handwriting of the monks is considerably bigger than a typical newspaper print run."

Maureen had been scanning the layout of the manuscript throughout the last few interchanges and looked up with a curious expression on her face.

"You're sure all four extant copies have sixty-three clauses, John?"

"That's correct. The variations are minor blemishes—misspellings, punctuation—nothing which could create possibly be a legal point of contention."

"What if I told you the last clause on *this* document—right next to the king's mark—is number sixty-four?"

CHAPTER THREE

KEVIN LOOKED BLANK. John Midler froze in the act of lifting his water bottle to his lips. Maureen flushed bright scarlet: the silence her question had caused became unbearable.

John blinked.

"My first reaction would be to say, 'You must be mistaken,' or possibly, 'Are you sure?' But I know you well enough to be certain that you wouldn't make such an elementary mistake reading Latin numerals incorrectly. Let me see!"

With just the tiniest trace of reluctance, Maureen stood back and allowed John full access to the viewing glass. In the left margin, neatly aligned beneath the preceding clause numbers, the Latin characters listed a clause with the number LXIV: sixty-four.

John continued to scrutinise the entry for several minutes, prowling around the table to look at it from several different angles without saying a word. Eventually, he straightened up and ran his fingers through his hair.

"This is going to raise further complications in establishing whether or not the document is genuine," he said. "This, to my knowledge, is without precedent or comparison. If this document is genuine, if it can be verified, it will be right up there with the discovery of the Dead Sea Scrolls or the cave paintings at Limoux!"

Kevin gasped. "You can't be serious! What could possibly make it that important?"

"Let's not get too far ahead of ourselves! First of all, we have to find a way of establishing beyond all possible doubt that this scroll is authentic—not a forgery or someone's idea of a joke—

though I have to say, from my own experience of working with ancient documents, it feels authentic!"

A sudden thought struck Maureen. She frowned. "I remember hearing somewhere that carbon dating isn't accurate enough to date artefacts that are mere centuries old. It's only really useful to measure in geological terms where millennia are involved. Is that true, John?"

"Hmm. I think the jury's still out on that one, Maureen. I'll check when we get back to the uni, but what we need as our first priority is someone with a background in forensics—someone we can trust to keep his or her mouth shut until we're ready to go public. There must be other ways of establishing how old something is—look at the Turin Shroud, for example. There's general agreement about the date of that, and we're talking about a timeframe of two thousand years or so."

Maureen glanced at her watch. "Time's getting on, all the same. Have we got time to look over the wording of Clause Sixty-Four before we roll this manuscript up?"

"Being honest, I don't think I could bear the thought of waiting a minute longer. I have a feeling this could be big—*really* big—assuming it's genuine. What possible reason could there be for adding an extra clause to such an important document unless King John had something specific in mind?"

"And how did it finish up buried in an underground chamber in Liverpool city centre eight hundred years after it was signed?" Kevin couldn't keep quiet any longer: his instincts told him this was a major news item.

"We're getting ahead of ourselves again! This is raising too many questions and no answers at all!"

"You're right, John," Maureen said, "but perhaps you should have a look at Clause Sixty-Four before we pack the document away and head for home? Your Latin is surely better than mine..."

"Cos I'm an old fogey? Maybe I should take that as a compliment."

"No, Sir! That's not—"

"What you meant? Hmm…let's have a look. It's not as long as some of the other clauses, but we have to assume it has some special significance for either a local lord, perhaps the town?"

John hunched over the scroll once more and studied the minuscule handwriting.

"*Ego Iohannes*…why is he repeating himself? He began the preamble to this document with the same formal statement!"

"Could be because he wants to underline something—like a codicil, a postscript?"

"Possible, Maureen, though I don't know that would carry any weight if a point of law was involved—something else we have to check as soon as we can. But listen to this!

"*Ego, Iohannes, hodie primo Augusti anno regni nostri sexto decimo ad municipium Liuerpul nominem urbem concordo*…"

The Latin was lost on Kevin, but he reacted when John spoke the name of his hometown. Likewise, Maureen gave a gasp of amazement, which caused John to pause.

"Today, the first day of August in the sixteenth year of my—our reign, confer on Liverpool the name city."

John paused.

"I'd be inclined to translate 'name' as something more formal—perhaps 'the rights and privileges of a city'?"

He waited a moment for Maureen's nod of acceptance before continuing.

"Let's add the phrase for the time being. It's implicit in the context of what comes next, anyway. Listen to this…"

"'…confer on Liverpool the rights and privileges of city as granted in our Royal Charter in the eighth year of our reign. Liverpool's residents shall henceforth elect a Senate'—the writer has used a capital for Senate—'with power to pass local laws and raise taxes. The elected Senate shall be considered Freemen.'

"'This right is granted to the city *in perpetua*'—I'll leave that phrase in Latin, as it's still used today with the identical legal meaning—'in recognition of the support shown by its loyal citizens for our royal person. The Powers and Privileges stated in this City's Charter, granted in the sixteenth year of Our Reign, are hereby confirmed.'"

Given this day under my hand and seal
Iohannes, Rex Britanniæ
1 Augustus 1215

Several seconds of stunned silence followed. Kevin's nerve was the first to break.

"I don't for a moment doubt your translation, Professor Midler—and I think, in this instance at least, I ought to be allowed to use your title—but would you please confirm for the tape record that what you've just said is a true and accurate translation of the words on the scroll? This will be vital in the chain of evidence. I need to make a note of the time and date it was first made. And I can assure you, there is no way I'm going to bring another reporter in on this, not while I can do the job myself!"

Maureen had jockeyed for a closer look at the text while this conversation had been going on. John nudged her for an agreement before nodding to Kevin.

"With the one subtext I mentioned before about the implication of the rights and privileges that a city could expect under Roman law, the words on this document are exactly as I read them. Maureen, are we in agreement on this?"

"I can't argue with a single word, John. I probably wouldn't dare, even if I had the slightest doubt about the text—which

I don't. I'd also support your rephrasing of what the use of the word 'city' implies, from a legal and constitutional viewpoint. By this period of their history, the Romans were fond of using a form of shorthand when they put together important legal documents."

"And didn't I hear somewhere that Magna Carta—assuming you can prove this is a valid copy—is the nearest we've ever come to putting together a written constitution?" Kevin asked.

"That's correct, and I'm glad you've heard that one, Kevin. I can quite easily imagine that particular point being the biggest single stumbling block when we attempt to verify the manuscript, establish some sort of provenance."

John looked at his watch once more and began to pack tools back into his swag bag.

"Let me do that," Kevin said, angling in to take over. "There's precious little I can damage!"

"There's one more thing." There was an odd inflection in John Midler's voice. Everyone froze and held their breath, waiting for him to continue.

"The reference to the Royal Charter, which in the words of Good King John, was granted 'in the eighth year of our reign'—in plain-speak, that would be 1207."

He paused and looked around to be certain he had everyone's full attention.

"Technically, legally, any which way you want to define it, this Charter *predates* Magna Carta by eight years. That's significant! It means that the rights and privileges contained in *that* document have precedence over anything of a later date. So, if—as Kevin said a few minutes ago—Magna Carta is the nearest we have to a written constitution, Liverpool's Charter—"

"—is as near as makes no difference the city's Declaration of Independence!" Maureen interrupted, forgetting for the moment her usual deference to her professor. John Midler didn't seem offended but nodded his agreement.

"In a nutshell, Maureen, I believe that's the case. Have any of you actually *seen* the Charter? It's under glass in the town hall. It can't be more than a six-inch scrap of vellum."

Maureen had seen a photograph of the document but not the document itself.

"Professor Midler, can you arrange for us to view it sometime?" Kevin asked, having completed the mundane task of packing away the tools.

John shrugged. "I'm sure you can go and see anything that's on display at the town hall, and I'm absolutely certain you don't need my permission, but I'll ring and make an appointment if you want me to."

"Thanks, that'd be brilliant. Makes it a bit more, you know, official, like!" He closed the tool bag, adding, "I'd feel a lot easier if you two experts concentrate on rolling the manuscript and protecting it. You're best placed to know how to handle it, and I doubt very much it will roll tight enough to go back in the tube, even for a short jaunt across town!"

***

Kevin led the party back along the *Echo* corridors and down through the open-plan reception area, eerily silent and empty at this time on a Saturday afternoon with no further editions due to be produced until late Monday morning. The only person they encountered en route to the main entrance doors was the security guard on the mezzanine floor of the reception area.

"Have a good one, Kevin!" he said as he unlocked the door and let them out. He looked at John and Maureen but didn't seem inclined to question their right to be in the building along with a member of staff he recognised, and Kevin was astute enough not to offer any information he wasn't specifically asked for.

"We'd best stash this in my car before we do anything else," he suggested. "I'm assuming you want to speak to Billy and the navvy gang before we leave?"

John was so engrossed by the implications of their preliminary studies of the manuscript, he'd relegated the labourers who had come across it to the back of his mind. As if on cue, Billy popped his head out of the trench.

"We're just about ready to secure the tunnel and finish for the day," he said.

"Kevin says we should leave this, erm, material in his car..."

John looked around to see if there was anyone within earshot. They had Old Hall Street to themselves at this time of day, and Billy grinned at John's reaction.

"The site's blocked off. We'll keep an eye on it tonight and tomorrow, don't worry! Want another look before you go off to do...whatever you academics do with old stuff?"

"We've got Kevin's photos of the site, and plenty of work on the manuscript itself. I doubt we can learn anything significant by going back underground today," John said, raising an eyebrow in Maureen's direction. She was quick to agree. "But the offer to keep an eye on the site is appreciated, and I'll make sure you get paid for it," he promised. "Give me a quote on the hours you've worked so far by Monday morning. There are funds set aside for research, and the provost owes me a couple of favours."

***

"Would it be easier to set aside my area of the room and keep all the evidence in one place?"

Maureen had been sharing John Midler's research office space since the beginning of the academic year, and they had both benefitted from the arrangement. She was neat and tidy by nature, and her corner of the area was immaculate.

John looked across at the sterile, scrubbed-clean surfaces on offer and nodded his approval.

"It certainly won't take you long to remove your personal effects from that corner. If you're serious, it would make our research easier to keep under wraps. The less people who know about it, the better."

Kevin cleared his throat. "You've not forgotten our arrangement, I hope?"

"Relax, Kevin. I'm a man of my word. Of course you'll be the *only* media hawk we deal with. Your *exclusive* tag is guaranteed, and you can book your ticket for next year's Pulitzer prize-giving, too!

"Best make a start. We've barely twenty-four hours to squeeze as much as we can out of this before we hand the manuscript over to the *Echo*."

Maureen pounced immediately. "John, think this through! We can't keep on moving this…this…priceless, unique document from one hidey-hole to the next and just hope it doesn't start falling apart! It's only survived since it was written because it was locked away in an airtight container, sealed against the elements and everything else. I suggest we photograph it from every possible angle and send the photocopies, along with an accurate translation and a copy of Kevin's photo file. The original should be in some sort of secure, controlled environment, but I don't need to tell my supervisor how to preserve historical objects."

"You're right, of course, Maureen. I think we have everything we need to protect the document at our fingertips here."

Using the heavy slice of clear Perspex John had already used to examine the document in the field and a sturdy piece of plain white card as an underlay, the ancient document was quickly and efficiently isolated from the effects of air and moisture. The seal was completed by the application of a thin strip of mastic around the perimeter, where glass met card.

"Is that it?"

'It' had been so simple and so swiftly achieved that Maureen couldn't believe the task was over. John caught the full flavour of the range of questions behind her simple query.

"We need to think about protecting it from light, and especially sunlight, but on this side of the room, direct sunlight won't be a problem. Air temperature will also have to be taken into consideration, but it never gets too warm in here anyway, and air-conditioning is standard throughout the building."

"Let's not get too far ahead of ourselves. We don't even know how long we can hope to hang on to this document!"

John and Maureen both turned to glare at Kevin, who immediately made a cross-my-heart gesture on his chest.

"You know I'd never, ever open my mouth to anyone. I'd be mad to contemplate it, as long as I've your word on an exclusive tag! But you're right about one thing. As soon as the story breaks, it's going to become nigh-on impossible to hang on to the manuscript. Security is going to be a nightmare. In fact, I'd suggest getting a bank box somewhere deep underground and heavily guarded. That would also solve the controlled climate problem."

"Calm down, Kevin!" Maureen said, laughing. "Neither of us is suggesting you'd be guilty of talking out of turn. John, what about a bank deposit box of some sort?"

"That sounds like a good idea to me. We can't do anything about that until they open Monday morning, anyway, but it's worth a shot. Now, perhaps we should be getting on with some practical tests in the limited time we've still got sole, exclusive access to this treasure trove."

CHAPTER FOUR

Kevin put the phone down and struck a line through the last line on his notebook.

"I can vouch for these people, personally. They're all pros, and none of them will want to be upstaged by anyone breaking ranks to release the news ahead of the rest. We need a voice in the media, both the newspapers and the radio, but we don't want a crowd at this first meeting. My boss—Marc Farrell—and the head honcho from Radio Merseyside is the absolute minimum, plus a senior member from the university to confirm the historical provenance of the document. We daren't risk inviting any more!"

He rubbed his hands over his face and stretched. Other than trips to the bathroom or to eat fast food and drink strong coffee, none of them had left the room since Saturday afternoon.

"Ten o'clock is a bit late for the main edition anyway. I'm surprised I managed to persuade Marc to agree to start the meeting that late—I had to work hard to persuade him it was a story which would blow him and all the opposition away!"

"I was impressed by the way you handled it, Kev," Maureen said. "You didn't give him the least clue of what it was all about, but it looks as if you've wangled us another twenty-four hours by promising he'd have a major story to break on Tuesday."

"I guess I'm lucky, Mo! I've got a pretty good relationship with Marc, so I didn't have to work too hard to persuade him to come along to this meeting. He also knows how important the cloak-and-dagger aspect of news gathering can be—especially where a possible scoop is on the cards! I wasn't too sure about Angie

Ross at Merseyside, though. Our paths have crossed once or twice, but I've had no personal dealings with her until today."

"But you got them both to come to a meet without even knowing what the story is? That took some doing, Kev!"

"Marc knows my track record for nosing out a good story, by which I mean one that is going to sell papers. I'm pretty sure he sold the idea to Angie Ross."

Maureen glanced at both her male companions, then lifted one arm and made an exaggerated display of sniffing something unpleasant.

"We're none of us going to make a good impression at a press meeting if we don't get a chance to clean ourselves up a little. John, there must be shower facilities or something close at hand?"

Working non-stop all weekend in the same clothes, on a diet of strong coffee and takeaway pizzas, had left its mark on their personal appearance. John made a couple of phone calls, then sent Kevin and Maureen off to clean up first, insisting that someone had to be on guard in the office/lab 'just in case'.

"And I was right!" he crowed when they returned. "You hadn't been gone more than two minutes when someone rattled the door handle. At first, I thought you'd come back for something you'd forgotten. But whoever it was scarpered when I called out, so I guess they were up to no good. I'll be as quick as I can!"

John returned in under five minutes and donned one of the pristine white lab smocks, which had been provided for him and for Maureen. Kevin had—somewhat reluctantly—declined the offer and opted to dress in his slightly stale street clothes.

"I'll never be a science boffin. Why try to look like one?" he said. "And anyway, Marc knows me. He'd bust a gut laughing if he saw me in a lab coat! Nah, I'm best being myself, and it also means I can go straight out on duty afterwards if necessary."

An internal phone sounded: John fielded it and spoke briefly to the caller.

"I'm going out to meet our guests," he said, "but I want you to stay here. You can watch on the CCTV. There's no sound, but you'll see why I'm going out there on my own."

With this cryptic comment, he slid out of the door and closed it firmly. Kevin and Maureen looked blankly at each other, then concentrated on the CCTV screen where John was striding purposefully along a deserted corridor.

The door at the end of the passage was locked: that much was obvious. The first thing John did after unlocking it was to wave away a posse of five or six hangers-on who had clearly expected to be allowed to accompany Marc Farrell and Angie Ross.

Opposite the door to John Midler's office/workroom was a plain, unadorned table. John halted before entering: Kevin and Maureen witnessed in dumb show as John indicated to the invited guests that every recording device, camera and tape recorder was to be deposited before they were admitted to the inner sanctum. Even without a soundtrack, it was clear that this demand was not popular with either newshound, but John folded his arms and just shook his head at every argument until they complied.

"You'll be able to keep an eye on your equipment through the CCTV link. Nobody will steal it!" he reassured them as he locked the door again. What was left unsaid was the fact that the same camera would also prevent anyone from sneaking up on them for an unauthorised viewing.

"You'll appreciate the cloak-and-dagger tactics we're enforcing when you've seen what we have to show you," John said as soon as the brief introductions had been made. "And I'm certain you won't regret coming, even though Kevin—at *my* insistence—told you nothing other than it was a major news item. Thank you for believing him."

"When he told me you were involved, Professor, I assumed it had to be something which also involves your academic background. Ancient history?" Marc asked.

"Early British history, yes. And one thing everybody knows about our earliest records is, of course, Magna Carta. Let me show you something..."

Twenty shellshocked minutes later, Marc and Angie were sitting with the conspirators around a table in a satellite side room that had served as kitchen and crash pad over the weekend. John had insisted on a strict no-food-or-drink policy in the research area to be absolutely certain there was no possibility of damage or contamination. Sleep had been out of the question, but they'd all taken a power nap from time to time in a padded armchair that had seen better days.

"You say the other copies of Magna Carta are all identical? Word for word?"

"Correct, Mr. Farrell. Different handwritings, of course, penned by different monks, and one or two spelling variations—the Anglo-Saxon equivalent of typos if you like—but other than that, the other four manuscripts contain exactly the same sixty-three clauses. This is the *only* document to have Clause Sixty-Four tacked on the end, immediately above the king's mark. He *must* have known what he was signing."

"And as the clause clearly relates to Liverpool, and Liverpool *alone...*" Angie sipped at her coffee then shook her mane of hair as if trying to rid herself of invisible cobwebs. Her hands darted to her bag, seeking the traditional reporter's standby pad and pencil before belatedly remembering the security restrictions John had insisted upon.

"Can't we please take notes? I promise, no tricks, indecipherable shorthand or secret codes, and you can proofread everything I write before we leave," she pleaded.

Marc said nothing but added the saddest brown puppy-dog eyes imaginable to Angie's request. John hesitated, unable to decide.

"Marc, this has got to be *my* story!" Kevin burst in. "You can't expect me to—"

"Calm down, Kev! That's not the way I work. You'll get full credit, I can assure you. It's not so many years ago I was the new kid on the block living in cheap digs on Upper Parly the night the Toxteth Riots kicked off. The cops set up roadblocks, nobody could get in or out, and I was the *only* reporter on the scene for the first forty-eight hours. Every street phone got trashed, of course, and although I had a radiophone in the car, I was terrified, as it was kicking off all around.

"Yes, you'll get your exclusive byline. You've earned it, Kevin, and as your boss, I'm proud of what you've done setting up this meeting. But we need to get some basic details written down, and Angie's right. This is far too important to let even the smallest detail get forgotten in the stress of the moment. I'll make the notes, and if you're happy with them, you can add your signature to every page after you've read them. Do we have a deal?"

Kevin offered his hand immediately.

"If I can't trust my boss—especially in front of witnesses—who *can* I trust?"

Marc grasped Kevin's hand sincerely.

"You show a lot of promise, kiddo. Welcome to the team! As soon as we get the chance, I'll be looking to give you a boost on the promotions ladder. Professor Midler—"

"John, please! We've also been thinking of ourselves as a team this weekend. First names all round, if that's okay with you?"

"No probs, John. Now, a practical matter before we go any further…" Marc paused and looked around the table to make sure he had everyone's full attention.

"You said yourself, Magna Carta is the closest thing we have to a formal written constitution in over eight hundred years of British history."

"Yes, that's the accepted view," John agreed.

"So now we could use a definitive legal opinion—or a ruling, more likely. This document must have enormous significance, legally speaking. I'm no expert in these matters, but it wouldn't surprise me if this Royal Charter actually gives Liverpool the right to declare itself an independent—what's the word I want? Fiefdom? Republic?—and with a clear mandate to self-government. We need one more member on this team. We need a lawyer."

CHAPTER FIVE

"THERE WILL BE a very important item in our next news broadcast at midday. This has been arranged with our respected local newspaper, the *Liverpool Echo,* to coincide with the exclusive story revealed in detail in today's edition. We advise everyone to make sure they obtain a copy of today's *Echo.* Our afternoon programmes will be rearranged to accommodate anyone who wants to ring in with their comments on what is possibly the most important news in the whole of Liverpool's recorded history. A panel of experts will be here in the studio to discuss what it may mean for the city and everyone who lives here."

The DJ cut to a popular—and lengthy track—from a local group and removed his headset. As he did, the switchboard instantly went into meltdown as the radio station's most avid listeners immediately and predictably reacted by trying to discover what significant news was about to be revealed. He looked from the solid red lights to the volunteers fielding the calls and finally to Roger Allyn, who was the station's most experienced phone-in jock and ran a two-hour live chat session every weekday.

"You think you can handle this, Rog?"

"I think I'm covered. I won't be on my own in the studio today, and the crew you and Angie have scraped together should be able to help me out with any legal points which crop up."

"Hope it's not going to get too crowded!"

Roger looked around the room and nodded. The original research team of three had grown to four. Kevin had recommended an old school friend, Steve Dunning, who had followed a family tradition and joined his father's law firm. Marc was representing the newspaper, Angie the radio station. With himself manning the microphones and the mixer desk, a total of seven was a comfortable limit for the studio.

"I don't envy the team on the phones their job," Angle said. "How are they managing to keep the callers happy and still tell them nothing?"

"I worked out a script for them to follow," Roger replied, "and as long as they stick to it, they'll be fine. They've only got to persist for another—" He glanced at the studio clock "—twenty minutes or so until today's *Echo* hits the newsstands and we can go live to discuss our city's future!"

He turned to John Midler.

"While we have a few private moments left, perhaps you can give me some idea of just how important the discovery of this document might be? Historically, for example, what's the significance of this extra clause?"

Before John Midler had a chance to reply, a red light on the studio wall began to flash.

"Sorry, John, we're on air in thirty seconds. We're out of time!"

"That's all right, Roger. I'd only have to repeat myself for your listeners anyway. I'm sure I can wing it. I prefer to lecture a hall full of students rather than picking over the bones of something in a small group."

The last few seconds were counted off by an anonymous female voice, followed by the radio station's current jingle as the flashing red light turned to a steady glow. Roger cut in smoothly and professionally as the music ended.

"Good afternoon, it's twelve o'clock on Monday, the seventeenth of September, and I'm Roger Allyn. In the studio with me today, I have some special guests. We're omitting the news headlines this hour, and when you've heard what my guests have to tell us all, I think you'll understand why.

"First, let me introduce John Midler, who is head of history and archaeology at Liverpool University. Professor, over to you."

"Thank you, Roger. Although 2012 has been officially designated Liverpool's Biennial, we all know that the town is considerably more than two hundred years old…"

John continued, giving a condensed history of Liverpool's existence from the earliest records in two or three sentences. In under a minute, he'd navigated his way from ancient history to the present day and the renovation work in Liverpool's oldest district, which had led to the discovery of the Charter. Beyond the soundproofed triple glazing of the studio, Maureen watched as the outside line switchboard became a solid wall of red lights, overwhelming the army of volunteers attempting to cope with the calls.

John Midler spoke without notes but with growing confidence and in simple, non-technical terms about the wording of the Charter and the importance of confirming its historical authenticity. Roger sensed that he was beginning to struggle for breath and posed a question to allow the professor an opportunity to recover.

"If this is a genuine document—and I know you haven't had the time to confirm that as yet—can you give us some idea of how important this might be for Liverpool?"

John put aside the bottle of water he'd all but emptied while the question was being asked.

"It's significant that these extra lines—Clause Sixty-Four—are *only* found on this document. It's also interesting that the date on the document is not the same as the date we've always associated with the signing of Magna Carta on Runnymede Green, which was the fifteenth of June 1215. The document we discovered appears to date from later in the same year—the first of August—

but there's also the phrase 'in the eighth year of our reign', which would actually mean it was written in 1207—in other words, *before* Magna Carta. But if you need a legal opinion, you'll have to ask someone who knows more than I do."

John turned to the clean-cut, soberly suited man sitting on his left.

"The *Echo* reporter, Kevin Wyatt, found someone he's known since they were at school together. Coincidentally, I was at school with Stephen Dunning's father. The family have been solicitors in Liverpool for many years. Stephen, perhaps you'd like to tell Roger something of your background and then give us *all* an idea of the legal implications involved?"

Stephen thought about rising to his feet as he would when addressing a courtroom but seemed to change his mind as if deciding this would be overpowering in the cramped confines of a recording studio.

"Thanks, John. In brief, law has become a highly specialised business in recent years. With the way legislation has become more and more detailed, that isn't really surprising. For many years now, I've specialised in corporate and business law, and I've been involved in helping a lot of small businesses get started in Liverpool.

"From time to time, I've had to perform historical searches for clients setting up a new business or service, usually to check on things like protected copyrights, and the term which comes up time and again is *prima facie*. Essentially, this means 'first occurrence', and it can be very important to establish if something is the first of its kind."

"The importance of this legislation—assuming it can be established that the signature and provenance are authentic—lies in the *date* of the document and the fact that it was signed by the king, the highest authority in the land at the time. Some would say this country would be in a better state if that were still the case today."

Although it had been delivered in a serious, lawyerly manner, Stephen's aside provoked a few chuckles around the room, loud enough to be picked up on the studio mics. A certain amount of tension that had been building in the room was now dispelled: Roger made a mental note to try to find out if it had had the same effect on the listeners while Stephen continued in a more relaxed, almost conversational tone of voice.

"As it stands, this Charter issued with what appears to be an authentic royal seal and in the name of King John has all the hallmarks of a genuine document. As such, it ought to be considered equally as binding as the other extant copies of what we call Magna Carta. The short answer to the most important question seems clear. Liverpool has every right to decide to exercise the prerogative implied in the document—the right to self-government as an autonomous region, in the UK but not necessarily of it, if you appreciate the difference."

"Oh, I think we can *all* understand that," Roger replied. "We've always known that Scousers *are* different! But more to the point, this document is clearly of great significance to Liverpool, and I'm sure it will be a major talking point when we decide how the city should be governed in future—or perhaps we should start referring to ourselves as a city state?"

"I don't see any reason in law that might prevent us, but perhaps a local referendum would be a sensible way of testing public opinion. There were funds set aside for this."

"True, Steven, but that was when we were testing the waters about the possibility of an elected mayor. This is a very different matter."

"Roger, if we're going to set up as an independent city state and establish our own autonomous Regional Government, we're going to need a leader of some sort. Whether you call him the mayor, the prez, King Billy or the Duke of Knotty Ash doesn't really matter, as long as the person who accepts the role is prepared to look after the region's best interests and represent us in our dealings with the rest of the country."

"I think you could reasonably say the 'rest of the world', Roger, but yes, we need a strong figure to show everyone we mean business."

Steven's voice suddenly became thoroughly professional. It was a subtle shift but enough to leave the radio audience in no doubt that he was now speaking of more serious matters.

"As long as we can achieve a high turnout and a significant majority voting in favour of an elected mayor, we've got a solid foundation to build on.

"I had time last night to do some preliminary checks. From existing records, I discovered that the Objective One funding we received from the EF to improve the infrastructure of the region is unquestionably ours. That's over £9 billion for starters, and as long as we use it on projects which enhance our infrastructure, there's nothing Westminster or anyone else can do regarding repayment."

Much ill will had been stirred by the 'Indian giving' parsimonies of the national coalition government when they had attempted to insist on the repayment of funds granted expressly to develop the derelict ground that still languished unloved at the northern end of Liverpool docks, parts of which still showed clear evidence of damage sustained at the height of the Blitz in 1941.

"We also need to elect our own regional body to support the mayor. One person can only achieve a limited amount, whoever they are," Steven continued.

"For the moment, titles aren't as important as a genuine work ethic. We can continue to call them councillors, or senators as the Romans did, or even government ministers. As long as they get the job done, nobody's going to be too concerned.

"We all know they were only bleating about returning the £5 million 'beer money' we were granted to develop a part of the docks because some of the bigger financial backers of Southampton docks were piling on the pressure to try and ensure they didn't lose a percentage of their cruise passengers once the job was done.

"But as a lawyer, I say they haven't got a leg to stand on, and the chickenfeed sum involved won't even be missed!"

"Steven Dunning, thank you for your valuable comments on the legal aspects of what is revealed in this unique document. Do you have any final words of advice for our listeners or our local politicians?"

"I think the idea which has already been mentioned, organising a local referendum, is the best way forward. If Liverpool is to make a successful transition to a form of self-government, it can only be done with the wholehearted support and backing of a significant majority of the local residents."

"Thank you once again. This is BBC Radio Merseyside. We'll just squeeze in some traffic and travel news, then we hope to have a comment from the city council…"

***

"Replacing my earlier guest in the studio, Leader of the Labour group in Liverpool, Councillor Joe Saunders. Councillor Saunders, what's your reaction to today's big news?"

"When I heard on one of your morning broadcasts that something out of the ordinary was to be announced, something of great importance to the whole of Merseyside, I picked up my phone and made sure that everyone would be available for an emergency meeting of the full council this afternoon. This will, of course, be the only point on the agenda, and I'm grateful to you for saving us debating time—assuming, of course, that they're all listening to this programme. I'll be going straight to the town hall when I leave the studio. It will be a closed meeting, I'm afraid. There wasn't enough time to make it possible for the press or members of the public to attend."

"In that case, Councillor, perhaps these documents might be useful and save you a few more minutes?"

Roger passed the council leader an envelope containing half a dozen sheets of printout.

"You'll find copies of the standard text of Magna Carta as it appears in all the other known examples, plus a copy of the Liverpool version with the extra paragraph, Clause Sixty-Four, and a transcript of my conversation with corporate solicitor Steven Dunning, earlier in this broadcast."

"Very efficient, Roger, as always, and much appreciated. I wish I could read through them all now, but you've certainly saved me a significant amount of work, and we can better use this air time to give your listeners as much detail as we possibly can."

"First of all, Councillor, will there be a full turnout for the council meeting this afternoon?"

"Roger, I made it clear that I will accept no excuses, and everyone I spoke to will be in attendance. We won't be leaving the town hall until this matter is thoroughly debated and a vote is taken. It's a turning point in our city's history and far too important to be treated in any other way."

"Councillor Saunders, I won't keep you any longer. How soon can we expect to hear the results of the meeting?"

"As soon as the vote is taken—and the meeting won't end until we have one!"

Despite the short notice, there were no absentees from the meeting that afternoon: one member who was in hospital demanded a video link and voted from his bed. The Labour group just about had a working majority, but on this single issue, as Joe Saunders had suspected, there was no difference of opinion. Questions were asked about funds and financing in the longer term, including one from a Green Party councillor who proposed the introduction of a 'Mersey Pound', which he claimed could be used by residents for goods and services that were exclusively used within the region. The point was debated briefly but seriously and eventually left 'on hold' until a later date.

"This is something I believe we can look at again, once we've established our primary goals," Joe said as the motion was narrowly defeated. As council leader, he'd decided to abstain on this point, and although the voting was close, his vote would not have changed the result for or against. He made this comment more for the purpose of having it recorded in the secretary's minutes of the meeting before moving on to the next point.

With an experienced council member as chair, the points allowed for debate were controlled and restricted to the day's agenda. The debate was lively and far from one-sided, but the result of the vote was never in doubt. With a handful of abstentions and no votes against, Liverpool's elected representatives decided to accept the modified Charter King John had offered their founding fathers as a mark of his gratitude for their support.

Dominic Ion, a young councillor with a background in banking, had one final question once the votes had been counted.

"Will the council consider a demand to the Exchequer for repayment of the taxes unlawfully collected from this region since August 1215?"

The council's immediate reaction was an amused chuckle, which rippled freely around the room, but even the least mathematically gifted of those present immediately knew that there was no way such a demand would even be considered. The number of zeroes marching across nine hundred years of account ledgers was impossible to imagine. There was also the indisputable fact that the country as a whole had been hovering on the brink of insolvency for several years: the prospect of being paid any recompense whatsoever for taxes collected, however unfairly and long since spent were, effectively, less than zero.

"I regret we won't be able to send such a demand to the powers-that-be in London," Joe said, once the proposal had had a few minutes' discussion followed by the inevitable negative vote, "but as they say, 'If you don't ask, you won't get,' and I'm going to ask Councillor Ion to prepare a document—couched in *very* diplomatic terms!—outlining the grounds we feel we have for our demands for recompense. However, I don't want him to think of this as an imposition from me personally just because I'm council leader. Can I ask for a show of hands from those who approve? Any against? Abstentions? Thank you!"

Joe turned to the young councillor, whose first name he'd just recalled.

"Dominic, it would seem you have a united council behind you. We look forward to reading a draft letter as soon as possible. Be creative, but make sure it's legal! Let's give 'em a scare, by all means. I doubt we'll get so much as a brass farthing from Westminster, but even an acknowledgement or an apology would be nice.

"Now, if someone will chase the scrum of media hawks from outside the front door and allow *one* rep from the *Echo* and one from each of the two *local* radios to come inside, I promised them an interview."

***

"Liverpool Town Council has voted to turn the forthcoming referendum about the election of a mayor into a referendum asking the electorate for a mandate to secede from the United Kingdom and become an autonomous, self-governing city state. A document conferring the right to this, signed by King John in August 1215,

was discovered recently during renovation work being carried out in one of the oldest streets in the town centre."

John hit the mute key: on screen, Kevin and Marc continued to hold centre stage at the press conference in the town hall reception room. Both were clearly savouring every moment of the occasion as they explained to the reporters of the national papers, radio channels and TV companies the details they had already released via the local media.

"I didn't realise how much of a kick a journalist gets from an exclusive tag!" John said as he watched the dumb show on the screen.

"They both deserve it. Think of the hours they've already put into this and how much time their connections with the media has saved us," Maureen pointed out. "I just hope things don't escalate too quickly, out of control!"

"That's something our local politicians will have to be careful about."

John scribbled a note to himself. "I'm sure they've got a wealth of experience between them. Hopefully, they'll think of it themselves, but it can't harm if I remind someone... and the nationwide publicity this is getting has *got* to be good for business!"

The TV screen changed to a standard news studio setting, showing scenes of a battleground somewhere far from Liverpool. John switched it off just as Marc and Kevin came through the door. Maureen looked surprised.

"That was quick! We've only just switched off the interview!"

Marc grinned. "They call it a live interview, but it was recorded about twenty minutes ago. That's pretty well standard practice, as it gives them a chance to redact the 'umms' and 'ahhs', make it look and sound more professional."

"Aw, that's another illusion shattered!" Maureen pouted. "Is nothing sacred? Can't we be allowed just a dream or two?"

"This is called real life—what happens to the rest of us while the dreamers dream!" Marc offered but without rancour. He'd recognised the twinkle in her eyes that told him she wasn't serious.

"What was the mood out there, Marc? D'you think we've a chance of a mandate, majority support?" John asked.

"For the idea of self-government? I don't think you need worry on that score! I've heard nothing but positive feedback from everyone I've spoken to."

"What, even the national media hacks who tried to gatecrash when I let you in?"

"I think they're hoping we'll take some sort of humiliating pratfall or run out of funds or something."

"Not gonna happen!" growled Kevin, flying high on caffeine. "You heard what Steve Dunning said. The law's on our side in this. The finances we've already been granted from Europe, together with whatever we can raise from local industry, will be enough to get us started."

John's mobile sounded off. He frowned, clearly not expecting a call.

"Hello? ... Yes, this is John Midler..."

Several seconds passed: John said nothing, but the non-stop squawk indicated that he was being told a great deal. The caller eventually paused for breath, and John had the opportunity to get a word in.

"I think it would be best if I put this call on the speaker. Angie Ross from Radio Merseyside is in the room, and Marc Farrell from the *Echo*, too. You'd better recap what you've just told me, so I don't garble the details...thanks!"

He docked the handset in the amplifier and introduced the speaker.

"Robin Stuart is the CEO of Core Holdings. He holds the purse strings for a lot of local industry, including John Lennon

Airport and Liverpool Waters. He has plans—I'll leave him to tell you himself."

"Thank you, Professor Midler. I've been trying to reach Angie Ross, but she's not picking up. I'd no idea she was with you until someone at the radio station tipped me off!"

"And I insisted on her surrendering her mobile before coming to this meeting—a simple security precaution, not because I don't trust her, but we've got to keep this under wraps as long as possible."

"As a businessman, Professor, I appreciate your concerns for security. I've been left severely out of pocket more than once by someone talking out of turn, but I have a business proposition which I believe will interest your Home Rule for Liverpool team, and I'm going to need both Angie Ross and *Marc Farrell on board for the PR angle."*

"Before you reveal all, Robin, can I just say that your proposition sounds almost too good to be true!"

"Believe me, I'm a businessman first and foremost. I take little interest in things from which I can't profit in one way or another. I'm keen to support anything I believe is in Liverpool's best interests, but I'm no Joe Williamson!"

Joe Williamson was a wealthy merchant who provided work for people in the early 1800s by encouraging them to dig a labyrinth of tunnels for no apparent reason other than to be gainfully employed and earn a wage upon which their families could survive.

"My idea is to develop the northern end of the docks. Simple, unskilled labour—at least, to start with—which anyone who really wants *to work won't find too difficult. Then there's also the Tramlink from the city centre out to the airport, and I know you've already mentioned that as a priority. That would most definitely make JLA the most attractive regional airport in the country."*

"It sounds to me as if you've been planning this for some time, Robin, and it's not exactly the sort of project that can be funded from the petty-cash account, either!"

"It's no secret that JLA has been making respectable profits every year for some time now. To me, this is as good a time as any to give the local economy a kick in the you-know-what and at the same time create some real, long-term job opportunities and make sure they go to local people.

"You can't take it with you, they say, so it makes sound economic sense to spread it around a little and invest in the town and its future. We've been isolated, financially and in terms of job opportunities and regional development, for far too many years now, and it's time we take a stand and show London we mean business!"

"Can I ask you how much you're prepared to invest in this development of the docks? There're some parts of the docks that haven't been used since the Blitz in '41."

"Core Holdings can and will match the £9 billion we've already been granted by the EU. That total will be more than adequate to refurbish the dock complex and *the river crossing between Runcorn and Widnes. I also believe we should call London's bluff, tell 'em we don't need their paltry £5 million beer money. We've got the skills and the knowledge to set up a proper turnaround cruise terminal here in Liverpool without their thirty pieces of silver."*

"So what's in it for you? You're a businessman, after all. You must be looking for some sort of profit."

"That I won't deny. But in this instance, for once, I'm willing to take my chances along with the city and its residents. Unlike some I could mention. When I *say, 'We're all in this together,' I mean it—sincerely!"*

Joe Saunders, who hadn't taken an active part in the discussions yet, stepped forward.

"Mr. Stuart, you and I have had our differences over what we each felt was best for Liverpool from time to time, but I'm in no doubt about your sincerity on this matter. Can I interest you in becoming my assistant on the town....council, senate, rood, parliament—whatever we eventually decide to call it? I'd be grateful if we might benefit from your experiences and firsthand knowledge of running a successful venture such as JLA."

"As long as it's me *you want, and not just my chequebook!"* Robin chuckled, but without malice. *"Gentleman's agreement?"*

Joe had no hesitation. "Game on!"

"I'll drop by your office first thing tomorrow to make it all official, Joe. Can you have someone type up an official, legally binding contract of some sort?"

"Consider it done, Robin. Shall we say, ten o'clock?"

CHAPTER SIX

"STEVE, WAS THAT strictly kosher, what we just witnessed in there? Joe Saunders co-opting Robin Stuart onto the council that? Can he—as council leader or however you want to think of him—actually *do* something like that without a meeting or some sort of a vote?"

"Hmmm. Let's see." Steve paused and polished his glasses. "Now, I *could* give you a long, convoluted, every-angle-covered, and *expensive* cure for insomnia, full of legalese..." he murmured. "On the other hand, I can remember that we're friends and I'd prefer to keep it that way!" he added with a grin, swerving to avoid the mock-swing JRK—officially Councillor John R. Kirwan—took at his head as punishment for the idle threat of legalistic bombast that they both knew was never going to happen.

"Legally? Well, if we accept that Liverpool intends to establish itself as a de facto autonomous province or region and considering that the evidence of this Royal Charter indicates we *should* have been recognised as such since 1215, I'd say all bets are off on that score. If we take it to the letter, every piece of legislation passed by any central, London-based government since that date cannot be applied to Liverpool without being voted upon independently by the city, its residents or, the duly elected authorities, the town council itself.

"In the circumstances, I'd say that Joe as council leader can 'co-opt' someone onto the council—or whatever we decide to call it—at least on a temporary basis until such time as a vote can be called. There are precedents throughout history. It certainly wouldn't be a one-off situation, far from it! But legally speaking, we're in uncharted waters here."

"Spoken like a true lawyer. Always leave an escape route open," sighed John with a wry grin.

"What else did you expect?" Marc commented. "He's old school, and he was well trained by the Jesuits!"

"All the same, this is something we need to have ratified by a full council meeting ASAP. How soon can you organise that, Joe?"

Joe was already punching a number—the first of several—on his mobile phone.

"Tonight, with any luck..."

***

That evening, Liverpool City Council sat for what would prove to be the last time as a body. Robin Stuart was introduced, his credentials examined, and he was permitted to argue his case, which he did convincingly and well. Once his place within the council had been agreed, it only remained to agree on what format the replacement administration ought to have once a formal election had been held.

John Midler had given this some thought and forwarded a suggestion that the new body should adopt a name that did not have overtones of the old regime.

"I like the sound of a synod," he said. "It's got a good, solid, historical ring to it, and it's a term which definitely has no recent politically sensitive associations. It also sounds close enough to 'senate' for people to recognise it as a political body."

The archaic term hinted at a distinctly historical precedent and gave it an aura of respectability that appealed to the informal de facto steering committee who would be responsible for organising the required ballot. Liverpool's Synod would consist of one hundred representatives, twenty from each of the five boroughs on Merseyside, and work towards a true 'common wealth' for the region as a whole.

***

John Midler managed to bluff his way past Joe Saunders' receptionist on a pretext of something both urgent and personal. Joe ended the call he was on as John entered. Before replacing the handset, he called through the open door for the stack of waiting calls to be diverted.

"If this is a bad time..."

"No worse than any other, John. I'm glad of the break, to be honest. What's on your mind?"

"Practical matter, really, nothing major that could affect you or the referendum, but all the same!"

He sat down and accepted the coffee Joe had already poured.

"My assistant, Maureen—don't know how I ever managed without her—has asked me about completion of the dig site where the Charter was found. I'm not sure I even told you at the time. Her dad, Billy, was in charge of the team of roadworkers who found it."

Joe could see where this was leading. "And they won't get paid for the job until it's finished, am I right? But they can't fill in the hole they've dug before everything's been investigated, excavated, catalogued and removed to a place of safekeeping, right? And of course, you'll need specialists, museum experts and the funds to carry out a full-scale operation..."

"Which is why I've come to you. The museum can't afford to—"

"Say no more! I'm sure we can find a few bob somewhere that's not earmarked for something else."

"Thanks, Joe. Billy's waiting outside with Maureen, but I know he's keen to get back to Old Hall Street and get on with the job in hand."

Joe Saunders stood and stretched.

"Can't remember the last time I was outdoors. I feel like I've been locked in this office for weeks on end! I'd like to meet Billy, thank him for everything he and his team have done already."

Billy stood puffing nervously on a fag as Joe came out to the steps in front of the town hall. The bright early morning sunlight took Joe by surprise, and he had to shield his eyes from the glare before he could offer Billy his hand.

"You've done the whole city a massive favour, Billy. And you needn't worry about being suitably rewarded for your efforts, I'll make sure of that!"

"Me'n the lads appreciate that, Mr. Mayor, Sir—"

"Skip the titles, Billy! We're all on the same team here, and everyone else calls me plain, simple Joe! And you, young lady, d'you answer to Maureen or Mo?"

"Mo's fine."

"You've also done a great job so far. I'm sure you'll be an asset to the organisers—I might even poach you from John Midler if he'll let you go! Any questions from either of you?"

Both shook their heads and Billy glanced at his watch.

"Thanks for everything, Mo! Now, I should be cracking on. I know you're also mad busy, but if you could follow me back to the dig and help me fill in the details for the lads...

"Billy, I'm grateful you and your team stood Dixie over the weekend and made sure nothing disappeared or got damaged. The museum's team know their stuff—they'll be along to give you a hand. They'll have everything we need removed, photo'd and catalogued before you even know it!"

Billy and Maureen walked around the corner to join the other navvies at a table outside the coffee shop opposite the *Echo* offices. Temporary barriers had been placed at both ends of Old Hall Street, which was now completely traffic-free. Museum staff wearing hi-viz bibs soon arrived to supervise forty or more volunteers as they worked swiftly but with meticulous care to remove and catalogue every artefact found in the subterranean chamber.

"What can you tell me about the Charter?" Billy asked. "I mean, I've heard what's been on the news and so on, but I never got a good look at it. Is it in good nick, for example? Has it been damaged? Is it easy to read? You've actually had the damn thing in your hands!"

"That's a bit odd from you, Dad. When did you get interested in reading?"

"Don' be cheeky, kiddo! I'm asking cos I really want to know! What's the point o' havin' a kid with a good job if I can't get a bit o' gossip 'bout summat what's in the news—'specially when it's something that's so important to all of us!"

Maureen couldn't let that opportunity go either.

"As long as you're not just gonna leg it down the bookie's an' lay some stupid bet on the election or something, I'll tell you—if you're *really* interested, that is?" she said with an acid tone Anne Robinson would have approved of. Billy was unimpressed.

"Mo, I read as much as most anyone I know, and it's not jus' the racin' results in the *Echo*! I like to know what's goin' on round town—you wouldn't believe how many times I've sussed out where a job's gonna turn up just from reading something in the paper! My point is, I'm Scouse through an' through, an' it seems t'me that things are about to change here in the 'Pool—change for the better! I want to be in from the start, do me bit f'r the town and maybe make a few bob fer meself! Nothin' wrong wi' that now, is there?"

Maureen studied her father carefully. Despite the constant sarcasm and sniping typical in every family, she didn't doubt his sincerity for a second. Billy returned her frank gaze: the teasing laughter disappeared from his eyes and he continued in a more serious tone.

"Nothin' wrong in me bein' a great softie an' wantin' t' see Liverpool get the break we all deserve for once, is there? Poke in the eye with a sharp stick for the fat cats as live dahn saaff in London? Do I need another excuse?"

Billy rarely took life seriously, and Maureen knew it.

"Fine, Dad, I believe you—honest! Since you ask, the text of the Charter was in simple, Classical Period Latin, which worked in our favour. We have lots of experience of translating documents of similar nature and antiquity, and almost no chance of any misunderstandings or fluffed translations."

Yozzer appeared at Billy's elbow. "The museum team's getting all excited about something they've come across, Gaff. You better come an' have a word—you too, Miss. It must be something historical they've found!"

Two tunnels had been discovered leading roughly east and west at the southern end of the underground chamber. Extra lighting had been installed, but so far, none of the volunteers had attempted to enter either shaft.

"We decided we'd wait for you, Professor. It only seems right that you or your assistant should be first to set foot in there!"

"Risk our necks, you mean?" John joked. "Do they look stable, Billy? Any signs of cave-in?"

"The tunnel leading west slopes down and looks pretty straight. It's man-high and looks like it's heading directly towards the river."

"Bolt hole, maybe? Or some sort of escape route?"

"Or even used by smugglers. There's been a lot of that going on down the years, but don't forget Wilkinson's job-creation scheme—the tunnels he had dug through town centre to give local unemployed men some money to live on. What about the other tunnel?"

"That seems to slope upwards. I'm guessing it's aimed at—or maybe started from—Everton Brow."

"Okay, here's what we do. One volunteer, roped up and wearing a wire, in each tunnel with whatever cameras he or she can manage. Stills and video shots, please, and a running commentary. No risks! If it looks dodgy or there's any sign of collapse, you're to get the hell out ASAP! I appreciate your offer, and if I were a younger man, I'd grab it, but we have to be practical, and I'm not the nimble goat I once was. Photos on my desk as soon as you're through, please! I'll be waiting."

"I get the impression the tunnels are from a much later date," Billy said. "I don't see these wooden support beams being in such good condition if they'd been there nearly nine hundred years."

"Hmm. You mean Josh Williamson or someone just burrowed into the chamber by sheer luck, then carried on digging through the opposite wall without bothering to explore the chamber itself? Sounds very unlikely, and if they'd stopped to look around, you can be sure they'd have found the scroll."

"I'm not convinced both these tunnels were necessarily dug at the same time or by the same people. The materials used to seal off the tunnel leading uphill and west are definitely not as old as the scroll. It's going to be interesting if we can determine whether the tunnel was started from this end or finished here."

***

A few hours later, John Midler laid aside his magnifying lens and took off his glasses.

"These photos are all very well, but I'm not getting a *feel* for the materials. Get a message to the team in the tunnels. I need some samples. In particular, I need to examine the brickwork used in that end wall. That could give us an idea of the date it was built."

"What would be the significance of that, John?" Maureen asked.

The senior historian shook his head and sighed. "You come across so many tales and rumours, myths and legends when you research history, it's sometimes difficult to separate truth from fiction. Now, the tunnel leading off towards the river is easy enough to understand. Whether it was originally a smuggler's route in and out of the town or whether it served another purpose isn't the issue here. There are probably a couple of dozen just like it, forgotten under the streets of Liverpool alone, and in every other major port in the country. Avoiding customs and excise isn't a new game. It's been going on ever since taxation was first invented.

"It's the other tunnel that bothers me. There has to be some reason why that one was ever dug. At the moment, we don't even know where it leads or where it starts from, which, in my opinion, is more likely to be the case. I can more easily understand someone digging a shaft which slopes *downhill,* especially towards a hidden spot somewhere on the banks of a river, but starting here and working *uphill*—and in all likelihood, keeping it secret—would be far more difficult, especially if it's being dug by hand, using very basic tools.

"I've come across some rumours of tunnelling in Liverpool, other than Williamson's famous job-creation project. I just can't recall the details. I'll have to check it out on the internet this evening. For now, I say we call it a day."

***

"Good morning, Professor. What happened to *not* risking your neck?"

Emerging from the tunnel, John Midler didn't reply immediately but slid something he'd been studying intently into a specimen bag and stashed it in a canvas sack before turning to Maureen.

"Working in the field is something I really miss, and I never seem to get the chance these days—one of the drawbacks of being a lecturer. And I think what I have here will answer your question from yesterday."

He climbed out of the trench and led Maureen over to a table outside Costa, where Billy Lynch was waiting. As they approached, Billy signalled a passing barista to bring more cups.

Once they'd been served, John took out the specimen bag.

"I told you there was something nagging in the corner of my mind," he began, "and once I knew what to look for, the rest started to fall into place."

He smoothed out a few wrinkles in the plastic bag.

"This is from the brickwork sealing off the tunnel that leads inland—uphill, that is—back towards Everton. As I suspected, it's considerably younger than the chamber, dating from the mid-1600s. And the rendering is on the *inside*."

"Meaning that the tunnel must have been started uphill from here!" Maureen blurted out, then flushed crimson and apologised for the interruption.

"No need! All that does is prove once more I've got the best research assistant I could hope for," John assured her. "I heard a story when I was growing up about some kids skulking around basements along Scotland Road after a heavy night of bombing during the Blitz. They came across some tunnels, but they didn't explore too far into them because they didn't have a torch, and the walls looked a bit unsafe, but they did tell their parents when they got home.

"Unfortunately, the houses themselves were declared uninhabitable, and the whole row of terraces had to be bulldozed a day or two later."

He paused for a moment, then turned to Maureen with a curious gleam in his eye.

"Maureen, tell your dad what was happening in Liverpool in 1643."

Maureen wasn't expecting this, and for a moment, she was thrown by the apparently random non sequitur nature of the question. *Why's he asking me this?* She was about to accuse him of trying to make her appear foolish, but suddenly she realised his real motive was almost the reverse.

"My special-interest field, of course! The English Civil War!"

"Exactly, Maureen! And once again. Liverpool proved themselves true Royalist supporters!"

"An' even I've heard of Roundheads an' Cavaliers!" Billy nodded, not to be outdone.

"And you think there's some connection?" Maureen asked.

John nodded. "I did my homework on the internet last night, and there's a persistent rumour dating from that time. It claims that King Charles wanted to slide a large stash of cash through Liverpool to Ireland to buy more weapons. One of his nephews, Prince Rupert, is supposed to have been responsible for the transport of a huge fortune in gold, which somehow went missing before it reached its destination."

"And you think it's possible this bedtime story you heard as a kid might somehow be connected?" Billy was impassively rolling a cigarette as he spoke. There was no trace of scepticism or disbelief in his voice: the question was carefully phrased and posed in a serious manner.

"Prince Rupert gets an honourable mention in 1642 for his part in a 'no score draw' battle in which his Cavaliers fought the Roundheads to a standstill at the Battle of Edge Hill—that's Edge Hill, Warwickshire, by the way, not Edge Hill, Liverpool. But never mind the coincidence of the name. Prince Rupert escaped with his life, and presumably his fortune, but the gold never seems to surface again in any later accounts of the period."

"Suppose it *is* there, though," Billy said. "The gold, I mean. Would it be finders, keepers or what? Cos I'm pretty handy with a shovel meself. I wooden mind—"

"Without knowing the rules about treasure trove, Billy, I couldn't give you a definite answer, but there *would* be a guaranteed reward."

"We'd have to ask our legal eagle Steve Dunning about who actually owns the gold after all these years, assuming that's what we've found here," Maureen added.

"My instincts say, if Merseyside's recognised as an independent city state, there's a better than even chance the gold could belong to the regional Exchequer," John said with a small shrug as if this were a matter of little importance.

"Well, as long as everyone remembers who *found* the damn document in the first place!" Billy growled. "It always seems to be the lawyer types never fail to find a way of makin' money out o' situations like this!"

"I can tell you this, Billy!" John said seriously. "Steven will advise caution, but I guess that's no surprise, coming from a lawyer. However, the translation itself is very clear. Liverpool has the right to self-government, and there doesn't seem to be anything *anyone* can do about that. It seems to me there isn't a lot *anyone* can do to stop us making a legitimate claim to ownership of anything else we might dig up—and for once, I mean that literally!"

He took a sip from his coffee.

"But there's something else on my mind. Joe Saunders has been chewing my ear off this morning. He's decided to throw his hat in the ring and declare himself candidate for leader of the Synod. He asked me if I'd run as his deputy, but I told him Steve Dunning would be a better choice. I've never been that interested in politics."

Maureen nodded. Working closely with the professor for almost twelve months, she'd noticed that he was outstanding in his specialist field but often came across as a perfect example of the absent-minded academic dreamer portrayed in fiction.

"You're probably right in that. Steven's experience in the cutthroat world of the law courts and making speeches would be very useful. D'you think he'd be interested, though? Would he even have the time? Solicitors are generally rushed off their feet—especially the best ones."

"Joe seems to think he can persuade him. We'll have to wait and see."

***

Most of the staff in Steve Dunning's firm were family members. This made it much easier to delegate his workload to a deputy solicitor who already had some insight into the needs of the clients involved. Steve was formally co-opted as Joe's partner, and the short, intensive campaign of public information meetings began in earnest.

"The most important thing is making sure everyone out there has access to *all* the facts," Steve said at a late-night session on the third full day of campaigning. "Look at the last few years. Liverpool's had an average turnout of less than forty per cent in each of the last five local elections and only just crept in at forty-two per cent for the last general. Better than a lot of other towns and cities, but these aren't exactly the sort of figures we want to see for something as important as deciding if we're strong enough to make the break!

"More PR, more press and media involvement—we have to be sure we carry people with us on this! In effect, it's a single-issue referendum. There's no room for different shades of what you can call traditional party politics. It all boils down to doing what I think we all feel is the best thing for the whole community!"

In each of the ninety wards in Liverpool and also in the other political regions collectively designated Merseyside, volunteer campaigners set aside their political rosettes as they travelled the streets, doorstepping in a manner that had fallen into disuse for a number of years. Public meetings in church halls and libraries at selected times of day ensured that all the facts were presented for as many people as possible.

As the week progressed, the possibility of Liverpool declaring itself an autonomous, self-governing province within the British Isles became almost the sole topic of conversation in bus queues, hairdressers, pubs, outside school gates, more or less anywhere two or more happened to meet.

"The crunch question, as usual, is how we finance this, and we've got that covered with a combination of what we've already been granted in Objective One European funding combined with the funds Robin Stuart is making available through Core Holdings."

"True enough, Steve," Joe Saunders said amiably. "Cash backing is nearly always the deciding factor. But the way I see it, there's so much needs doing around Liverpool, so much that's been neglected, allowed to rot and fall apart."

"Things have changed a *lot* since Maggie's bully boys stuck the boot in on us!" John Midler growled. "I can still hear that auld bugger Howe talking about a 'managed decline' of Merseyside as if he'd decided we had no future whatsoever and the kindest thing to do would be to bury the town, cement over it and build high-rise flats nobody can afford on top of it!"

"Just the sort of riff-raff we'll be looking to keep out of this fair city once we have an effective passport control up and running at the Runcorn Crossing!" Joe said reassuringly.

"In one way, Joe, that's exactly the point I was trying to make," Steve interrupted. "We have to decide our priorities, some form of triage like they do in hospitals, from walking wounded through contagious diseases and up to most urgent and serious RTAs and major traumas. So many projects—how do we choose?"

Joe looked around the room before answering: it seemed clear he had a planned response ready. His opening words confirmed this.

"I've given this some thought over the last twenty-four hours, and I say don't bite the hand that feeds. According to Robin Stuart, Core Holdings has a decent-sized pot to contribute. Perhaps we should consider making the restoration of the Tramlink out to the airport our first project. It's labour-intensive, so it offers long-term employment possibilities, and God knows, we desperately need a few of *them* in this area. It'll also make JLA much more accessible. More to the point, Core Holdings stands to profit from this as well."

Steve Dunning was the first to react.

"There are several reasons that would be a good move. Maybe even several hundred! I agree with your point. The Tramlink Project is a perfect opportunity to create hundreds of long-term, secure jobs for local people—construction jobs, which anyone who's prepared to use a bit of muscle can apply for. Basic unskilled labour, no need for high levels of qualification, and it will do wonders for our employment stats.

"Don't get me wrong. Construction work is going to be a very important aspect of our local economy, both in the short term and for the foreseeable future as we build on the goods and services we provide both for ourselves and to have something to export to the rest of the UK and further afield. But look at it this way. We have a large pool of local people out there, available to start work tomorrow as long as we have the jobs to offer them, and anyone who's been out of work for any length of time is going to jump at the chance."

"It's also good PR," John Midler added. "Being able to kick off as a self-governing state with some independent funding already available is all very well, but having a range of *real* jobs to offer right from the start is even better. And with the amount of arable and pasture land in the region, there's no reason we can't feed ourselves and still have a surplus to sell on."

A number of voices were raised as plans, proposals and ideas for strengthening the new region's finances were aired around the room. Joe Saunders sat quietly and allowed the delegates to let off steam for a minute or two before he stood up and banged on the table to regain control of the meeting.

"As chair, I have to insist that we carry out our business in an orderly fashion! I'm grateful for the input from each and every one of you. It means I don't have to think of *everything* myself!

"But we need some formal structure, so I'm suspending this meeting as of now, and we'll reconvene in the morning. Can everyone be here for ten o'clock? Good!

"Now, I assume someone took notes? Thanks, Mo! I knew I could rely on you. Can you also be available tomorrow morning? Professor Midler's already been co-opted, and you've been involved from the very first, so you'd make an excellent PA—at least while we get started. Maybe I can persuade the prof to release you for a couple of months..."

CHAPTER SEVEN

"I'M IN WILLIAMSON Square, Liverpool city centre. It's eight a.m. on a bright but not especially warm September day and there's such a crowd, it's difficult to move! Let's find out why so many people are here in a city which this week announced its intention of seceding from the United Kingdom and managing its own affairs!"

The outside-broadcast camera pulled away from the BBC reporter and panned to a wider shot of the scene. Two more cameras had been positioned on the edges of the plaza, one high on the roof of the Playhouse Theatre commanding a bird's eye view. The unit producer cued in a shot from the overhead camera, sending the same TV image to several million living rooms the length and breadth of Britain: one of a patient, orderly queue three or four wide, stretching along three and a half sides of the open square before disappearing around a corner. A strategically placed mobile camera, currently parked on the opposite side of the square, showed that the queue continued past the Sayer's cafeteria on the corner and as far as the pedestrianised Church Street about two hundred metres further on.

"There are reports of similar scenes all around Liverpool this morning, all caused by the same local news item, all of them focusing on their nearest Job Centre. It's still almost an hour until Job Centres all over the country are due to open their doors, but these people don't seem to mind the wait. I'm going to ask a few people why they're here today."

The reporter moved away from the *Superlambanana* sculpture she'd chosen for background fill while delivering this spiel and approached the front of the queue outside the still-closed Job Centre doors.

"Can I ask you, sir, why did you decide to come here today, and why did you come so early?"

The three men at the front of the queue clearly belonged together as a group: the reporter was about to ask if they were friends when she noticed how closely they resembled each other, and realised they had to be siblings of some degree, probably brothers.

The man in the centre—the man she'd chosen to address—answered her as spokesman for the group, sparing her the embarrassment she was feeling. "Me 'n' me bros was out an' had a few scoops after what they mentioned on the telly last night about work—guaranteed proper jobs!—for anyone prepared t' pick up a spade an' use it!"

"An' the buildin' trade's been quiet f'r a while now..." Brother Two interrupted.

"Quiet?! S'been dead fer years!" the third said scornfully. "But we're not afraid to put in the hours, nor the muscle. We'll make a go of it, see if we don't!"

"So you went out for a drink, and decided...?"

"No, we decided first, *then* we went out," explained the spokesman patiently as if dealing with a child.

"We were pretty sure it'd be an immediate start, so we got our last night o' serious drinkin' out o' th' way!" Bro Two added in what seemed an extremely reasonable, persuasive tone.

"An' when we were finished, it seemed like too much bother t' go home f'r an hour or two an' come back out."

"An' there was no buses, so it was peg it or gerrina cab, an' we didn't fancy that!"

"So we come 'ere instead, an' found we was first in the queue."

"Yeah, but only *just*!"

The reporter's head snapped from one brother to another as they constantly cut across each other like a well-rehearsed stage act. Other jobseekers close enough to hear what was being said began to laugh and offer further comments and wisecracks, but it was all good-natured. The reporter's professional control of an interview situation was beginning to slip but was salvaged when the door of the Job Centre was suddenly opened, and a clerk began to give out tickets.

"Oi! I come 'ere cos I was promised a job, norra bleedin' lottery ticket!" shouted one unidentified voice from several rows back.

"If this turns out t' be another gov'ment snow job, promises, promises an' all o' them lies..." The rest of the sentence was lost under a sudden, unmistakable rumble of discontented voices. As the happy, positive mood of the crowd appeared to waver on the cusp of a bipolar switch and possible violence, another member of the Job Centre staff appeared at the door. He was suited and booted, suggesting senior management. More significantly, he had a microphone and carried a small speaker unit under one arm. He clearly intended to be heard, but would the now-restless crowd *listen*?

"Good morning, everyone! I hope I haven't upset anyone by not using the usual form of greeting, 'ladies and gentlemen', but I can see the gents are in the majority today!"

Even distorted through the microphone and portable speaker, the light touch of humour in his voice came across loud and clear. It had an immediate, positive effect on the queue as the tension dissipated: there were a number of low but audible chuckles from the crowd. The manager continued.

"We were expecting a good response to yesterday's job news, but I'm sorry to say we hadn't anticipated quite so many clients and so early in the day!

"I've asked my staff to distribute numbered tickets, and I can assure you all that everyone who wants to speak to a jobs advisor *will* be seen. This Job Centre and every other Job Centre in Liverpool will stay open today until the final client has been interviewed.

"Once you've been given a ticket, you won't need to stand in a queue. Just stay close enough and listen for your number. We'll try to call them in blocks of ten at a time, so we don't get overcrowded. Any of the vendors in Williamson Square will supply free hot drinks to anyone who shows them a ticket."

This gesture was well received and sparked a spontaneous, sincere cheer from the assembled crowd. The queue swiftly dissolved into knots and groups of threes and fours who made a beeline for the nearest coffee stall, café or restaurant. The BBC reporter had by now had enough time to recover her aplomb and succeeded in cobbling together a positive, polished voiceover résumé of the scenes the camera had captured.

***

The main evening news had reached the point at which someone makes a fool of himself, attempting to second-guess the next day's weather. Joe Saunders muted the sound and turned to face the guests he'd invited to his office.

"It's been the same in every Liverpool Job Centre today. They say they've been rushed off their feet, and none of them closed at the usual time."

"But did everyone who signed on get seen?" John Midler asked.

"More to the point, did everyone who wanted a job get one?" said Robin.

"No need to worry on that score. There's plenty of manpower out there, and these first few weeks, we'll need every man we can hire for the donkey-work phase of the Tramlink Project, digging down to the buried tracks.

"Some of them have a decent amount of experience in construction, according to their CVs. They'll be going out over the weekend with a couple of engineers to drive the route from city centre to JLA. It's a busy road, and there's going to be some disruption once we start digging, but that can't be helped. We need to get down to where the original rails are still in place, and all we can do is complete the job as quickly and as efficiently as possible."

***

Monday morning dawned bright and clear. The derelict site of the Liverpool Garden Festival, which had lain unloved, unwanted and brutally vandalised for over twenty years, had been commissioned as a combined storage depot and parking zone for the Tramlink Project.

"Ninety acres should be more than enough for all the works vehicles and still leave plenty for employee parking."

Robin had picked up an eerily accurate feel for just how much space was needed to park and store large vehicles, a sixth sense he'd acquired over the years he'd spent developing airports and similar large-scale projects.

"You sweet-talked someone or other into letting you have it in double-quick time, all the same!" John countered. Robin hesitated, then nodded.

"One small catch," he said. "As you seem to have guessed, there *was* a sweetener involved, but nothing dodgy, nothing underhand. I said that when we've finished the Tramlink, we'll restore it as close as we can to what it was like when it was used as the festival site, and I shook hands on a target date of June next year for the handover."

"Nine months? You think we can build this bloody railroad—"

"Tramlink."

"Same difference, Robin. Let's not split hairs."

"Relax, Joe! We've got the manpower. It's not as if we're building the line from scratch." Robin put an arm around Joe's shoulder and sat him at the table.

"Look at the positives we've got going for us already," he said as he booted up his laptop, "Even I was surprised. We can skip past all the paperwork generated by route-planning permissions and land acquisitions. Then there's laying out the route—that's already there, in place once we dig it out. We won't be laying foundations, bedding in each length of track, and off the top of my head, that's just a few of the things we *don't* have to do in order to see this job through."

Joe hadn't seen this side of Robin Stuart's business acumen before. The down-to-earth, common-sense logic of his arguments couldn't be faulted, and Robin wasn't finished yet.

"It just so happens that only a mile or so down the road, there's a stockpile of rail track bought expressly for this project, which has been rusting away in a corner of Garston docks since before the festival site was even opened. And before you ask, that was a figure of speech. I've had a gander at the tracks over the weekend. They're *not* rusting away. In fact, they're in good nick considering how long they've been in storage."

John Midler had been sitting listening to all this and feeling a bit of a fifth wheel, not qualified to comment on practical matters of this nature. Now, suddenly, he stirred as an idea occurred to him.

"You talk of handing over the site and also about attempting to make some running repairs before you do so. I'm assuming you're going to have other projects for the navvy gangs to carry out when this Tramlink has been built?"

"General idea, John! There's the whole of the docks to look at, for starters, both sides of the river, naturally, and there's many years of neglect to put right."

"My thoughts exactly. So, how about having another team, with a different set of skills, all trained up and ready to take over? A team of landscape gardeners, maybe? Right now is the start of a new academic year. We could fast-track students through one of the higher education colleges around town—they'd be qualified by next summer."

The pebble John had tossed into the pool with his suggestion appealed to Joe and to Robin for different reasons. As an experienced politician and passionate for anything which promised to be beneficial for his hometown, Joe could see the positive PR value of a second opportunity to reduce the local unemployment statistics, with the creation of genuine, long-term job prospects for large numbers of local people.

Robin was less interested in the positive spin that could be gained from how the PR element of the situation was handled. For him, the most important thing was the way in which one job could create two or more. A bowling ball flashed before his mind's eye, striking the lead pin squarely, toppling both the pins immediately behind and scoring a clean strike of all ten skittles by setting in motion an unstoppable chain of events.

Robin's vision ranged further. His mind's eye captured and built upon scenes of the dry docks at Cammell Laird filled once more with ships of all sizes being built or repaired while a flotilla of cruise liners and cargo ships competed for quay space along the northern bank of the river. High above the city, he seemed to soar, riding on the shoulders of a gigantic Liver bird patrolling the skies above her native town. For one lucid, intoxicating, almost terrifying instant, he saw clearly every available square foot of the northern docks complex built upon, with full production at each and every business that had been established north of the Pier Head, stretching as far as Formby Point without encroaching on the protected woodlands or threatening the world-famous Royal Birkdale golf course. Suddenly, the possibility of full employment in Liverpool—and jobs to spare for anyone prepared to apply for them—didn't seem quite so unlikely.

CHAPTER EIGHT

There were a few minor hitches and delays on the first day of operations. These could, for the most part, be excused as an inevitable part of a bedding-down process due to the unique nature of the work and the scale of the operation.

What impressed Robin more than anything else was the fact that in seven days of three eight-hour shifts involving over five thousand construction workers, no time had been lost through accidents or injuries.

"Nobody's rung in sick, either! Not so much as a sore throat or the perennial excuse of a dodgy curry!" Maureen confirmed as she looked back through the desk diary to check the notes she'd made each day during the first week. She'd put in five twelve-hour shifts herself, so most of the diary notes were in her own minuscule but perfect handwriting. There were shorter but equally efficient notes here and there from the two part-time women who manned the office phone when Maureen was off duty.

All three shifts had been informed that their first pay packets would be handed out at noon on Friday, in acknowledgement of the fact that many of them had been out of work for some time and would have found it difficult to work the traditional week in hand.

"We've decided to pay this first wage in cash to give anyone who hasn't already got a bank account time to set one up. Come along to the depot any time after noon to collect. You've earned it, every penny!"

Robin Stuart had repeated this statement several times to each of the shifts to be as sure as he could that everyone was aware of the special arrangements for the first payday. On the day itself, outside caterers had been hired to set up a snacks and soft drinks marquee next to the double Portakabin, which served as the Tramlink office.

The press and media were formally invited to cover the occasion, although they had never been far away all week. They'd been allowed to film every aspect of the work and to speak to anyone who'd agree to give them a few moments to share their thoughts and impressions of the project. The only proviso was an absolute insistence that health and safety regulations were not compromised: the success of this was evidenced by the lack of accident reports that Maureen and other senior members of the management team had already noted. Robin could be forgiven the praise he lavished on the whole workforce in a brief speech he made just before the pay office opened, although it was intended for the eyes and ears of the TV and radio reporters rather than the navvy crews themselves.

He had a further surprise up his sleeve.

"We can learn a great deal about ways of improving our work environment and practices from some of our European neighbours," he said, looking over a crowded, cheerful assembly in the refreshments marquee.

"Friday was always payday many years ago, before bank accounts were even invented. And even today, the working week still ends at midday on Fridays in parts of Europe. Unfortunately, time and targets won't allow us to do this every week. However, today, as a thank-you for the incredible work you've all done in getting us off to a flying start, you can clock off once you've received your pay packet. Have a great weekend!"

For two or three impossibly long seconds, you could have heard a pin drop. An audible gasp followed as the entire workforce drew a breath into their astonished lungs: one voice from somewhere towards the rear of the tent was a nanosecond faster to react.

"Cheers, Boss!"

A roar of approval swelled from the throats of every employee, captured in film and on the microphones of the press and TV reporters, echoing back and forth without losing intensity, accompanied by applause and snatches of song. Robin tried several times to restore a semblance of order, but his audience was determined to show their appreciation of this most unexpected gesture.

Eventually, the applause and cheers diminished as the audience's collective throats became hoarse and dry. Robin seized the initiative and called Joe Saunders to the mic.

"We mustn't forget someone else who played a very important part in getting the Tramlink Project off the drawing board. He isn't actually paying you all from his own personal bank account, but if you'll listen for a moment, he *will* tell you how far we've progressed in our first week, and then we'll go through a few practical details, which will help us to get your pay packets to you as quickly and as securely as possible. Feel free to raid the snacks and drinks. My nose tells me someone's also lit a barbecue out there, somewhere..."

***

"Two *miles*? In the first week of ops? Jaysus, Billy, you kept *that* under your hat!" Steve Dunning's courtroom Oxford English delivery faltered momentarily. He took a breath and continued, "I don't doubt your word, but are you sure of the figures? You must be nearly halfway to Garston already!"

Even without the advantage of being involved from the outset, Billy Lynch would have been an automatic choice for works foreman in most people's eyes: his track record was all the recommendation he ever needed. He nodded a confirmation of the first week's progress report, glanced at a vacant chair and raised one eyebrow.

"No need to wait for an invitation, Mr. Lynch. Please, sit down."

Billy pulled a sheaf of papers from his pocket but didn't need to refer to them. Instead, he placed them on the table.

"The figures are all in there, but to put them in context, working around-the-clock shifts has helped enormously. There isn't a lot of domestic property on the section of road from Jericho Lane heading for the Garston Interchange, so we haven't disturbed anyone's sleep by working through the night. That's something we'll have to deal with when it crops up. We'll be going through residential areas pretty soon, but we'll cross that bridge as and when.

"It helped to have some accurate schematics, which told us to within centimetres where to find the tracks and how deep they'd be. Every section of rail so far has been in good condition—no rust, no obvious damage, no sign of warping or twisting. You'll have to get a rail-track engineer of some sort to look them over. I'm no expert, so I couldn't comment on the condition of the tracks, especially when public safety's going to be an issue."

"Thanks for the reminder, Mr. Lynch. We'll make a note of that."

Maureen was scribbling notes at lightning speed. Billy knew his daughter had taken the trouble to learn an effective Pitman shorthand before beginning her university studies, much to the amusement of her classmates, who had instead chosen to rely on the internet and the latest cutting-edge technology. They can't do *that* with a memory stick, Billy thought to himself and continued his report.

"Two miles is correct, by the way, all bar a couple of feet. It might be as much as a hundred yards short of the distance, but no more. The digging has been easy, the weather's been kind, and digging up the central reservation means we're not hindering traffic—or perhaps I should turn that around and say, the traffic isn't hindering us!"

"That *is* good news!" Steve Dunning commented. "We can use this to give ourselves a pat on the back in the Considerate Constructors' nominations—and it's also good PR in a more immediate, local sense. We need to have the people most affected onside.

"What can we expect in week two, Mr. Lynch? Any problems you're aware of?"

"Nothing other than being called Mr. Lynch. I'm half-expecting t'see yiz put on a judge's wig! Billy, please!

"We'll have to trim back the twenty-four-seven shift pattern as we get closer to peoples' houses, and we'll also have to be careful as we pass the cricket club. Lancashire are playing all their home matches in Liverpool this year while Old Trafford's being refurbished." He shrugged. "For the moment, nothing else comes to mind," he concluded.

Steve's mobile beeped discreetly: in the temporary silence, it sounded louder than it normally would. Steve frowned and apologised.

"Sorry, I thought I'd turned it off. Hello? ... Marie? I'm in a meeting, I can't—" He stopped mid-sentence. A continuous squawk suggested a long stream of information being passed on: the expressions chasing across Steve's face suggested the information was not positive.

"Thank you, Marie. Sorry if I was a bit short! Yes, you did the right thing to call me straight away. Keep a watching brief... and in this case, yes, I mean that literally!"

He ended the call and addressed the room. Suddenly there was no trace of the casual, relaxed tone of voice he'd used at the meeting up to this point. The man on his feet was the professional solicitor Steven Dunning LLB.

"Joe, is there a television in this office? BBC News Channel, right away..."

Local and national media coverage of events around Liverpool had intensified as the first week progressed, following the navvy crews at a discreet distance.

Angie Ross was on screen. As she spoke, the camera panned back to a middle-distance shot of the Aigburth Road junction with Jericho Lane. There were no vehicles in the shot: instead, the camera revealed a large crowd filling the carriageway from kerb to central reservation, approaching the camera from the direction of town centre.

"...about four hundred, perhaps more. They don't seem to be organised in any way or by anyone. The group was first reported gathering near the lake in Sefton Park and has grown rapidly as they moved through Aigburth Vale. They're heading towards the Tramlink work site but don't appear to be heading for any specific target. Some are carrying bricks, staffs and other weapons. There are reports coming in of vandalism and looting from shops and private houses along the route. We'll keep you informed as we get more details. This is Angie Ross, reporting for Radio Merseyside and BBC outside broadcasting."

"That's our Angie. A real pro—never misses a trick!" muttered Kevin Wyatt, torn between envy of his radio counterpart for being on the scene mingled with a certain amount of relief that he was in a safer environment. He'd been out in tense 'mob scenes' several times and knew from experience that they could easily turn nasty, especially if alcohol was involved. And if there *was* some looting going on, the off-licences were usually the first target for any unruly rabble of protestors.

Billy was out of the Portakabin and sprinting for a JCB parked close to the perimeter fence of the compound.

"Billy! What the hell?!" Joe shouted.

"He's protecting himself!"

Maureen knew exactly what her dad was planning and laid a restraining hand on Kevin's arm when he made to follow the foreman's lead.

"Let him have his head! Let Billy take the controls of a JCB and he's untouchable. He can make a rig sit up and beg if it suits his purpose."

Billy vaulted into the driver cage: the engine roared to life as his butt hit the seat and he spun it on the proverbial sixpence. Gravel flew from the enormous rear wheels as he floored the throttle and headed out of the gates. The front scoop was raised above the cab, resembling the gaping mouth of a furious cobra as he turned right and accelerated towards the vanguard of the advancing mob, now less than two hundred yards from the compound. The powerful engines drowned their chants and catcalls. They slowed, then came to a stuttering halt, blocking the whole carriageway. A few tools were raised and shaken in token gestures of defiance. A few optimistic bricks were tossed long before the JCB was close enough to be in range, but Billy ignored them and showed no intention of stopping or even slowing down. As he closed to under fifty yards from their front rank, they began to fall away in a belated attempt to get out of his way.

The navvy crew had parted to allow the foreman free passage and flowed into a solid phalanx, trotting behind the site workhorse with their spades, picks and assorted implements of destruction over their shoulders in a military full port. The would-be assailants had been concentrating on the bellowing, larger-than-life mechanical monster bearing down on them and totally failed to notice the danger following in its wake.

Billy changed to a lower gear scant feet from the panicking, disorganised rabble as they dropped their stolen cans of cheap lager and scurried haphazardly in every direction. He floored the throttle once more as he double-declutched and carved a rubber-burning 'doughnut', gravel spewing under his handbrake turn.

This had the inevitable effect of spreading utter and complete intimidation. As one, the mob turned tail and began to run, all thoughts of mindless violence forgotten. Billy stood up in the cab, towering far above the retreating tide of the city's flotsam and jetsam like a modern-day Finn MacCool. The image was reinforced when he lost his Scouse veneer and began to curse and insult them fluently in his native Gaelic. Meanwhile, the navvy crew flowed around the JCB, intent on delivering a healthy portion of summary justice.

Joe Saunders and the remainder of the discussion group sat open-mouthed, watching the scenes being relayed on the television screen. Angie Ross had fallen silent, but any commentary of what was happening on screen would have been superfluous.

"This looks like it could turn ugly," muttered Kevin.

"Why aren't the camera crews moving in closer? They're not keeping up with—"

"I don't think they can. Look!"

The current screenshot—presumably from a handheld camera—had become shaky and disoriented as if the operator was finding it difficult to hold a steady footing. The shot cut to a different camera, which showed Angie Ross standing alone outside the works compound gates.

"We seem to be having difficulty with our reporting of what's happening a few hundred yards away from here. I can tell you that a large crowd, which, until a few moments ago, was heading for the Tramlink depot, has been turned away by construction workers. From where I stand, I can see that one group of construction workers has split away from the main party and has turned around. They've linked arms and formed a solid wall of bodies, denying camera crews the opportunity to record whatever is happening further down the road. A number of trucks and other vehicles are being driven onto the carriageway, presumably to reinforce the barricade. I'm going to see

if there's anyone at the site depot who can give us some information about this unexpected development."

She tucked away her wireless mic and sashayed across the puddles and coarse gravel of the parking area. The camera she'd been addressing followed her every inch of the way. Despite the straightforward angle, the cameraman wasn't quick enough to identify the person who opened the door a split second before she arrived.

"Kevin! What's happening?"

Angie Ross nodded her acknowledgement of the existence of the other people in the room, but she seemed most interested in hearing a fellow professional's assessment.

"Looks like the navvy crew has decided to block the media from recording events, but figuring out what's happening off-camera isn't exactly rocket science! They were shown the error of their ways, and I think that's all that needs to be said on the subject."

***

Billy Lynch dodged the bullet yet again. Angie Ross had a reputation for coaxing information out of many people, particularly those who might have any number of valid reasons for saying as little as possible about their private lives, but it appeared she'd reached an impasse.

"Perhaps you could at least inform our viewers whether the emergency services were needed—or not?"

"Miss Ross, I hope you're not suggesting that there was a degree of...unnecessary *violence* used by my workforce this afternoon?"

"Can you answer the question, please, Mr Lynch!" She was closer than anyone had ever seen to losing her professional sangfroid in an interview. Billy had answered every question put to him about the navvy gang's confrontation with the would-be troublemakers without hesitation, and with a convincingly innocent expression in his eyes, but she knew he wasn't telling her the whole truth, and she also knew that Billy knew that she knew. She hated not being in total control of any situation.

He caught the look in her eye and appeared to offer an olive branch.

"I can tell you that ambulances weren't necessary. Those who hurt themselves by stumbling and falling as they ran were all perfectly capable of reporting to A and E as walking wounded and under their own steam."

"Why were the media prevented from following the group which was dealing with the demonstrators?"

"Can I just say that, to the best of my knowledge, no group has yet claimed responsibility for organising any demonstration? So until we're told something different, it's to be assumed that this was a spontaneous event. Not organised, not in any sense of the word."

"But there was no question of anyone trying to prevent the media carrying out their indisputable right to observe and report upon the news as it happens! That is, after all, one of the major benefits of living in a free, open and democratic society!"

Angie's eyes narrowed with suspicion. Billy was getting the better of the exchange, but even with all her years' experience of the rough-and-tumble of interviewing the slipperiest of politicians and the smartest criminals, she had no handle on Billy. It's like battling the wind, she thought. She'd already been blown some considerable distance from her pre-planned course. This interview wasn't going the way she'd intended.

She paused a fraction of a second too long before firing off a further question intended to distract her jousting adversary, as she now thought of him. Billy beat her to the punch.

"When I got a brief phone call warning me that there might be a problem developing on the approach roads, I left the planning meeting I was attending and went to assess the situation myself."

Billy had always had a keen sense for the mot juste, and his confidence was clearly growing with every second. He took charge and began to run the interview. His diction had already shed almost every trace of his Irish background and Scouse upbringing: his accent was now indistinguishable from Angie Ross's BBC-approved Oxbridge speech patterns.

"As soon as I arrived, I could see that something had to be done immediately. If I may be allowed to paraphrase, to my mind, there was a clear and present danger of someone being injured, and so as the foreman, and therefore responsible for public safety, I instructed the navvy gang to place themselves *between* the media crew and the oncoming crowd, whose intentions were not clear at the time. I couldn't be certain that their intentions were hostile, of course, but in the circumstances, I believe it was a reasonable assumption, and subsequent events seem to have confirmed that my decision was justified. In reality, it was a basic health and safety issue, and I'd like to praise *all* the men on duty this afternoon for the part they played in whichever group they were attached to."

He's done it again! Angie thought to herself furiously. He's gone and stolen the limelight: how *dare* he! Belatedly, she realised that Billy had finished speaking, and the silence on the recording tape was going to need some pruning before it went out on TV.

"Thank you, Billy Lynch. It's good to know that simple health and safety standards are there to protect us all. This is Angie Ross, in Liverpool. Now back to the studio..."

***

"So what *did* happen off camera?" Kevin demanded as the deftly edited news clip dissolved back to the BBC News studio for a summary of the rest of the day's headlines and the latest guesswork about the next day's weather.

Billy stared back at him and shook his head.

"I wasn't *there*. You can't quote anything I tell you. It would only be hearsay at best! If I told you anything, I'd be breaking the trust my members have placed in me by telling me things in confidence."

Kevin raised his empty hands above his head. "No names, no pack drill, no notes, no quotes! You have my word on that. This is strictly off the record, between friends."

"Fair enough. Mo seems to think you can be trusted, which has to count for something." Billy looked around the others gathered in Joe Saunders' living room, waiting to add their own thoughts and assessment of the local news item, which had been promoted to a three-minute spot on the national news.

"There was a few strong words spoken—or so I'm told!—and it seems that some of the protestors didn't understand what they were being told. They had to have a few things...explained to them."

"And these explanations somehow caused panic and alarm, and a number of the protestors needed hospital treatment for the injuries they sustained as they... ?"

"Stumbled on the uneven footpaths?" John suggested on Billy's behalf. "Shocking business. The council really ought to be doing something about it—I heard something about local residents turning up uninvited, with mops and buckets, cleaning up as soon as the streets emptied..."

"I heard that too, John," Jo said. "I'll see if I can find out a few more details when the council meets tomorrow morning." He rose, bringing this informal and unofficial sub-committee meeting to a natural close.

CHAPTER NINE

IN LESS THAN a month, the Tramlink track had been laid along the A561 to the spur road that served John Lennon Airport. A few days of exceptionally heavy rain slowed the overall progress, but it highlighted a drainage problem which nobody had known about, and they had the opportunity to rectify the problem while the excavations were taking place.

Work along the final mile from the dual carriageway to the airport was carried out for the most part during hours of darkness, causing the least possible disruption to flights. As a further bonus, JRK managed to bully and sweet-talk a number of local and national bodies into providing extra funding, which in turn meant that more workers could be hired. Nobody was entirely sure how it came about, but the crews soon adopted the term 'navigators' to describe either themselves or the job they performed. It was clear that they wore this particular badge with pride.

"What's the timetable for the rolling stock, Jim? How soon can Cammell Laird deliver?" Joe Saunders wanted to know. It was part of his daily routine to call in at the Tramlink Project and check on progress.

Jim removed his hard hat and pulled out his mobile. "I haven't had the chance to call them yet this morning… Hi, Trev. Joe's asking for a progress report on the earliest date you can let us have at least one tram. We'd like to start testing… Really? That *is* good news. I'll pass it on!

"There are two at the stage of being fitted. Upholstery, chrome work, curtains, the last few details to make them customer friendly, so to speak. He reckons he can have them shipped by Tuesday at the latest—on barges, if you think we can lift them with a jib crane or through the Tunnel, which will probably take longer. Any preference?"

Joe didn't answer immediately: he appeared to be thinking through the pros and cons very carefully.

"I hadn't thought about delivery options," he admitted, "but since the dry dock's near as dammit exactly opposite the airport, perhaps that would be best. Using the Tunnel and driving through town with an abnormal-load transporter is bound to create traffic problems, especially during what's laughingly referred to as 'rush hour'. I'd say let's opt for the barge, even if coming through town would be a great photoshoot and hand us the opportunity for some good PR! But I have a feeling that bringing them over Runcorn Bridge might actually be quicker than trundling through the Tunnel and the narrow streets of city centre."

***

At one o'clock that Friday afternoon, a hooter brayed. All the navigators completed the tasks they had in hand before packing their personal gear and heading for the marquee that was their refreshment centre and doubled as the pay office. The time-honoured convention of paying wages 'over the barrel' had been modified so that each man received a printed payslip rather than actual cash in hand, but the custom had found general approval from the workforce. It was as good a reason as any other to have a chat and a soft drink to take the dust off the throat before heading for the showers and the nearest hostelry.

Jim Burke, in sweatshirt and jeans rather than business suit and tie, stood patiently in line to be served at one of these. He wasn't exactly trying to pass himself off as a navigator: in truth, he would probably have found it difficult to explain why he opted to do this when he got the opportunity on a Friday, but he felt he had an obligation to understand what made the team tick, sense any potential problems before they became an issue. His face was known amongst the crews, but he tried to visit different pubs each time and kept a low profile.

The pub he chose that Friday was a few bus stops from the airport and had a decent cellar of real ales: it also boasted a superb chef and an excellent choice of meals. Naturally, it was crowded, including a large number of hungry navigators enjoying the sunshine on the patio, where they could smoke while waiting for the Friday special menu, which for most of them was a variation on the fish-and-chips theme.

He took a long pull from his Liverpool One bitter, appreciating the slightly unexpected lemony back taste. Someone with a pint in one hand and a set of cutlery in the other was at his side, optimistically looking around for a non-existent empty seat at a table. He didn't seem too concerned but shrugged and grinned.

"I guess a vacant table was too much to hope for, but at least the beer's drinkable. I really like this idea of an early dart on Fridays, too. It makes the weekend seem much more than just three or four hours longer!"

"Yeah, I agree with you there," Jim replied, unwilling to admit his management role but reluctant to deceive by silent omission. He was relieved when the as-yet unidentified crew member took another healthy gulp of his beer and changed the subject.

"'Nuther day or two, we'll be signing off on this Tramlink. You intend stayin' on?"

The way the question had been phrased, Jim had no qualms of conscience, answering it with hundred per cent honesty and certainty.

"I'm in this for the long haul. I think the bridge sounds an interesting challenge."

"Yeah, better than rebuildin' the Seaforth docks. I reckon that's what I'll be signing up for, too! An' if it's true, that they're really gonna set up passport control to keep the riff-raff out, so much the better!"

A waiter came out on the patio carrying a loaded plate. "Fifty-seven."

"That's me!" Jim's companion emptied his glass and took the cutlery out of his shirt pocket. "Good talking' t' you, mate. Have a good one!" He disappeared indoors, following the waiter's lead. Inwardly, Jim was more than a little relieved to avoid having to lie—or at least dissemble—before such a genuine, friendly guy.

***

"I'm telling you, the mood on the shop floor—the chatter, the general tone, what the men are talking about on their tea breaks—is very, very positive."

After his brief encounter with a single, unnamed hand, Jim had drifted around the pub and struck up casual conversations with a number of other people. Every conversation followed similar lines to the first chance encounter.

"The idea of building a passport control and customs facilities on the new river crossing appealed to every navigator I spoke to. They *all* thought it was highly amusing!"

The Usual Suspects—John Kirwan, Paul Freeman, Dominic Ion and his sister Nuala—were holding an unofficial cabinet meeting around Jim's kitchen table.

"We can start winding down operations at JLA next week," Jim said, "so we can offer an extension of contract—or whatever you want to call it—for anyone who wants to transfer to the Runcorn–Widnes crossing.

"Paul, I want you to see if it's possible to set up a free shuttle bus to serve the new construction sites at Widnes and Runcorn. Maybe we could section off a part of the parking area and operate a park-and-ride service from South Parkway."

"Mmm. I'm wondering if it might be an even better solution to park a couple of Portakabins on both sites, use them as dorms. If we did that, we'd also have twenty-four-seven security on site."

"Dom, crunch me some numbers. I like the sound of Paul's idea. Nuala, can you do some phoning around, help your brother with the costings?"

***

"Ever done any bridge-building work?"

"'Fraid not."

"You're in good company—not much call for bridges in recent years. Still, I have to ask just on the off chance there's a few amongst the crews have some experience. You were with the Tramlink job from the very start, I see, so I've got your recent work stats. Job's yours, if you're up for it?"

This conversation, with a few variations, was being replicated at a large number of temporary interview desks spaced out around a sports hall in Garston village, hired for the day. Very few of the familiar faces from the navigator crews who had completed the Tramlink within the target time and *under* budget had not resurfaced to sign on for the river crossing, but as he gazed around the room, Paul decided that there was still plenty of time for more job applicants to arrive. Every seat was occupied by men patiently waiting their turn to be interviewed, and it was still early afternoon. He'd already interviewed half a dozen who hadn't been involved in the Tramlink job but had applied this time around on the strength of a word-of-mouth recommendation from a friend. He had no doubts that this would be a common thread when he checked with the other interviewers at the end of the day.

The next candidate who eased himself into the chair opposite had no bridge-building experience either, but several years of cutting peat and building defensive dykes to hold back the waters of Irish fens and bogs would prove as useful as his superb physical fitness and willingness to work.

"How did you hear of the job?"

"Sure, me cousin rang and told me. He was on y'r Tramlink Project."

A few keystrokes confirmed the cousin's existence, and an excellent attendance record.

"See you on Monday, Mr. Mullins. Be at South Parkway by eight a.m., please."

"We're back in Liverpool again this morning. Or, to be correct, just *outside* the city limits but comfortably within the region known as Merseyside.

"This seems to be the place to follow for good news, in recent weeks!"

Angie Ross was wearing a ridiculous custard-yellow hard hat which a shrivelled shrimp of a health-and-safety exec had insisted she wear to report from the Mersey Gateway site just above Runcorn. She detested not being in total control of everything, from the smallest details of her personal life to the glossy, airbrushed perfection of her professional image. Nothing would have given her greater pleasure than eating the grinning H&S exec alive before breakfast, but to make a live broadcast from the mudflats on the Widnes side of the Mersey, she was forced to go by the rulebook.

"Behind me, you can see the first shift of the day starting work on the £530 million Mersey Gateway bridge. When it's finished, it will also become one of the new customs, excise and passport control facilities, which will process road and rail traffic entering the autonomous Merseyside region from the South and East of the United Kingdom."

An off-camera hand signal directed the camera to pan 180 degrees slowly, clockwise out over the river. Framed by the high double arches of the existing road/rail connection downstream from the present location, a brace of tugs could be seen towing a barge from the Cammell Laird shipyard. The river ran still, the quiet time between tides: the early morning sky was the palest powder blue, a perfect backdrop for the vehicle secured centreboard. It had been finished in the purple and gold livery of Liverpool City Council: even chained down, it seemed to chafe at the bit, anxious to run free.

"Downriver, we can see the first of four tram units being delivered from the shipbuilding yard Cammell Laird, who have diversified and adapted their engineering skills to build the rolling stock for the Tramlink Project. The remaining coaches are near completion and are expected to be available within the week. In the meantime, this one will be undergoing trials and testing on the new-laid tracks between the airport and city centre."

The cameraman took his cue, scripted by Angie Ross, and panned slowly north, pausing for a dramatic shot with John Lennon Airport in the foreground and the distinctive twin towers of the Liver Building filling out the frame, surmounted by the iconic Liver birds. He counted slowly to five, then continued his sweep along the shoreline until he had Angie's head and shoulders back in shot. He was acutely conscious of how short his career as a cameraman might be if his hand slipped, revealing the fact that Angie Ross was slowly sinking into the muddy foreshore and the three-sizes-too-big wellingtons she was wearing were engulfed almost to the knee. No matter how quickly she signed off, she was going to need the assistance of at least two or three 'beefsteaks' from the construction site to haul her out of the mire.

The BBC cameras didn't catch the scene as the coach was smoothly transferred from the barge to the pier that existed purely to service John Lennon Airport from the riverside. Thirty or forty volunteers—most of them with some practical experience as stevedores and dock hands—had opted to remain at the JLA site to perform this operation while the remaining navigators transferred to Runcorn and Widnes in shuttle buses to break ground on the Mersey Gateway Project.

"Tell you what, this liftin' gear makes it a doddle t'get the load ashore!" one old-timer commented. He was close to retirement age, one of the few who'd served his time on the docks when every vessel was loaded and unloaded by hand, and his experience had proved invaluable several times already during the few crucial minutes needed to transfer the load from barge to quayside.

"Did you actually handle this sort of cargo manually, Gramps?" one of the younger men asked. The nickname was used automatically and without disrespect: if anything, quite the reverse.

"If it wasn't nailed or welded in place, we found a way o' movin' it!" the ancient replied. "All y' needed was yer 'ook, an' keep yer wits about yiz!"

The carriage swung gently thirty feet over the heads of the crew: all they had to do was guide the carriage by leaning into ropes, which had been secured to strategic points along the coachwork to keep it in line and level. Inch by inch, it sank towards the spur of track laid along the pier to make it possible to transport bulky equipment and other cargo to and from JLA without using the busy A561, causing traffic delays.

Despite the careful calculations, calibrations and constant checks and double-checks which had been carried out in preparation for this delicate operation, everyone present instinctively held their breath as the wheels touched, then settled firmly onto the virgin track. The ropes were slackened, then released. Several of those closest to the line instinctively took a half pace backwards, as if they expected the beast to awaken, rear up and roar off towards Speke without human intervention. It simply oozed power as it stood in the early morning sunlight. An inner beauty shimmered around it as the polished surface caught and reflected every stray sunbeam. The River Mersey chose this moment to come alive, giving the lie to the 'dark lake' its ancient Norse name hinted at: every ripple was suddenly transformed into a tiny living flame.

The assembled crew stood in awed silence for a moment, then reacted in exactly the same way a primitive tribe might have reacted to the sudden appearance of a twentieth-century artefact in the middle of a Peruvian jungle. A rag appeared in every hand: every inch of the coach was polished with a love which verged on reverence.

A people carrier with darkened windows drew up. The rear doors opened, and a camera crew was decanted. In seconds, they had their equipment in place and ready to roll by the time two passengers emerged, wearing crisp airline-style uniforms in the distinctive purple-and-gold livery of Liverpool City Council. They posed briefly for a formal publicity photo before making their way across the tarmac. They halted once more for another set of shots before climbing into the driver's cab and working through a document, which appeared to be as detailed as an airline pre-flight checklist.

With a final photogenic thumbs-up gesture from the crew to the cheering crowd of stevedores and navigators, the powerful engines purred wakefulness. The golden vision sighed gracefully into life, with a triumphant tarantella of airhorns announcing her maiden voyage to the refurbished main entrance gate of John Lennon Airport.

"You played that one close to the chest, Robin!"

Jim Burke sank into a seat in the people carrier next to Robin Stuart for the short trip in the wake of the tram. Robin grinned like a mischievous schoolboy.

"I promised the *local* media exclusive access. The nationals were all told to go to the front entrance. They're going to be right miffed when the early editions hit the streets before they get a chance to post their reports!"

"I didn't see Kev Wyatt or Angie Ross back there."

"I sent the details to both of them last night, but I saw Angie lurking with a mic in her hand and Kev rang me to say he was sending someone to cover for him. He'd already promised to be at the main entrance."

"Chancing your arm a bit, aren't you? The main national press—*and* the BBC—could prove dangerous enemies if you rub them the wrong way."

"Jim, it's entirely possible they might find out before much longer that they're not as welcome 'oop north' as they used to be! Even their financial clout might not be enough to save them—"

He stopped so abruptly, Jim shot him a sharp glance.

"Something you're not telling me, Robin?"

"Nothing you need worry about, but we're nearly at the main entrance. I need to speak to someone else first, but we'll continue this conversation in private later."

John Kirwan's PR team had ensured blanket coverage of the opening ceremony at John Lennon Airport. As the tram drew up outside the main entrance, it was met by a fusillade of flash guns.

"Well done, John. This is an excellent turnout!"

"Thanks, Robin, but it was a team effort. I had very little to do myself! Now, as you already know, I've made sure the local guys 'n' gals have got a head start to bang their stories in with an exclusive tag. The plan is to drag things out here—without anyone getting suspicious—so the *Echo* and local radio can get maximum PR value out of breaking the news ahead of everyone else!

"It looks as if we've got everyone's full attention," JRK continued. "Let's strike while the iron's hot, shall we?"

The media scrum continued to jostle and dodge for photographs: they were being held in check by a solid line of airport security guards. The tram drivers emerged from their cab, and JRK mounted the steps to join them, setting off a further frenzy of flashbulbs as the media recognised a familiar face entering the lists. He raised his arms in salute and allowed the applause to continue for a few moments longer before lowering them gradually as if conducting Liverpool's famous Philharmonic Orchestra, cajoling them into a *pianissimo* passage of music.

"Ladies and gentlemen, thank you for being here today as we launch Liverpool's Tramlink service! The project has taken less than six months to complete, from drawing board to this point, and will provide a swift, reliable service to City Centre for every passenger using the John Lennon Airport. At peak times, we'll be aiming at a timetable of a tram every fifteen minutes, serving every flight arrival..."

JRK spoke confidently and, as usual, without notes. His speech was peppered with statistics and other details but delivered in a relaxed manner, which made it all seem very genuine and spontaneous. It wasn't, of course, but the speech had been designed to give that impression. When JRK ended by asking for questions, there was a slight lull, perhaps more than suggesting that he had, in fact, covered all the bases and there were no areas of doubt, no hidden skeleton bones for the hungry jocks in the crowd to seize upon and chew.

"*Daily Express.* Can you give us some idea of how the Tramlink Project has impacted on the local community?"

"Thank you, good question!" JRK meant this sincerely: it presented him with an ideal opportunity to demonstrate the value of regional as opposed to national development policies.

"First and foremost, let's take a look at local employment opportunities. From being an unemployment black spot for many years, Liverpool has become a major success story, almost overnight. The Tramlink Project has been central to this, and the spinoff of work being carried out by sub-contractors—such as the rolling stock produced at a local shipyard, which now has full order books—has also been significant.

"So the most visible impact the Tramlink Project has had on the local community has been to restore pride and a sense of purpose to the community. We can hold our heads high and say, 'There's work for them as wants it,' and know it's not an idle boast!

"Our future plans include using the enhanced powers for regional planning and development granted to Merseyside by Clause Sixty-Four of Magna Carta. This is in keeping with government policy of regional devolution of power, and I'd like to place on record sincere thanks on behalf of every Merseyside resident to every Coalition Government MP for making this possible!"

There was a round of spontaneous applause at this opportunistic rapier thrust, and JRK was obliged to pause for a moment before carrying on.

"There's still some cosmetic work to be done here at JLA, and that will be carried out over the next few days. There's no such thing as half a job—it's either finished or unfinished, and we Scousers don't leave jobs unfinished!"

This produced further deafening applause. JRK was in his element, playing the crowd as skilfully as any politician with many more years' experience than he had.

"We're now in a position to begin our next project, the construction of the Mersey Gateway at Runcorn and Widnes. Once the customs and excise facilities have been created at this site and at other locations, the future of Merseyside as an autonomous, self-governing region will be assured.

"In just a few short weeks, this has already been noticed by a number of influential authorities and potential customers outside the region. It has also attracted significant inward investment in the form of EU finances. This, in effect, means that the Mersey Gateway Project will be self-financing."

"But where's the cash coming from right now? Who's bankrolling you?"

The question came from two or three rows back: the questioner was an authentic George Cole lookalike, right down to the hack jacket with leather elbow patches, a trilby-style titfer and an anachronistic card with the text 'News International' tucked into his hatband.

In direct contrast to the enthusiastic applause that JRK's speech had prompted, the instant reaction in the room to this question was a frigid silence. Those closest to the questioner shuffled away from him as if he'd announced that he had an advanced case of leprosy.

"The invitations to this opening of the new service included News International as a matter of courtesy. Are you attached to one specific title?"

JRK's question was posed carefully and without undertone, but everyone knew the reason behind the question. A certain red-top title in the News International stable had made itself persona non grata in Liverpool with a vindictive attack on Liverpool's football fans in the aftermath of a tragic accident that had cost ninety-six supporters their lives.

"Will you answer my question or not?"

An uneasy murmur sighed around the crowd. JRK sensed that this could turn ugly and needed sensitive handling.

"I don't have a problem answering your question, but I have to assume that you are, in fact, reporting back to a certain newspaper which, shall we say, doesn't sell many copies locally."

A slightly nervous ripple of laughter suggested that JRK had defused the situation, but the tension still remained.

"In answer to your question, the council has nothing to hide," he asserted. "Our finances are a matter of public record, as the law requires, and are available for inspection online. The funds currently in our account are a mixture of public funding and a surprisingly large amount of voluntary donations from individual supporters. Further funding has been agreed in principle by a number of businesses and individuals who would prefer to remain anonymous for the moment, and I will, of course, respect their wishes. They will no doubt choose the time and place to make their support for the party *and* this region public knowledge. Questions from the room? No? We can proceed with the original question, which was about the impact of our activities to date on the local community..."

Briefly, JRK ticked off a few more boxes, naming the border control facilities planned for both Mersey Tunnels, the East Lancs Road and Switch Island. This exposé was received in silence, which suggested either intense concentration or total shell shock on the part of the seasoned news media reps outside the airport's main entrance. Even JRK, with an excellent overview from the footplate of the tram, didn't spot the moment when News International's representative was discreetly escorted from the scene by a pair of conscientious security guards.

The first Tramlink trip from JLA to the Pier Head terminal was fêted and cheered by crowds, who had gathered all along the route with flags and bunting. The fifty-six available seats were mostly reserved for local dignitaries and some of the senior media circus, but JRK had insisted on tickets being reserved for the winners of a free draw offered to the passengers of an early morning arrival from Dublin.

"We're providing a service that is intended to enhance the experience of visitors to Liverpool. What would be the point of not having a guest or two on our first journey?"

Nobody could argue with this, and the family of four who were the lucky winners were impressed.

"It's our first visit to Liverpool, but it certainly won't be our last!" was the comment from Kieran O'Gara to the interviewer as the family luggage was transferred to a taxi for the short journey to their hotel. The publicity value of such a comment from someone who clearly had no personal involvement in the project was immense and more than justified JRK's insistence on setting aside places for ordinary members of the public.

The news was syndicated and covered extensively by BBC and ITV by lunchtime. Both were playing catchup by then, as the local BBC station had been allowed an exclusive tag on the morning's events as they happened. Both nationals were also miffed to discover that a retainer fee was required before permission to transmit footage was granted.

"We've never been asked for this before!" exploded one senior CEO when presented with a release document for his signature.

Steven Dunning gave him his most solicitous professional courtroom smile.

"That's because you haven't been dealing with a fully autonomous, independent region until today! It's quite simple, really. We must now make sure that we cover our costs and generate capital for our own enterprises and future projects."

Monitors at strategic locations around the Mann Island terminus reminded the day-trippers from London and other regions that BBC Radio Merseyside was continuing to transmit live coverage of everything that was happening, including the debate regarding payment for transmission rights: there were also a couple of cameras, their tripods emblazoned with the Mersey TV logo, being trained on the discussions. Nobody was quite sure where or on which channel Mersey TV could be received, but the possibility of receiving some measure of negative reporting encouraged the reluctant CEO to sign the document Steven Dunning was continuing to wave before him. The movers and shakers from the remaining TV companies capitulated immediately rather than be left behind and forced to report yesterday's news.

JRK's phone burred in his pocket as the last of the signatories scrawled his name on the agreement document and turned to bawl his frustration at the nearest of his camera crew.

"John, you're needed ASAP at the dig in Old Hall Street."

"Billy, you're lucky. We're just wrapping up at the Pier Head. Is there a problem?"

"Can't talk about it on the phone. There's something you need to *see*."

CHAPTER TEN

JOHN PULLED PAUL to one side.

"I'll have to ask you to tidy up here. I've had a phone call from Billy Lynch—says he's something he needs to show me up at the dig. I'm going to slide off quietly, no fuss. Join me when you can—it sounds as if he's found something significant."

Sliding away unnoticed was easier than JRK had expected it to be. There was a lot of bustle and confusion, with some camera crews jockeying for that special shot while others were packing up and decamping. Old Hall Street was barely two hundred metres away, not even worth hailing a cab for, so he opted to make the trip on foot.

Billy had commandeered a table outside Costa: Professor Midler and Maureen were there, waiting with Billy's crew and a sufficiency of coffees.

"What's the score, Billy? You said you couldn't talk about it on the phone."

Billy looked up and down the road before replying. It was still blocked to through traffic, and for the moment, there were no pedestrians within earshot.

"The prof asked me to have a shufti up the tunnel we uncovered. The one leading uphill towards Everton Brow."

John Midler nodded.

"I did some reading at home. I had a feeling there might be something more. So I asked Skinny-Ribs Yozzer if he'd go in and have a look-see, him bein' the runt o' the litter."

"An' seein' as 'ow youse is all too fat to get in there!" Yozzer growled without malice. He took up the tale.

"It wasn't as tight a fit as I was expectin', but I couldn't stand up. It's about three foot wide, four foot high and well secure. Joists an' rafters every ten foot or so, I'd say. I took some photies on me mobile. We can lookit them inna minute."

He waved the phone for a second or two, then laid it on the table and dug a fairly clean handkerchief out of his pocket. It hit the table with a solid *clunk*.

"I'd wriggled my way about fifty foot into the passage before I couldn't go no further. The tunnel's filled with a load o' sacks an' boxes, but even in poor light, I reckernised what I'd come across straight away!"

He unfolded the handkerchief to reveal three large coins, which glowed with the unmistakable pure lustre of gold.

"There was a split in the nearest sack. I grabbed these and backed out with my mobile."

John Midler broke the stunned silence.

"Yozzer's photos will give us some idea of how much is down there, but I believe we may have stumbled across Prince Rupert's gold."

A brief phone call confirmed that Kevin Wyatt was on duty at the *Echo* offices.

"Yes, it'll be a bit of a squeeze here in the broom cupboard, but at least it's private! I'll meet you in Reception..."

Billy left the rest of the gangers at the dig site with instructions to extend the trench around the entry tunnel and shore up the walls with what came to hand but without attracting undue attention.

"Keep a lid on this, lads. We don't want the world an' his wife lookin' over our shoulders if what Yozzer found is what it seems to be! I'm leaving him in charge until I get back, even if he *is* the new kid on the block. He's the only one skinny enough to crawl in there, an' he deserves the credit—along with a decent bonus, come payday! Fair enough?"

Norman and Eddie had no arguments with the gaffer's decision and began assembling a canvas shelter to place around the tunnel entrance. Yozzer nodded his thanks for the field promotion and began stuffing items into a small shoulder bag.

"I won't try to bring anything else out. It's safer to leave it in place for now, an' gold weighs a ton. It's too 'eavy to shift, and I don't want the walls collapsin' on me neither! Seems to me, best thing to do is take some more photies an' check what I can see o' the walls. We're goin' to be in an' out all the time, they'll need shorin' up anyway before we can start bringin' stuff out."

As far as Billy was concerned, Yozzer's attention to these practical matters was confirmation enough of his suitability for the job in hand. He turned to suggest to John Midler, Maureen and JRK that it was time to adjourn to Kev's cramped quarters just as Paul Freeman joined them.

"Nicely timed! I'll give you the details once we're off the street. It's too public here, and Kev said we can use his cubby hole. I just need to get out o' these overalls an' boots so I don't traipse mud all over the offices."

Kevin was right. Six people in the room he'd been allocated as a junior reporter wasn't just a squeeze, it was a flagrant violation of at least a dozen different health and safety directives. Nobody cared, but by the time Billy and JRK had summarised the most recent developments, they were all fingering their collars and panting heavily as the temperature in the room soared.

Paul had been scribbling notes. Suddenly, he dropped his pen and ripped off his tie.

"I can't think straight in here, and there are too many unanswered questions," he grumbled.

"We could all do with a drink," Kevin agreed, "but it's strictly soft drinks only here at the *Echo*, and you'll need a pocketful of change for the machine."

JRK looked at his watch. "I make it pub o'clock. Any objections?"

"There's a pub us hacks use. I can get us a private room," Kevin offered. The vote was instant and unanimous.

The meeting reconvened around a table in the Lady of Mann with much-needed liquid refreshments close to hand. Billy had detoured via a supermarket to purchase 'emergency supplies' for the navvy crew keeping a watchful eye on the dig site and was last to seat himself.

Paul took the lead, following his notes.

"Has anyone thought of the *legal* questions we might have to consider? I mean, assuming we've stumbled on something which is valuable, we have to ask ourselves who it actually belongs to. Does anyone know what the law says about Treasure Trove, for example? Is it a case of 'finders, keepers'? Are there specific rules about precious metals—if that's what we're dealing with—and other items that have some cash value? Gold, for example, has always been the recognised international trading marker."

"Good point!" JRK had his mobile out, speed-dialling. "Steven? Glad I caught you. We need some legal advice... Yes, professionally. Of course nobody expects you to do pro bono work every time you're called for an opinion! Listen, how quickly can you get to the Lady of Mann on Dale Street?"

***

"Matter of fact, the rules were amended quite recently."

Steve Dunning's fingers blurred as he entered data on his laptop. In seconds, he grunted with satisfaction and leaned away from the screen.

"From your description of the size of the find, it's certainly more than three hundred years old—that seems a very arbitrary age for defining treasure, but I suppose you have to settle on a figure, somehow. But it goes on to say, if the object—or objects—

contains more than ten per cent gold or silver, the person *in possession* of the item is obliged to inform the authorities within fourteen days or risk a fine and possible imprisonment. Seems a bit draconian to me, even from a lawyer's viewpoint!"

He took a sip of beer and looked around.

"Previously, it was the *finder* who was under a legal obligation to report findings. The main difference is, if the finder sells it to a dealer, for example, that's not the end of the story. The dealer is—at least, in theory—still obliged to report the find.

"A coroner is then appointed to try to determine if it was lost—in which case it automatically belongs to the Crown—or hidden with the intention of recovering it at a later date."

"What difference would that make?" Paul frowned, then hastily apologised for the unintended interruption.

"No worries. Perfectly natural question," Steve assured him. "The difference is this. If the coroner decides it was hidden rather than lost, he must then conduct an investigation to establish if there is a traceable heir to the treasure. And guess what?" He paused dramatically before completing the sentence.

"If no heir can be found—most unlikely, since almost a thousand years have passed—then the treasure *becomes* the property of the Crown."

"Hmm. Sounds to me like a 'heads you win, tails I lose' situation. Typical bloody government protectionist legislation," muttered Paul.

"Actually, I believe it could work in our favour," Steve countered. He'd had a few seconds longer than anyone else to read the text several times, and his legal brain had already come up with a possible solution.

"We agree that it was found by someone working *for* Liverpool Council, yes? And the *change* in the law absolved *him* from any obligation to report it. That's very specific, and in this case, it's also going to be important. Yozzer has nothing to worry about, and I'm sure he can be rewarded appropriately, but that's a separate matter!

"It was found buried underground, here *in Liverpool.* And since Liverpool is now a self-governing, autonomous region—or realm, or city state or whatever other title we adopt—then as the Crown, the treasure automatically reverts to is…?"

Without thinking, everyone suddenly found themselves on their feet, glass in hand. The same word came from each thirsty throat as they toasted:

"Liverpool!"

CHAPTER ELEVEN

"PROF, MO! CAN you hear me?"

"Go ahead, Yozzer!"

"The coins I brought out before. They were in the nearest sack or bag—some sort of cloth. They spilled out of a rip. I haven't moved it or poked about inside yet. You can see it if I back out…"

He suited action to word. Powerful flashlights were trained on the bag, about ten feet from the end of the tunnel.

"I thought the container itself might be just as important to a history buff as whatever happens to be inside it, but it's bound to be heavy, and I don't see us getting it out undamaged. You need to make a decision before we carry on."

"I'm not exactly crippled by arthritis," John murmured, "but I think Mo should be the one to wriggle along the passage rather than me. It'd be a tight squeeze for me, and she's always careful in her handling of artefacts."

It had been easy enough for the history/archaeology experts to clamber into the underground chamber. There was adequate headroom, and they had both pulled on denim boilersuits. Maureen stuffed several pairs of disposable gloves into her pockets and eased her way into the narrow passage.

"John, the bag itself is a woven cloth of some sort. Not surprising it's starting to fall apart after all these years."

Maureen's voice was only slightly muffled, and every word was clear, distinct.

"I'm going to start excavating. I can see more very similar bags a little further along, so if we have to tear this one apart to retrieve the contents, it won't be a total disaster."

"Your call, Mo. I trust your judgement! I think we'll go for the contents this time, but try not to do more damage than necessary to the fabric."

"I've got a couple of scalpels and some sharp scissors, so I won't rip it to shreds, anyway, and I'll take a few shots of what I can see before I start."

Maureen took a series of photographs before switching to video mode and adding a running commentary, which she continued as she began to enlarge the tear.

"There don't seem to be any air currents, so this passage has probably been blocked at both ends, creating a hermetically sealed vault or chamber. No evidence of decomposition or rot in the material. Definitely hand woven, panels stitched together.

"There are more coins inside, different sizes, very similar to the three you've already seen. Can you find a tray or a box and something soft to line it?"

Thirty minutes later, Maureen backed carefully out of the passage with her first findings. The haul consisted of forty-three coins in a variety of sizes. All of them were uniform in colour and density and were unquestionably gold. Most of them appeared to be in mint condition, as if they had not been circulated or changed hands more than once or twice before being packed away.

"That's to be expected," John Midler commented. "Think about it. Large-value coins would only be needed for large transactions between wealthy individuals. Your ordinary man or woman would barter goods and services. Very few could read or perform the simplest of mathematical tasks."

"And what we have here is probably less than a tenth of the one bag that was close at hand," Maureen continued from the professor. "As I said before, I can't see how far along the passage this hoard goes. There are six sacks—all bigger than this one—and then solid boxes filling the passage three wide and four high. If they're all filled with coins, jewellery and other valuable items, it's going to take weeks of heavy lifting to remove it all and *years* to catalogue it all and trace where it all came from, and why it's hidden here!"

"We'll get nowhere fast unless we can bring in some equipment," Billy said. "I never realised just *how* heavy gold is until today, and there's no way we can shift it by hand!"

"Which means we have to have a team we can trust operating the equipment," Maureen added. "John, at least part of the team will have to be historians. Can you vouch for your best final-year students? I'm sure Billy's crew will supply the technical know-how."

"Let's not get too far ahead of ourselves," Steve cautioned. "If we're keeping this under wraps, we want as few people in the know as possible. Even if nobody talks out of turn, someone's bound to notice the increased traffic in and around what's supposed to be a straightforward road repair."

"We're going to need your advice on the legal aspect of this too, Steve," Paul said. "You said we're obliged to report finding treasure trove within fourteen days. Perhaps we could report finding something of 'historical significance' rather than disclosing what it is? That would surely be enough to justify increased activity *and* explain the comings and goings of academics as well as the road repair crew."

"Mm. Historical significance might or might not be sufficient grounds for failing to declare the find straight away. That's also a bit of a grey area. Personally, I'd be a lot happier if we could keep this under wraps on the grounds that it might be a threat to national security—or our own regional security. Let me have a think about that."

"The most urgent problem's a practical one, though," Paul cut in. "We've all seen that there's a significant number of objects to be removed, inspected and catalogued. We know from the few things we've moved so far that they're all very heavy, despite the individual items not being particularly big. Manpower's going to be a major headache. The more people involved in the job, the more likely a security breach. You can't stop people talking about something like this!"

Billy Lynch leaned forward.

"How many men d'you reckon we need to get the ball rolling? I've got contacts, men who've worked for me before, men I'd trust with my life! I know for a fact I could go out right now and find a dozen strong bods who can keep their mouths shut and at least the same number again by tomorrow!"

"Billy, if you're prepared to vouch for these guys personally, that's good enough for me," JRK said. "I've a feeling we can trust your judgement."

JRK looked around the underground chamber. He was in his element here and seemed to grow an inch or two as he took control of the situation.

"Billy, I'll leave the hiring of extra navvies in your hands. I assume you'll get a better mobile signal if you go outside and sit in your van? You can do me a favour, drop into Costa and tell them I'll be out with an order in a few minutes. Steven, do you need to plough through reference books back at the office to check on the legal position?"

Steven nodded.

"Okay, I'll phone you tonight for a progress report. Mo, I'm not having you crawling through the muck in that tunnel. You can start making a catalogue of the items we've already unearthed, and I'll get someone to help with that as soon as possible. Everyone else can concentrate on passing things out of the passage into the chamber and stacking them until they can be added to Mo's list."

***

When JRK returned to the trench with a tray of assorted coffees, he had Billy and Yozzer with him. They carried in a portable generator and other equipment needed to install more lighting in the outer chamber. Once this had been installed, the room seemed twice as big, and JRK nodded his approval.

"I've a feeling we might be short of space before we're finished. There seemed to be quite a haul stashed in the tunnel."

"Well, John, we *are* talking of a King's Ransom—literally!" Paul reminded him.

"True enough, and if it was intended as a bribe for the hire of a private army from whoever was king in Ireland at the time, it would have had to be a goodly sum anyway! And speaking of which..."

JRK pulled three copies of the day's edition of the *Liverpool Echo* he'd bought while waiting for the coffees to be poured and passed them around.

"Look at the front-page headlines."

The vital and potentially very profitable West Coast train link from London to Liverpool and beyond had been put out to tender, following government policy. It had been run efficiently for many years by one particular company, Jomfru Trains, the brainchild of a well-known and respected businessman, Rik Hines. Many people were surprised when a rival bidder, ClearTrack, was awarded the new contract. They were due to take over from January, which was now less than three months away.

Rik Hines had immediately appealed against the decision, and questioned the figures quoted by ClearTrack, claiming they were over-optimistic and could never work. Rik had a no-nonsense personality. In a ridiculously short period of time, he'd achieved cult status as a self-made businessman, almost as popular as a pop star. An independent commission had been looking at the nuts and bolts of ClearTrack's tender for several months.

The commission had concluded that there were serious procedural flaws in ClearTrack's tendering and also that there was evidence of financial kickbacks and bribes involved. According to the *Echo*, the contract had been set aside and the other bidders—with the exception of ClearTrack—were invited to re-submit.

"He's so popular, and with a sympathy vote from those who see him as unfairly overlooked in the original round of tenders, I'd say it's a shoo-in for Rik Hines this time," was John's opinion, and everyone nodded their agreement as they glanced at the half dozen pages the newspaper had dedicated to reporting the item.

"You know, I've always had enormous respect for the guy," JRK murmured. "He'd be a great addition to the team if we could get him on board!"

"Maybe, but he's a Londoner, innee?" Paul countered with a grossly exaggerated 'cor blimey, guv' accent. JRK seemed about to protest but was distracted when his phone rang.

"John Kirwan speaking... Yes, that's right. I'm in a meeting at the moment, and we were just discussing the problems you're having— Tomorrow? Yes, of course! How will you be travelling? ... Ten o'clock, at John Lennon Airport? Yes, I'll meet you there. Looking forward to it. ... Bye!"

JRK snapped his mobile closed.

"Talk of the devil, they say! That was Rik Hines. He's steaming about the West Coast contracts, and he wants to meet with us tomorrow morning."

"Just don't let him drive the tram from the airport!" Paul grinned. Rik had caused a minor sensation when he'd insisted on taking the controls of a Jomfru train on a recent trip to Liverpool. The driver of the train confirmed that Rik had brought the train to a successful halt at Lime Street and obviously knew what he was doing at the controls. The media circus had had a field day with headlines on the theme of 'Little Boys and Big Toys'.

CHAPTER TWELVE

"Rik Hines, welcome to Liverpool! Good flight?"

"Fine, thanks. I didn't realise there was a helipad at Liverpool Airport. I thought I'd be using either a police facility or beg a favour from the coastguards. Those are about the only options available in London."

"I could say that we're a bit better organised in Liverpool, but in all honesty, it's probably nearer the mark to look at land prices here. You could probably buy a four-bedroom detached house in Crosby cheaper than a broom cupboard in Central London."

"Really? That's definitely worth knowing!"

JRK had opted to greet Rik Hines at John Lennon Airport's Arrivals lounge, accompanied by Paul Freeman. Rik had flown in a private-charter helicopter and arrived in a Jomfru livery crash suit, which he quickly stripped off and handed to one of the pilots with a sincere word of thanks as soon as his ticket had been processed. Beneath the shell suit, he was dressed in his usual smart-casual attire consisting of a leather jacket, open-neck shirt and blue jeans. His only luggage was a bulging holdall with a shoulder strap.

"So, this is the famous *Merseytram*? It looks even more impressive than it does on TV."

"Yes, and I've been warned not to let you drive it!" Paul chipped in with a grin.

"Hey, I promise you I really *am* qualified. I wouldn't have asked the engineer to let me bring that train in otherwise! I've never asked anyone who works for me to do anything I can't do myself. Hands-on experience of every aspect of a job, that's always been my way of doing things, but I won't ask—not *this* time, anyway—as long as we can ride in the cab with the driver?"

"I don't see a problem with that," JRK said, shaking Rik's hand as they strolled out onto the concourse via the staff entrance, where the two drivers were waiting to greet them. Fifty yards away, the first few passengers to clear Customs from the latest flight to arrive were coming through the main entrance. JRK glanced at the clock on the information board.

"Next departure time is in fourteen minutes, Rik. We've time to have a look around the controls if you like—and as long as you'll give us the guided tour?" he added, turning to the two drivers, who nodded cheerfully.

"We're running a half-hour service at the moment because we've only the one tram in service, but the second tram should be delivered before the week's out, and we'll be able to run a fifteen-minute service once that's in place. The whole system will become easier to run once all four power units are available—hopefully before the end of the month. That will give us three in circulation and one in reserve."

"And there's the Cammell Laird dockyard, where the carriages have been assembled." Paul pointed across the river: even at that distance, there was clear evidence of bustle and activity.

Rik nodded, and Paul continued.

"As a matter of fact, they've already got orders waiting to be filled as soon as there's capacity in the dry dock. These are orders which have been placed during the last few weeks, almost certainly as a direct result of the Tramlink Project being completed ahead of time *and* within budget."

"That in itself is pretty impressive. I can't think of any major work I've had completed on time!" Rik remarked. "What's your secret?"

"No secret, Rik. It's what *we* call Scouse attitude. Jobs have been hard to come by up here for far too long, so anyone who's got a job wants to keep it! Get the job done, do it well, and you'll still have a job next week. Maybe a tad over-dramatic, but it's not that far from gospel truth!"

JRK turned to Rik as the tram slowed and pulled up at the Mann Island terminal. The cross-river ferry had just left the quayside: a few hundred metres downriver, the first few passengers were beginning to board a large cruise liner.

"Listen, John. I want to ask a favour."

"Rik, you're our guest. You only have to ask."

"Can we stay here, in the cab, while the other passengers get off? Granted, I'm here on business, you and I know that, but it'd be so nice to play the tourist, avoid the press for once, be myself."

"Fine by me. Okay with you, Paul? And the next departure time's not for another half hour or so. The tram will be leaving on time anyway."

***

Maureen had once again secured the back room at the Lady of Mann and ordered a substantial buffet lunch. She was waiting as the taxi brought them the short trip from the ferry terminal, with an unmistakable look of excitement in her eyes.

"I've got some more detail about... about our *discovery*," she said and stopped. She glanced at Rik Hines, then back to JRK. He realised the grounds for her hesitation and took his cue.

"Can it wait until after we've eaten, Mo? Rik's taken the time and trouble to come up from the Smoke to speak to us, and he's got first dibs on today's agenda. And if it's something *sensitive* you want to tell us, it's only fair to listen to what he has to say first, in the circumstances. Because if I'm right—" he placed his hand on Rik's shoulder "—I have a feeling we might be discussing a business deal which could be in everyone's best interests. Now, drinks. Who's having what?"

***

"...and in view of the way government departments are all accusing each other of taking backhanders and who knows what else, I'm pulling Jomfru out of London altogether. There'll be an official announcement tomorrow morning, but I'm telling you now because I think you're doing the right thing. There's too much self-interest and corruption in London, and I'd like to throw my hat in the ring, support the stance you've taken."

"Rik, what can I say? I admit, I had a good feeling when you called last night, but I didn't expect this!" It wasn't often Paul Freeman was caught short of something to say.

Steve Dunning leaned forward to make his point. "Have you thought about the practical side of things, the legal implications, how your employees might react?"

Rik was ready with an answer.

"The way I work, I'd never dream of making such a major change without talking it through with my staff. They're more like family to me—many of them have been with me since not long after I pushed my first barrow round Camden Market! They've all given me their word there won't be any leaks to the press, and I believe them. Everyone I've had a chance to speak to personally, by the way, has told me they'd jump at the chance to relocate away from London. The cost of living's got beyond a joke, and when I checked a few figures last night, I discovered that less than ten per cent of my employees actually live in London. Logistically, relocation wouldn't be that difficult to accomplish. They'd be a damn sight better off with housing costs for a start. Have you *seen* the prices in London nowadays?"

"You've come a long way from pushing a barrow, Rik. Trains, planes, videos and electronics—you've got something of a Midas touch. If you choose to relocate, it's going to throw a cat amongst a *big* flock of pigeons!"

"I've been lucky, John. And since we're talking privately and *in confidence*..." He paused and fixed each in turn with a stare that demanded and received acknowledgement. He nodded and continued.

"I'll be announcing the latest venture within the week, but this is so sensitive I've got to insist on absolute secrecy. Not a single word must leave this room until I announce it publicly! Do I have your word? I'm deadly serious, and it will definitely be to *your* advantage as well as mine if we can work together!"

There was total silence in the room for several seconds. When his chest became painful, JRK discovered he'd actually been holding his breath. He refilled his lungs and glanced around his assembled team, looking for the smallest signs of acquiescence. He nodded, then stood and offered Rik his hand.

"Something tells me to trust my instincts on this, Rik, but anyone in this room will tell you, it'll be the first time I've ever given an unqualified 'yes' to anything without even knowing what I'm agreeing to."

A rumble of wordless encouragement rippled around the table.

Rik looked at each in turn. This time, he had a bright, comradely smile on his lips.

"Six weeks from now—on the first of November—I plan to launch Jomfru Cash."

"What? A *bank*?" Dominic looked as if he'd just been kicked above the heart by a police horse.

"It won't be run as a bank, and I don't want anyone to think of it as a bank, more like a cross between a building society and a credit union owned by its members.

"But the bottom line is the funding is already in place, thanks to the profitability of the businesses trading under the Jomfru banner. It's clear to me that I'd be much better off with all my businesses registered on Merseyside, where I'd be very happy to pay the tithe—that's ten per cent—income tax, or whatever you decide to call company tax in the new republic of Merseyside.

It simply *has* to be less than the ridiculous rates I'm paying to Whitehall at the moment."

"Can you really control the movement of the amounts of cash...credits, collateral or whatever would be involved...in setting up any sort of financial enterprise as quickly and easily as you're suggesting?" Dominic sounded far from convinced. Rik grinned.

"Good question. John told me you're the financial brains of the group, and you're entitled to ask it! This isn't a knee-jerk reaction. I've been looking at ways and means of getting out of London for months now. I've discovered that one of the biggest advantages of the internet is the speed of business transactions. The fact of the matter is, you can literally 'point and click' at just about anything, and it's done, there and then! It doesn't matter how many zeroes there are on the page or where in the world you've stashed the cash, you can move it from London to Liverpool, Lisbon or Timbuk-bloody-too if you want, and the transaction's done before you can blink!

"But to set everyone's mind at ease, the net profits of the combined Jomfru business interests for the past twelve months is more than adequate collateral for the financial wing I have in mind. Let me put it this way. I thought seriously about buying out Northern Rock when they had to throw in the towel, but then you made the news, and I knew straight away that this would prove a far more interesting proposition."

"Rik, have you thought this through? D'you have any idea how much it would cost to buy into something the size of the Royal Bank of Scotland? Telephone numbers don't even come into the frame!"

"Dominic, I've done my homework! And yes, I know we're talking of a deal involving billions, not millions! Every business under the Jomfru brand name is doing well and has done for years. Profits *and* growth figures have improved every year, and all the indications are that this year won't be any different.

As they say, you can't take it with you—and none of us are getting any younger."

"You think they're going to let you waltz in and cherry-pick their best branches? Somehow, I don't see that happening..."

"Fair point, Paul. So I make them an offer for the whole shootin' match, warts 'n' all. If they're not happy, maybe we can negotiate something, but my sources think they might not have much of a choice. The bank *they* tried to approach last week turned them down this morning, and as far as I'm aware, there weren't any alternative offers."

Dominic's fingers flew as he consulted his iPad: seconds later, he looked up and nodded confirmation.

"That news has only just broken. You must have *very* good sources!"

"I heard it from my financial gnomes before the chopper left London," Rik replied. "After all's said and done, I pay them to tell me today's news, not yesterday's. I've left a sealed bid with my financial advisors. One call from me, and they'll put it on the table. I like what I've heard so far, and I'm prepared to toss my hat in the ring. So, do we have a deal?"

"It wouldn't be the first bank to be started in Liverpool, guys—and gals!" JRK murmured, belatedly recognising the presence of Nuala and Maureen. "Martins bank started here, remember?"

"I hope this won't be interpreted as insider trading," Rik hedged, "but it seems to me that anyone with a few quid to spare could stand to make a few bob by buying *any* Jomfru shares at today's closing prices before the announcement is made tomorrow. I won't send in the dogs—or call in my gnomes—before today's closing bell. I can't say fairer than that!"

"Seems reasonable to me," JRK said. "Thanks, Rik. Okay, is there any other business on today's agenda?"

Rik had been so casual, he could have been discussing the price of fish or a disputed free kick in last week's football match, and it took a few seconds before the assembled group realised that a major financial coup had just been trumped through by their invited guest. On the other hand, he was the only one who had the right to make a decision of that nature, and it was, technically at least, his money, to use as he saw fit.

Maureen cleared her throat. "Mr. Hines, I—"

"Rik, please! You make me sound as old as my grandfather!"

"Rik, then. Maureen Lynch—or Mo—assistant to Professor John Midler, head of history and archaeology at Liverpool University."

"Thanks, Mo! I noticed you've been excited about something all through lunch. Is there a formal 'chair' to this meeting or can we hear what Maureen has to contribute before she explodes?"

"We're pretty flexible here. I think we can let Mo have the floor," Paul said with a quick glance around the table.

Maureen pushed her notepad to one side and took a small, soft velvet sack out of her handbag. Something chinked faintly as she placed the sack carefully before her and loosened the ribbon around its neck.

"John, you were there when we pulled the first few things out of the tunnel. I took a couple of the coins from the split sack home with me and cleaned them very carefully—and yes, John, I kept all the grime and gravel I brushed off each coin in separate envelopes, each clearly marked."

John Midler said nothing, but there was an unmistakable light of approval in his eyes as he nodded for her to continue.

"Once I could see the engraving on the coins, I started looking through internet pages to get a better idea of what we've found. The dates helped—between 1630 and 1643..."

"Not from the same time as the Charter, then?" JRK sounded puzzled, even slightly alarmed.

"Don't panic, John! All that means is at least two different people decided that this cavern, and one of the tunnels leading to or from it, was a safe place to leave something they considered valuable.

"They're almost identical in weight—surprisingly close, considering they'd have been produced by hand rather than on a production line, like modern coins.

"They're also consistent in the fineness of the gold, twenty-four carat, as close to pure gold as makes no difference, and they all have the same design on the obverse side—an angel fighting a dragon. The design was used during several consecutive reigns. The coins are called Angels, and they were last minted in the time of Charles the Second."

"You say there's a lot more to be retrieved and catalogues in this hoard of—well, we have to consider it treasure, I suppose?"

"That's right, Rik."

"And we can be pretty certain whatever else we find will also be valuable. As Dominic said, if we flood the market with what's been found, it will certainly affect the price of the artefacts themselves. First, though, we need to get them out of there and somewhere safe where they can be examined by experts."

"There's a team already working on that, Rik. My dad's in charge, and he's hand-picked a crew who can be trusted, but we're going to need more. It's heavy work, and eight hours or more down the hole isn't practical."

"Mo's dad is an experienced contractor—a good old-fashioned navigator," John Midler explained. "And from what I've seen, he's a good judge of men. If he vouches for someone, I'm certain they won't be talking out of turn."

"And I think we can leave him to organise that," JRK chipped in. "From what I've seen, he's got the job well in hand."

"He should let me know if he needs more bodies. I'm not without a few connections when it comes to people who can be trusted to keep schtum," Rik said with a grin.

"This has been a very interesting meeting," Paul said, in his best summing-up voice, "and we seem to be in a far stronger financial position than I dreamed possible! I suggest we give Rik a whistle-stop tour of the work that's going on at Garston and the new Mersey Gateway at Runcorn..."

Maureen's eyes suddenly flashed with fury. When she spoke, her voice was spiked with ice.

"I hadn't finished!" she snapped in a tone nobody present had ever heard her use before.

She paused, closed her eyes briefly, and took a long, shuddering breath to calm herself.

"Sorry, I didn't mean to lose my rag there, but these coins aren't the only things I found in the first tunnel I crawled into, the one leading uphill towards Everton Brow."

She delved into another padded cloth sack and brought out an object which was clearly a man-made tool of some sort and definitely not made of gold. She placed it reverentially on top of the specimen bag.

"Gentlemen of the jury—and Nuala. I believe we have here, on this table, the seal with which King John validated Magna Carta and also, in all likelihood, Liverpool's Royal Charter in 1207. It's not gold or jewellery, but in historical terms, its value could be completely off the charts!"

CHAPTER THIRTEEN

WHEN THE MINIBUS reached the Mersey Gateway construction site, the foreman was waiting to meet them.

"I've got hard hats and overalls for all of you. It's a bit chaotic out there, but as long as you stick close to me, there won't be any problems. If I can have some shoe sizes, I'll get some wellies from the store room..."

The site swarmed with activity, but the chaos foreman Gerry Burns had warned them of seemed quite well organised. JCBs and tractors criss-crossed the site on signposted tracks.

"We decided we had to enforce a strict no-pedestrians policy and create separate safe walkways," Gerry explained in response to a question from Rik. "So far, it seems to be working. We've over two thousand workers on site at any one time and no accidents reported in the first seven days of operation—and I mean a total lack of either traffic or construction incidents, which for a site of this size and nature is an excellent record!"

Suited and booted, they left the changing rooms and followed Gerry's lead to the top of a hill, which hid the site from the service road.

"We had to stash what we dug up somewhere," Gerry explained. "For the moment, this keeps the noise and disturbances to a minimum, and a lot of it will be replaced when we're finished. It'll all be properly landscaped."

There was a clear view over the whole site, which bustled with activity. Although it was too far for voices to carry, it was easy enough to imagine shouts, song, light-hearted banter and insults being exchanged in every direction. There was an unmistakable atmosphere of drive, ambition and personal pride in the job.

Within thirty minutes, they were back in the site office, stripped out of boots and hats but still wearing their coveralls. Gerry turned to a flipchart, which stood in one corner.

"The top sheet is simply an overview of the whole site. The only details on it are the existing bridge structure and some topographical notes about the subsoil compositions, the layers of rock, how it's layered, that sort of thing. Anyone feel they need the details? No? Good, that saves us time. We can get into the good stuff straight away!"

He flipped to the next schematic. The existing structures were still clearly identifiable, reproduced in stark, sharp, black lines.

"On this one, you can see where we've started work on digging out the ground where the new build will stand. The area hatched in red has been cleared and trenches started. We aim to have the foundations laid by the end of next week."

The 'hatched area' was a generous circle south of the bridge. Looking out of the window, a cheerful press of humanity sang, swayed and shouted good-natured insults to each other as they negotiated the site, apparently aware of each other's relative positions on the dance floor and able to avoid collisions.

"This map is updated at shift change each evening, so what we have here is the progress as of six-thirty or so yesterday evening—you can probably add another ten per cent to the area covered. I can see a surveyor team lining up some markers for our first foundation trench. Excuse me one moment."

Gerry left to intercept a group of three men wearing distinctive yellow hard hats. As he spoke, two of them turned and strode away from the office, each carrying a fistful of long rods in one hand and either a mobile or a short-wave radio in the other. The one who stayed put was busy setting some sort of equipment on a tripod.

Not a camera, Rik told himself. He knew the correct name for the special instrument surveyors used, but for the moment, he couldn't recall what it was: he had a vague idea what it was used for, and that, for the moment, was enough.

"There's a lot of activity on this site—I've never seen anything like it before! Do you have an overall timescale? How long d'you think the job will take?"

JRK exchanged a glance with Paul, who shrugged.

"Gerry Burns is probably the only one who could give you even an approximate guess on that. All I have to go on is the crew's track record to date, if you'll forgive the pun. Most of these men worked on the Tramlink Project from City Centre to John Lennon Airport. Seven miles, near as makes no difference, and they managed it in about four weeks. Mind you, the roads were already there, and the biggest part of the job was excavating tram lines which were still buried there from the old docklands light railway."

"That's still impressive! And getting the carriages built on time must have taken some doing, too!"

"The chassis and the plans were already in place. Cammell Laird only needed to have a guarantee of payment in order to hire the skilled workers they needed. The rest..." JRK shrugged. "The rest's history. Job done. None of us can claim any special credit for that, either. It's what we Scousers do best!"

He paused with a glint of humour in his eyes, then continued with a deliberately coarse, exaggerated accent. "Roll yer sleeves up, mate. Y'r at yer grannie's!"

Nobody had noticed Gerry Burns re-entering the office, but he'd clearly been present long enough to hear Rik's question.

"As far as time scale goes, it's still too early to think about guarantees, and I don't want to be hung out to dry for promising something we don't deliver! But every man on each team is pulling his weight, and looking at the first week's work, we're already well ahead of target. Now, if I could take on more men…"

"Do it!" JRK, Paul and Rik spoke as one. Each looked at the other, and Rik seemed slightly embarrassed.

"Sorry, it's not my shout. Not this time, anyway! But I still do a lot of interviewing and hiring myself on behalf of Jomfru. Some things become a habit!

"On the other hand, this is something practical which I can do without referring to any stuffy set of suits sitting on a board of directors, which I always thought was spelt b-o-r-e-d, but that's another matter!"

He fished in his pocket and produced a wallet.

"Nobody seems to use a chequebook anymore, but I'm ready to put my money—or my plastic—where my mouth is. I'll be happy to back you financially if you want more staff."

***

"…but there's nothing to see yet at this end. We still have to look at the layout, buy some land, get planning permission and so on."

Paul was giving a from-the-hip summary as the minibus rolled south across the Runcorn–Widnes bridge in the light noonday traffic.

"The rail connections will have to be extended, and there will have to be some parking for road traffic, a sort of holding pen for non-local traffic, customs *clearance* and so on. We can use the time we've got today to pay Cammell Laird a flying visit and then go on to the next project at Seaforth docks."

"The *next* project? You've only just started work on this one!" Rik protested.

Paul grinned.

"You aren't the only person who's offered financial backing, Rik, and Seaforth has been waiting for an investor since Jerry flattened the old docks in north Liverpool in 1941. In a way, he did us a favour. There isn't a lot of demolition and clearance needed, and making a start is going to be that much easier."

He summed up the conversation he'd had with Robin Stuart about installing a deep-water dock complex capable of handling large commercial and cruise vessels. With the exception of JRK and Nuala, this was the first time he'd had the opportunity to bring the rest of the group up to speed.

"...and Robin's prepared to make £300 million available to set the ball rolling. Only problem is, the manpower. The way things are going at the moment, we've more potential work available, and nobody available to hire."

"Who'd have believed that of Liverpool, even right up to a few months ago?" Dominic asked as he shook his head. "Still, it's a nice position to be in. We just have to find an answer to the problem."

"Cammell Laird might be prepared to offer some skilled workers," Paul mused. "They made their name from building ships. How hard can it be for someone with that sort of background to transfer his knowledge and skills to building a state-of-the-art dockland for the ships to use?"

"It might not be quite as simple as that," JRK replied, "but we can at least ask, see what they think."

Rik Hines' name and reputation had been enough to support JRK's telephone call asking the management at Cammell Laird's to grant a brief informal meeting on site. A senior shop steward met them at the gates and acted as tour guide as they circled the dry docks and other facilities before disembarking from the minibus outside the main office. The shop steward—Derek, according to the tag embroidered on his pocket—had remained with them as JRK and Paul had outlined the plans for Seaforth docks and the offer of financial assistance from Robin Stuart. The existence of the as-yet uncounted millions represented by

Prince Rupert's gold was by unspoken agreement airbrushed out of the overall picture.

The coffee pot circled the table once more.

"We've recently had some much-needed orders here at the yard, and it's true we're taking on skilled workers to fulfil them. It's also a fact that there are certainly many families who have seen generations of menfolk work most of their lives here at Cammell Laird. I have it on good authority that some of them have even looked enviously over the water and seen what's been going on in Liverpool for the last few months. We could certainly do with some good news regarding jobs on *this* side, too! It sounds as if the financial backing is in place.

"Derek, how quickly can you take a straw poll on the shop floor, find out what sort of spare manpower might be available in-house—brothers, cousins, uncles, that sort of thing? With the new orders, I have to say we can't really afford to lose any of the experienced shipbuilders we have on the books, but anyone who has a relative looking for work can say that I'm prepared to write references myself—as long as whoever works here has a good record himself, of course!"

"Hmmm. The Job Centre might consider that a bit iffy, but as this discussion *isn't* being minuted, and is therefore not *really* happening, we can safely ignore what *they* think." JRK's opinions about government bodies in general, and Job Centres in particular, were, for the most part, unprintable.

Nuala cut in to smooth things over. "Mr. Hines hasn't a great deal of time to spare, and he hasn't had the opportunity to see Seaforth docks for himself as yet. We do have a couple of spare seats in the bus outside if anyone would like to join us. I believe Mr. Hines has plans to return to London this evening if it's possible, and we really ought to be on our way..."

Derek left his deputy to pass on the call to arms and had an extra spring in his step as they returned to the minibus. One of the managers insisted on tagging along: Paul shot a questioning look in Derek's direction and received an almost invisible nod of approval before accepting the offer. The CEO ducked into an office on the way, emerging seconds later with a hard hat under his arm. ALAN was stencilled above the peak.

"My PA keeps telling me I should toss it. She thinks it makes the office look untidy. So I tell her, 'Over my dead body!' I like to remember what I did to get where I am today. Why should I act as if I'm ashamed of it? And it's a good excuse to get out of the office.

"The approach roads to the Tunnel can cope with peak-hour traffic already. They were brought up to motorway standard years ago, and creating a parking area won't be a problem. There's already some wasteland adjoining it, and most of it already belongs to the council anyway."

The toll booths at the Tunnel entrance kept the mid-afternoon traffic moving smoothly, and the shortcut Dock Road exit was open for use at that time of day.

"It means we don't have the hassle of threading through the one-way system in Liverpool centre. Paul, maybe that's something we need to take a long, careful look at. I've had a few people moan to me about getting snarled up in rush-hour traffic."

"Leave that with me, John. I'll get someone onto it. We really ought to look in on the dig site before going on to the docks, if only to introduce Rik to the navigator crew."

"And I can nip into the office with some copy," added Kevin. "Don't worry! I've been careful not to give anything away."

***

Eddie was standing sentry in the trench when they pulled up and radioed immediately for Billy to crawl out.

"We've heard a lot about you, Mr. Hines. Pleasure to meet you!"

Billy wiped his hand on a relatively clean towel before giving paw to their visitor.

"How are things down below?"

Billy looked at JRK before replying.

"Rik's been briefed. You can tell him anything you'd tell the rest of the team."

"Thanks, Boss! All the same, I think it'd be best if we all go 'downstairs'. We don't want to draw too much attention, and the offices along Old Hall Street'll be emptying out soon."

Kevin was back from the *Echo* news desk by the time Eddie had shepherded the group through the much larger and efficiently shored entrance.

"We managed to move a load o' tables in on Thursday night, on the QTs," said Billy. "There was plenty of room round the edges o' the room, but some of the jewellery an' stuff is a bit heavy. Some o' these folding tables are saggin' a bit in the middle!"

There was an absolute minimum of space between the tables—a grudging two inches, on average—and even those not showing signs of stress or strain were filled with neat rows of items extracted from the upper tunnel. By and large, each table was filled with either coins or personal trinkets such as rings and necklaces: some had been reserved for chalices, chests and other larger ornate items. A considerable number of unopened sacks and boxes stood in the centre of the chamber, awaiting inspection and classification.

"Carry on, guys. I'll be round to introduce yiz t' th' boss in a few minutes, but we need to keep ploddin' on. We need everything catalogued before we can do anything else."

"How far into the tunnel have we got?" JRK wanted to know.

Billy glanced at the notes he was carrying. "So far, we've cleared everything in the first hundred and fifty yards of the passage. Most of the boxes and moneybags we've come across so far have been undamaged. The tunnel's still filled floor to ceiling, and there's no way of guessing how much more there is."

"Or how much it's worth," Dominic added, clearly speaking as a professional accountant. "There's a considerable fortune sitting on these tables based purely on the current market prices of precious metals. What a collector would be prepared to pay over and above that to reflect their perceived value as works of art is anybody's guess!"

"I believe we're safest holding onto this treasure trove as collateral to establish a line of credit from Europe and other sources," JRK said. "The more we go around asking questions about the artistic value of the individual pieces, the more likely we are to run up against awkward questions—many of 'em querying the true provenance of what we've found, even disputing who actually owns it."

Paul looked at his watch, then at Rik.

"If we're going to look at Seaforth docks and give Rik a chance to fly back to London tonight, we really ought to be on our way."

***

"The access roads are in pretty poor condition."

"No need to mince words, Rik. They're knackered. Anyone who lives this side of Liverpool or has to commute into town from the north knows that. As far as road maintenance is concerned, we've been robbing Peter to pay Paul for years now, and there's never enough in the kitty to go around. With this set of docks being in such poor condition, almost deserted, we've had to use funding on roads in other parts of town."

"And as a result, these have gone from bad to worse. Yes, I can appreciate that."

The minibus bumped along a side road, which seemed to be more repair patch than original tarmac, and across a patch of uneven cobblestone fronting an open pair of cast-iron gates that had seen better days. A short section of worn rail tracks ran through the cobbles, almost hidden by weeds and scrub grass. A uniformed security guard checked the vehicle's registration on his clipboard, spoke briefly into the radio he carried and waved them through.

"Let's do the Time Warp again!" Rik suddenly warbled, very unmusically for someone whose first fortune had been dependent on the entertainment industry. He looked around as if expecting something.

"Just having a gander. You said yourself earlier on, this section of dockland still looks more or less the same as it did after the Blitz in '41. Listen carefully—there's no significant background sound at all. We're the only vehicle around. You can *see* the main road, but you certainly can't *hear* traffic passing…hell, there isn't even any birdsong! And did you see the brick the guard's using as a mobile?"

At JRK's nod, the chauffeur killed the minibus's engine. It was true: the silence that flowed over and around them was alluring, dreamlike. Paul couldn't help it: immediately, he yawned, setting off a chain reaction, which affected everyone, even the hired driver.

JRK made a conscious effort to establish some sort of control. He slid open the side door, stepped out onto the cobbles and cocked his head.

"It's true. Even the bloody gulls aren't close enough to be heard! We could just as easily be standing here during the Blitz. It's like having the place to ourselves."

He turned to Rik.

"And for the record, the security guard *wasn't* using an early 'house brick' of a mobile phone. It was a walkie-talkie! We've used them for years. They're all but indestructible, but I guess they'll be replaced by mobiles as they wear out. Still, I grant you it adds to the old-world effect.

"Anyway, if we all climb back on board, we can take a Cook's Tour around the buildings Jerry didn't manage to destroy. Robin Stuart and I got a good overall view of the site recently from the riverside. We took a ferry trip and discussed its potential..."

JRK summarised the main points he'd been through with the Core Holdings boss as they drove unhurriedly through the deserted docks. His enthusiasm brought the desolation around them to life. By the time he finished his pitch, it was very easy to imagine the hustle and bustle of a busy yard straining to burst out of the shadows lengthening around them as the sun approached the horizon beyond the mouth of the river.

"That was some vision, John!" Rik Hines was clearly impressed. "Listen, I won't ask my pilots to fly back tonight. They deserve a night off, anyway, and there's nothing that won't wait a few hours until I get back to deal with it. Any chance of a hotel room and somewhere we can all go for a decent meal?"

***

"John, I swear I'll be poaching your PA, first chance I get. Whatever you're paying her, I'll double it!"

Nuala had called in a favour or three and found luxurious—and theoretically impossible to come by—accommodation for Rik and his pilots at the Hard Day's Night Beatle-themed hotel. She'd also booked a table at a quiet out-of-town restaurant, and they had just reached the coffee and liqueurs stage. JRK caught the head waiter's eye and indicated they wanted some privacy. Seconds later, the serving staff had dematerialised, leaving the diners undisturbed.

"No need for that, Rik," JRK countered, not that he believed for a second Rik was serious in his threat. "You're joining us as a full and equal member. You've as much right to make use of Nuala's talents as Paul does—*and* myself!"

"Maybe I should be expecting *two* pay packets next month—or even three?" Nuala purred, blinking at each in turn with an innocent look in her eyes totally at variance with the wicked grin on her lips.

JRK looked around the table and tapped his glass. The quiet chuckle inspired by the pantomime comedy died away at once. He half-rose to address the group but appeared to have second thoughts and settled back onto his seat.

"I'm not going to pontificate or give a lecture, but there's been a development—something which is clearly to our advantage—and Robin, who negotiated it for us, is in the best position to explain. Robin, the floor's yours."

Robin nodded his thanks but remained seated.

"Core Holdings has negotiated a financial package with a number of backers, which will provide £5 billion pounds for the redevelopment of the docklands. The deal has been agreed but won't be announced just yet. There are a couple of things that need to be clarified before we can go public."

"How long have you been keeping *that* under your hat?" Dominic wanted to know.

"I've been leaning on the Marine Management Organisation for a couple of months now for permission to carry out a thorough dredging of the river to make it possible for the next generation of super-tankers to use our terminals. This is in addition to finally getting permission for cruises to start and finish in Liverpool. Once the MMO give their permission for the dredging, and I can't think of any valid reason for them to refuse, we can go public on this. That's all we're waiting for!"

"Whoa!" Rik protested. "Slow down a bit. You're losing me."

JRK took pity on him.

"Sorry, Rik. Things have been a bit hectic for us over the past few weeks. You'll have to get used to it, mate. It's par for the course."

"Perhaps a summary of the current state of play might be useful?" Steve Dunning suggested. His professional, logical lawyer's tone of voice had a calming effect. JRK nodded to Paul and sat back.

"You've seen the results of our Tramlink Project, which was set up to provide work for local people, people who'd lost their self-respect and their hope of any light at the end of the tunnel.

"Most of those men have now moved on to our next construction project.—the new bridge near Runcorn, our link with all points south. In fact, I think I'm right in saying we've lost no more than one or two of the workforce—they call themselves navigators, by the way, Rik. Did I tell you that?"

"I don't remember you saying it, but I've definitely heard that somewhere or other recently. As in the origin of the more usual 'navvies', I suppose?" Steve nodded.

"Thought so. Sorry, Paul. Carry on!"

"We've taken on more men for the Mersey Gateway Project. We'd already received Objective One funding from Europe to improve road and rail links, so nobody could object to that, and we did a bit more damage to the unemployment stats at the same time.

"We're using this opportunity to incorporate further construction work on the site, and build a customs hall slash passport control, with a decent-sized marshalling yard for HGVs. Local residents will all be issued with SmarTag ID chips for their vehicles, which should mean they can drive through a dedicated local-traffic lane without undue delay, and more importantly, they'll be exempt from paying toll charges.

"We will coordinate our efforts to make sure that customs and passport control facilities are also introduced at both Mersey Tunnels. These will go live on the same day the Mersey Gateway opens, provisional date fifteenth of June—the date Magna

Carta was signed. This will in future be an extra public holiday, Liverpool Day.

"All traffic from the north will be filtered through Switch Island, where similar facilities will be installed. This will go hand in glove with the regeneration of the docklands."

Rik had been scribbling on a notepad throughout Paul's *résumé*. Now, as he paused to sip from his coffee, he raised his pencil.

"You seem to have covered all the bases, Paul, but I'm finding it hard to see how you're balancing the books. The work you've already set in motion can't have come cheap! The navigator gang's wages alone must have come to a small fortune."

"I'll cover that one," Dominic cut in. He turned to Rik. "Paul's an excellent agent, but I'm the number-cruncher on the team."

"Dom means he can make numbers jump through hoops or even disappear if it suits his purpose," Nuala offered, raising a general murmur of agreement. Dominic habitually understated his talents, but his sister was invariably there to remind others how valuable he was to the group.

Dominic nodded his thanks for the moral support and continued.

"You know what they say, you have to 'speculate to accumulate'. Well, it's true. Money makes money, and we've had our fair share of luck, how the timing of certain things has panned out. For example, on the strength of the Objective One funding we were granted, we were able to approach other sources and use it as collateral to raise more funds elsewhere—for the moment, I won't say who, but it's all kosher, there's nothing underhand or even slightly dodgy involved. We sold the same idea twice over, and all of a sudden, we had more than three times the funding we started with."

Rik tapped his pencil against his notebook. "I'm beginning to understand your finances actually draw on deep resources that the casual observer might not appreciate! And you haven't even mentioned what you've stumbled on alongside Magna Carta..."

"Mainly because we have to go public on the find itself before we can hope to get even an approximate idea of its value."

"True enough, Paul," Dominic interposed, "but even so, there's going to be a considerable difference between the basic market price of the precious stones and metals themselves, and the presumably higher value that museums, art galleries and other private collectors are prepared to place upon them as objects of art."

"There's also a delicate question of *meum* and *tuum*, which has to be resolved before we can even consider what these items may or may not be worth to *us*," JRK cut in. "Steve, I know it's early days as yet, but have you made any progress to establish provenance on this treasure trove? Who actually *owns* it, considering how long ago it was...mislaid?"

"Legally, the answer's very simple. So simple, I've never had the slightest doubt about it." Steven's response was calm, confident and immediate, but there was a certain gleam in his eye, as if he were enjoying a private joke one last time before sharing it.

"No matter how you phrase it, treasure trove found anywhere—in the UK, in Europe or even worldwide—automatically reverts to the Crown, the country, the nation, the Government. However..."

He paused and looked around, favouring everyone present—including the two pilots—with a personal moment's soul-searching glance. The pilots seemed shell-shocked, hearing casual reference to unimaginably huge amounts of money bandied about in such cavalier fashion.

Suddenly, the effort became too much: Steven's lips parted, and a genuine smile cracked his face in half.

"However, the Charter specifically names Liverpool and Merseyside as a separate, independent, self-governing region, state, realm—the actual mot juste isn't so important. It's the intent, the authority the monarch of the time invested in the town and its residents.

"The treasure trove clearly belongs to Liverpool and the residents of the town. In other words, there is no possibility of any legal counterclaim. Whatever Prince Rupert's gold may eventually prove to be worth, nobody can prevent us laying claim to it and using it in any way we see fit!"

CHAPTER FOURTEEN

THIS CALM STATEMENT from the in-house legal expert drew involuntary gasps from all present: some in amazement, but for the majority it was the automatic release of a tension they'd each felt without consciously realising it.

Dominic Ion's fingers were already working overtime on a number of different calculators he had within arm's reach, scattered randomly in a rough semicircle on the table in front of him. He was oblivious to everyone and worked in silence for several seconds longer. A brief murmur of comments was just making itself heard when he stopped and looked around. All conversation stopped immediately.

"I've attempted, over the last twenty-four hours or so, to catalogue and assess the artefacts Billy and his crew have found so far, but I have to admit, the most recent report was handed to me late last night, and my figures could easily be well out of date.

"We have to bear in mind, I'm not in any way qualified to say what the true market price of any single item might be. Like every form of art, especially from such a long time ago, the historic value's usually decided by what the buyer is prepared to offer—and that's generally well in excess of its intrinsic value—Troy ounces or carats, degrees of fineness and other methods of calculating the prices of precious metals and the like."

"Yeah, but, Dom," Paul interjected, "that'd be like saying the *Mona Lisa*'s a scrap of old canvas and some homemade oil paints and it'd fetch no more'n a fiver down on Paddy's Market!"

"Maybe not that, Paul, but I take your point anyway." JRK grinned at the thought and continued more seriously, "I can't claim to be a legal eagle or a history buff, especially in the company of those who *have* chosen to specialise in those two fields. But it seems pretty clear to me that, since Liverpool's Royal Charter predates the document signed at Runnymede Green in 1215, and the one which includes Clause Sixty-Four is dated *after* the accepted date of Magna Carta, we're home and dry, historically. There doesn't seem to be any possibility of counterclaim or legal challenge regarding the provenance of this treasure trove, for want of a better term. Will that put your minds at rest?"

JRK directed his question to the whole floor but was most interested in the responses from John Midler and Steve Dunning. He was relieved to see that both reacted instantly and without doubt.

"It's an open-and-shut case in any court of law," was Steven's comment.

John Midler nodded his agreement, rubbing his hands together in anticipation. "Maureen, we're going to be busy preparing a careful, exact translation of this document. It will have to stand up to line-by-line scrutiny by all and sundry, and we'll have to convince a lot of people that we've got a legitimate claim."

John and Maureen commandeered a small office with a door, which meant they could concentrate on a translation of the document that would stand any legal challenge. Glass panels meant they could still see and be seen while they worked.

JRK turned to Paul.

"D'you happen to know how close we are to getting a local TV station? I heard there were a few groups preparing tenders."

"Kevin's probably the best one to ask about that. I'll give him a bell..."

***

Kevin didn't even need to consult his diary: this was a number he had in his head and on speed dial.

"Hello, Phil? ... Good man, listen, this could be a good time to scratch each other's back. You still looking for seed money for your TV plans? ... Suppose I could point you in the right direction, how soon could you launch? ... No, not over the phone. Can you meet me outside the *Echo*? I'm at a meeting near there. I can introduce you. ... Okay, twenty minutes? I'll be waiting."

***

"Phil, you probably know most of the faces around the table. Folks, this is Phil Greene, Tik-Tox Productions. He's been trying for a couple of years now to start a local TV station to cover local issues, give us an extra depth and coverage we can't get from the newspaper and local radio broadcasts."

Rik Hines unfolded himself from his chair and reached across the table.

"Glad to meet you, Phil. I wasn't too happy being the latest noob on the team, but I'm only a couple of hours ahead of you. Welcome aboard!" He grasped Phil's hand and brought him around to a vacant chair next to his own. Phil looked across the table to Paul and JRK.

"Jomfru Trains? Is *this* the source of the seed money you hinted at?"

Paul shook his head. "No, Phil. Not directly, although Rik has already indicated he's prepared to put his money where his mouth is. But we have other sources of funding..."

Over the next half hour, Phil was bombarded with photographs of the most significant pieces of Prince Rupert's treasures that had been unearthed to date. A swift phone call resulted in Billy Lynch arriving at the door with a battered briefcase under his arm. This proved to contain a cross-section of small, easily carried objects that had come to light during the current shift.

"We're running out of space to set up tables, though, Boss, and no end that I can see to the crates and cases still up the northern tunnel. We're going to have to start repacking boxes and moving stuff out of the vault."

John Midler nodded. "I knew this would happen sooner rather than later. Being honest, I'm amazed we've got away with it until now. But I've given it some thought. Am I right in thinking we want to keep the excavation site itself out of the glare of publicity a bit longer? Good! In that case, we should be moving what's already been brought out and catalogued from the vault to a secure location—I'd suggest somewhere in the university, but I'm open to other suggestions—and most important, we should be moving it under cover of darkness, using people we know can keep their mouths shut."

"Me 'n' the lads can gerra coupla bodies we c'n vouch for!" Billy stated. "Big lads, chunks o' beef who'll keep schtum if *I* tell 'em!"

"Your word's good enough for me, Billy," JRK replied. "How many d'you reckon?"

"Six fer starters, right off the top o' me 'ead! Last I heard, they were all between gigs. I can prolly 'ave 'em report 'ere t'night, if yiz need 'em?"

"There's some from the graveyard shift at JLA didn't have transport to get to the Gateway site in Runcorn. I can make a few phone calls..." Paul had his mobile at the ready as he spoke and started dialling as soon as JRK nodded.

Billy insisted on walking back to the trench with Phil Greene and Rik Hines in tow, to show them the scope and nature of the gold coin and jewellery that had been unearthed so far. Even Phil, the last to arrive, was startled to discover that the relatively short late summer's night had fallen while they'd been discussing their next few moves. The trench looked unguarded, and Billy's hackles began to rise until Yozzer materialised out of a shadow that was slightly deeper than most.

"Bang, you're dead—alluv yiz!" he breathed, briefly playing a pencil-thin beam of light across three chests as if it were a powerful laser gun. Billy explained the purpose of the visit as they clambered down into the trench itself.

The entrance door was now strengthened, and the earth immediately in front of it firmly trampled by the passage of uncountable heavy work boots. Once through the short passage into the vault itself, the problem Billy had referred to regarding space for tables was easy to understand. Ten rows of six tables in each row left just enough room to walk around the vault and scrutinise what had been laid out for inspection.

"I'd guess we *might* have half the treasure out of the north passage," Billy said, "but no more than that. We can't really bring anything else out until we get shot o' this lot."

"You said there's another passage—south, leading down to the docks themselves?" Rik asked. "Can you re-pack and store some stuff there, start creating a bit of space?"

"Could do. We can begin with the tables closest to the southern passage. There's probably twenty-odd, maybe thirty yards of southern tunnel dug out, and we should have more muscle on the job in a couple of hours to clear the other tables. With any luck, we can empty the vault before daybreak."

***

"I knew it'd be handy to have the Trannie parked up on site!" Billy grunted as he pulled up in the staff car park behind Liverpool University. A dozen pairs of willing hands were lining up to play a careful game of Pass the Parcel from the van's rear doors to the service entrance of the adjacent building as soon as Billy had unlocked it.

The first load was emptied rapidly and without accidents. Before moving off, Billy requisitioned a few volunteers to supplement the workforce back at the trench. With a contemptuous disregard for Elfin Safety, eight men climbed into the back of the Transit and held on to whatever they could grab in the total darkness for the five-minute journey back to Old Hall Street.

"Figured we could use a few extra pair of hands at this end," Billy grunted to nobody in particular as he parked up as closely as he could to the trench. Yozzer had the rear doors open before the engine stopped running and directed the newcomers into the vault, where they were deployed to supplement the teams storing boxes in the southern passage or ferrying packed boxes along a line back to the van. The tables emptied rapidly with the extra manpower available.

"When you get back to the uni, Billy, ask the prof for more storage crates. We're going to need them to pack things in. Most of the treasure was packed in flimsy material, which has disintegrated over the years."

"There should be no end of plastic crates we can use for that," Maureen called out as she dragged another damaged sack out of the uphill section of the tunnel. "I can't get a signal on my mobile from down here. Phone him from street level before you drive off."

Billy gave her a cheerful thumbs up and disappeared into the night. He glanced at the sky, which was still encouragingly dark. It should be possible to make at least one more round trip after this one before dawn began to threaten their clandestine 'capital transfer' activities.

Maureen was right. The sturdy plastic crates that filled the Transit on its return trip to Old Hall Street were ideal for the purpose and swift to fill. Everything still on the inspection tables and a significant portion of the items stored temporarily in the part-cleared cul-de-sac tunnel leading towards the river was suddenly much easier to handle, and the last trip of the night carried a payload heavy enough to test the vehicle's suspension to its limits.

As dawn finally broke, Billy parked the Transit back in its accustomed spot close to the *Echo* offices, then opened the rear doors and sat on the sill. He reached into his shirt pocket, but instead of a pack of cigarettes, he pulled out a thick wad of banknotes and began to count them rapidly into the hands of the extra muscle he'd hired.

"See yiz all again, same time tonight, okay?"

With a chorus of "Orright!" and other nods of understanding, the crew dispersed. Paul caught Billy's eye as the Costa coffee shop opened its doors and raised an eyebrow.

"Some of the lads...don't know how to use a bank account," Billy offered. "And it's easier to pay 'em *all* in cash when that happens. This way, nobody gets embarrassed by being paid diff'runt to ev'ryone else, see?"

Paul did 'see', but he suspected the Inland Revenue might take a somewhat less liberal view of the informality of this particular form of wage billing. However, it was none of his business. And if it worked, why knock it?

"You've told them there's more of the same still to be done—at very least, tomorrow, maybe longer?"

"Yeah, that's sorted. They'll be here bright and early."

"And they know they're to keep their mouths closed?"

"They're not going to tell anyone they're working the lump, cash in hand, no questions, no National Insurance stamps..."

NI cards and adhesive stamps hadn't been used for at least a full generation of manual labourers or anyone else resident in the UK, but Paul deemed it politic to let the comment pass.

"Fair enough. You know how to get the best out of the workforce you're supplying. I'm not going to interfere. They've done a good job and I'm impressed, Billy. I'm sure we can find a way of giving them a suitable bonus once the job's finished."

CHAPTER FIFTEEN

"MO, HAVE YOU worked through the night again?"

John Midler's question was an automatic reaction: his eyes had already told him all he needed to know. Neat stacks of paper—mostly computer printouts—had been deposited on tables running the full length of the room. Four student types scurried back and forth, adding new sheets of data to one pile or another. The wall above and behind the row of tables was covered with a pinboard, which was being populated with more notes. Maureen sat at a desk scribbling furiously: she raised one hand in acknowledgement but didn't look up.

"I couldn't leave the night shift to catalogue the new artefacts. They're good, but they lack experience. One moment, I'm almost up-to-date..."

Her voice trailed off: the pen smoked across the page a further three or four times before she paused, read through her latest notes and put the writing block to one side.

"The notes describing the items that were laid out on the tables were a great help. That includes the descriptions written by others, not just those in your handwriting and mine. Seems your students have looked at your notes and tried to phrase their own notes in a similar style."

"Hmmm. Imitation being the least obnoxious form of flattery, I suppose that's a good thing."

"Don't knock it, John. It makes it easier for me to compare notes when there are a number of writers involved. The language they use in their reports is pretty consistent."

She reached out and picked up her own notes.

"That gave me a bit of leeway. I've been able to concentrate on making a preliminary assessment of some of the items which were stored in the southern tunnel but hadn't been catalogued. I've managed to look through two cases. I've identified most of the artefacts I came across, but I'm going to ask you for a second opinion on a number of items."

"Now I *am* flattered, Maureen, though I'm not so certain the sum total of my knowledge is any greater than yours these days. Two cases is a good start. How many cases do we have of these items which haven't been catalogued yet?"

"Twenty-five, plus the two I've had a glance through and made prelims of them. We'll have to recycle these plastic crates for whatever's still to be brought out of the southern passage and whatever is still to be excavated from the uphill tunnel. One consolation. The archaeology department's not short of storage crates!"

"I'll leave the practical details to you, then. Just keep the supply of crates ticking over. I'll make a start on examining the crates you've already looked at."

The professor's more detailed study of the artefacts Maureen had already examined was as thorough as possible, given the circumstances. The first case held only four items, all of a fair size and mass, and all easily identified.

"Box twenty-six, contents four objects. First object," he intoned into his memo pad as he reached for a measuring tape and a pair of callipers.

"First object is a chalice, appears undamaged. Height, 457 millimetres. Mouth of chalice, 762 millimetres in circumference. Total weight 7.3 kilograms, consistent with expected weight of an object of this nature made from gold of exceptional purity.

"Adornments. Around the lip of the chalice, twenty-four gemstones, alternately red and green. Assumed to be ruby and emerald, lab tests required for confirmation.

"Bowl. Hemispherical, roughly half the overall height of the chalice. Inscription runs left to right, font cursive, height approx. eight-millimetre caps, six-millimetre lower-case. INRI repeated three times, equidistant. *Iesus Nazarene, Rex Iudae*—assumed to be intended text.

"Base. Solid platform around twenty-five millimetres thick. Proportions consistent to rest of this artefact. No further jewellery evident, but some etched letters and designs...

"*Hic est enim corpus meum.*

"'This is my body.' From this, I must assume that the chalice was intended for use in church services."

He continued to add quiet, confident memo notes as he completed his visual examination of the chalice.

"Next item. This is a monstrance, designed to display the eucharist in services. Overall height, 610 millimetres. Weight, 4.535 kilograms. The display box is at the centre of a sunburst of alternate long and short rods, presumably gold, of 150 and 75 millimetres, respectively. The sunburst is approximately 356 millimetres in diameter—203 millimetres measured to the end of the shorter rods."

He studied the remaining items in the two crates Maureen had prepared in the same patient, methodical and professional, unemotional manner. Maureen seized the opportunity to assess the unsorted crates, assisted by some of the senior students she felt were up to the task. More crates arrived from the trench at staggered intervals. John had opted for the lecture theatre they were using because it was windowless and had only two access doors. Security, especially from inquisitive eyes, was his major concern, but there was also the added bonus of air conditioning and temperature control, which would make it far easier to preserve any delicate items they came across.

"Are you hungry?"

John flinched as Maureen touched him on the shoulder to get his attention. Automatically, he glanced at his wrist, but he'd removed his watch rather than risk damaging something while studying it.

"It's mid-afternoon, and you haven't stopped since early morning. I've phoned for sandwiches and drinks to be sent up—they should be here soon."

John scribbled a final note on the last item in a crate—a bracelet of some sort, Maureen noted absently—and straightened his back.

"Pass the word for everyone to down tools. We can sit up at the back of the auditorium away from the workbenches. I don't want grease and crumbs all over the treasures we have here. And I don't want strangers in here. The food can be left *outside* the doors for us to collect."

"I thought of that, too. There are two prop-forward hulks watching the doors," Maureen said with a grin. "They won't let anyone in."

"Great work, Mo," the professor and then addressed the room. "Anyone who has to leave us, thank you for your time. I know that sounds pitifully inadequate, and when my head's stopped spinning, I'll think of a more suitable way of thanking you properly. The one thing I have to insist on is, keep your mouths shut. Everyone's going to be asking what's going on, and there mustn't be any leaks whatsoever until we're ready to make an official announcement. Is that clear?"

The response was immediate and unanimous: those who, for whatever reason, were obliged to leave—a much smaller percentage than John had imagined—were happy to promise their silence.

Maureen had been juggling two or three mobiles and arranged for fresh bodies to replace those who had to leave.

"We're gaining more than we're losing. The team's growing."

"There's more than enough work to keep them all busy. We should be grateful," John commented as he dropped his paper plate in the bin. "See if it's possible to contact your dad—he might be above ground, you never know—and ask how many more crates he's managed to fill. We've got plenty of room..."

"And staff to process them," Maureen added as she toggled her dad's number. She heard a ringtone and gave John a thumbs up a split second before her dad answered, leaving no opportunity for niceties.

"We need more empty crates, so we do. We're soon down to the last."

His distinctive Belfast brogue lent an urgency to the simple statement. Maureen clicked on the 'speaker' button and passed the handset to John.

"Not a problem, Billy. There must be thirty or so empty crates taking up space here. Bring whatever you can cram into your van, and you can take these back with you..."

CHAPTER SIXTEEN

"MY EDITOR'S BREATHING fire. He *knows* there's something going down on the street, right under his nose."

Kevin Wyatt had fled his rabbit hutch of an office to escape the display of blinking red lights that told him how many people demanded his presence on the *Echo*'s internal phone lines. He didn't dare go out through the mezzanine foyer to the main entrance and had opted to take the staff lift down to the car park. He didn't drive and fervently hoped this would throw others off his tail while he made a private phone call.

"I'm sorry, Kev. I had no idea how big this was going to be."

Maureen was troubled by pangs of conscience. She cast around for something, anything, she could offer the news-starved journalist. She studied the latest figures on her notepad.

"Kevin, I can't tell you the exact nature of the individual items we've hauled out and studied so far, and any attempt to value them would be futile. What I can tell you is, so far, we've looked at the contents of two hundred and seventy-five storage crates, each about the size of a typical milk crate. Every item has been a piece of jewellery—mostly gold, and of a surprisingly good quality—and the vast majority have been decorated with a variety of gemstones. As you'll have guessed, their intrinsic value itself is almost incalculable, but their historical significance makes them unique. I defy *anyone* to put a price on them. And I know it's a glib phrase, a cliché, but in this case, we might literally be talking of a King's Ransom."

"I could really *use* that as a feel-good headline, Mo. Can you ask the prof or JRK or someone for permission? I can't see it doing any damage if I use it as a wow factor, and I can guarantee a front-page headline. The editor's having kittens here, especially knowing it all started in a trench he can see from his office window, and he can't do anything about it."

"Give me half an hour?"

"I'd be happier if it was twenty minutes..."

"Don't push your luck, Kevin! We don't know each other *that* well. Not yet, anyway."

"Hey, I had to try. You can't imagine what it's like to have an editor on your back day and night when there's a good story going begging."

"I'll see what I can do. John's just come back in, and JRK's with him."

***

"...goes deeper than that. The real *difference between the actual value of the find—as defined by what the precious metals and gemstones would fetch on the stock market—and the historical importance they represent can't be expressed in pounds sterling, dollars or any other currency. The most significant difference this makes to Liverpool, and Merseyside in general, is this. It means that we, as a region, are now in a much stronger financial position than we were even a week ago. We have collateral, which we can use to our advantage to apply to Europe and other sources of funding for major projects that might otherwise be impossible to complete if we had to foot the full bill from our own resources.*

"John R. Kirwan, spokesperson for Liverpool's Governing Council, said, 'Although this is incredibly good news for all the city's residents and businesses, nothing will be done without full consultation every step of the way. We have to be clear about what we want to achieve and how we want to go about it. Every decision we make will have significance for everyone living in the region, and there will be full, open and transparent dialogue with every resident

at every stage of development. Every full council meeting will be held in public, with full media coverage for anyone who cannot attend in person. Nothing will be undertaken without a clear mandate from a majority of the electorate.'"

JRK toggled the mute button and let the rest of the interview run in silence on one of the TV monitors.

"Okay, folks, they're the ground rules. We're aiming for full, open discussion at every step and a clear majority behind every decision. Paul and Kevin, how quickly can we establish the radio links for broadcasting council meetings?"

Paul nodded to Kevin, who glanced at his notes.

"The outside-broadcast unit is installing the necessary mics and cabling as we speak. There'll be some seating lost in the public gallery of the chambers, but there should still be room for about eight hundred to attend, with another two hundred or so seats available in other rooms at the town hall if required. I'd say we'll be ready to rock 'n' roll from mid-afternoon. Live feed from the chamber will be up and running by that time, too. But we need to let people know that they can follow the debate on radio and TV—"

"Which can be done with regular soundbites during coverage and a few words on the front page of the *Echo*, I imagine?" Paul cut in as Kevin paused to take a breath.

Kevin nodded confirmation and continued, "We should probably have some sort of police presence outside the town hall, at least for this first meeting. Not that I'm expecting trouble, but there may well be crowd-control issues. We've no idea how many people will turn up hoping to get inside."

"Better safe than sorry. There's always one idiot spoiling for a fight in any crowd," JRK said decisively. "Now, since I'm supposed to be chairing the meeting, this would be an awfully good time to give me a hint of what's on the agenda. Nuala, do you have one somewhere?"

"Right here. The media are already aware of the treasure-trove story, so that will *have* to be top of the list."

"I'll be surprised if we actually get as far as point two. But it's vital we establish the *facts* and make sure everyone knows what we plan to do with our good fortune. Professor Midler—I'm afraid you're going to have to accept a formal title this evening, at least for the televised events—do you have a ballpark figure that will give us some idea of the size, the value of what you've managed to examine so far?"

John Midler glanced through his notes and conferred briefly with Maureen.

"Almost every item passing through our hands these last few days has been a well-preserved object or ornament. Most of them are cast in gold and adorned with a wide range of jewels, diamond, ruby and emerald being the most common decorative stones. I've no idea of the current stock-market prices of any one of these materials, but I've never seen a collection of this size anywhere in Britain or Europe. Billy says the tunnel itself has been picked clean. I'd say each crate we've emptied must have contained at least a hundred pounds—or fifty kilos—of gold ornaments, coins and other objects. Maureen, what was the final tally of crates?"

"Eight hundred and seventy—plus the cloths, parchments and scrolls we haven't even looked at yet. Their importance lies in what's written or painted on them. We can't put a price on their heads the same way we can with precious metals."

"It's still four thousand *kilos* of precious metals!" Dominic Ion bounced to his feet. "Releasing *that* much gold or any other precious metal onto the market all at once would be a disaster. The selling price would hit rock bottom overnight."

"Which is why we won't be doing anything remotely like that," JRK snapped back. He took a short breath to control himself before he continued.

"Sorry, Dom. I wasn't having a go at you personally. But you're right about the effect it would have on market prices if news of the size and nature of our treasure trove becomes public knowledge. We can't avoid admitting that we have a substantial hoard, but for the moment, I propose we keep further details in-house. And, John, the fewer people who know just how valuable a gift Liverpool has received from Prince Rupert, the better."

Suddenly, Kevin Wyatt flapped wildly from a PC in the corner of the room where he had been monitoring news stories as they developed.

"I think you'll want to see this, guys."

His hands darted across the keyboard: a magnified Sky News broadcast marched across the wall screen at one end of the room.

The camera was trained on a reporter who looked barely old enough to shave.

"A think tank of academics at Sheffield University have published a paper which shows that restrictions, cuts and changes in the benefit system proposed in the last Budget is likely to cost Liverpool in the region of £850 million in lost funding. They claim this represents four per cent of the city's income in the current financial year, equivalent to the sum which had been set aside to encourage economic growth over the next two and a half years.

"Professor Stephen Hallam, you were in charge of the think tank. How significant are these figures?"

"We based our studies on a wide range of official statistics. Our conclusion is that the Coalition Government in London is pursuing policies which are designed to have the greatest impact on individuals and communities which are well outside their own comfort zone. In other words, certain parts of the country are highly likely to suffer cuts and deprivation. Those where traditionally they get little support from the electorate. These regions of the country are being starved of the support they need simply because they don't vote Tory."

"It's certainly a *long* time since the Tories had any successes here in Liverpool. That fits, I guess."

"That's a bit of a leap in the dark if you ask me, JRK."

"It's cheap-jack journalism, Paul, but it's the sort of thing people remember. Let's not forget the news channel we're getting the story from."

"Hmmm. I'd want a bit of corroboration from other sources before I ran it on the front page of the *Echo,"* Kevin muttered, then immediately flushed scarlet as he realised what he'd said. "Not that I'm likely to be making that sort of editorial decision anytime soon, but you know what I mean..."

"Calm down, Kev. Nobody here's going to grass you up to your boss."

"Thanks, Maureen. I wouldn't fancy the job, anyway—ahh, crud. Looks like I have to rush over the road."

The theme from *Z Cars* blared from his mobile. He was on his feet, pulling on his jacket as he spoke.

"Yes, Boss! I'm on my way—be there in five with the latest update."

He paused at the door and tapped his mobile phone.

"He's going to ask me for some facts and figures. We'll have to give something for today's edition—call me as soon as you decide how much I can tell 'em."

He tapped his phone again and put it back to his ear as the door closed behind him.

"Sorry, Boss. Must have been a bit of a dead spot in that lift..."

CHAPTER SEVENTEEN

THE EARLY SHIFT reporting for duty at the *Echo* the following day was startled by the presence of a cordon of uniformed Securicor guards surrounding the newspaper offices. They shared the premises with a number of other businesses, but nobody was allowed to enter the building without showing some form of photo ID.

Billy called in a few favours, and before nine o'clock, a flatbed truck delivered a large quantity of heavy-duty steel plates, which were laid across the trench: extra tentage was swiftly erected above and around the trench, and the battered Transit van disappeared from the scene. Old Hall Street was suddenly and without explanation closed to all traffic other than the *Echo*'s fleet of distribution vans.

By mid-morning, at least an hour ahead of the usual schedule, the vans were mobilised carrying Tuesday's edition throughout Greater Merseyside and further to the newsagents in North Wales. Both local radio stations had suspended their scheduled programmes all morning, replacing them with studio discussions involving a number of city councillors and political pundits.

***

Even before Radio Merseyside's midday news began, the switchboard was swamped by people who'd bought early editions of the *Echo*, frantic for further information.

"Anyone who has bought a copy of today's *Echo* will already know that, for once, there really is just one thing to talk about in today's news."

Roger Allyn's familiar bass-baritone voice linked smoothly into the end of an abbreviated news summary just after twelve o'clock.

"And before we continue with our studio discussion, I'd like to ask our listeners to give our switchboard volunteers time to breathe while our invited guests discuss the significance of the documents and other items which were discovered during what began as a routine maintenance operation in Liverpool city centre and has become... well, I'll leave it to our experts to tell us what that may be. Professor John Midler is a head of department within Liverpool University's Faculty of Arts and Humanities. John, you're far better qualified than me to inform our listeners of exactly what has been found and its importance to Liverpool as a whole."

"Roger, it's probably every child's dream to go digging and stumble upon some sort of treasure trove, and I can confirm that valuable items, including gold and jewellery, are amongst the things we've discovered.

"But the very first thing we found is far more significant that any of these items, despite the market value of the precious metals and stones used in the jewellery. The first item discovered in the excavated trench was a document, perfectly preserved from being sealed in an airtight container. Laboratory testing has established its provenance and authenticity, and what we have is a version of the first British Constitution on record, Magna Carta, which was signed by King John in 1215."

"When you say 'a version', what do you mean?"

"Until now, we've assumed that the four known copies of Magna Carta on display at various universities and museums were the only ones to have survived. However, although we can confirm the age of the newly discovered document and the king's signature, this one has an extra clause added immediately above the signature. Clause Sixty-Four in *this* copy of Magna

Carta doesn't appear in any of the others. It applies directly and exclusively to the city of Liverpool and its residents, confirming the right to become an independent, self-governing state while retaining the privileges and protection of the monarch, 'in recognition of the faith and support shewn to our good self' as he expressed it."

"So how did this document remain hidden, lost and forgotten for eight hundred years?"

"We can only assume that the war took a turn *against* the Royalist army just after this was signed and sealed. Perhaps accidentally dropped on the battlefield, or maybe deliberately concealed to be retrieved at a later date. We can't be sure after all this time, but we can be absolutely certain that King John, for all his faults, was a sincere and a generous man. There's no doubt in my mind that he fully intended this as his way of rewarding the town and people of Liverpool for their solidarity and support of the royal cause."

"Mayor Joe Saunders..."

Roger's voice was low, his tone of voice neutral, but it hinted at a deep, unshakeable no-nonsense air of authority. The remaining members of the group in the cramped studio sat back at once, accepting the senior reporter's decision on who had earned the right to speak next.

"Professor," the major began, "does this mean that Liverpool has had the right—delivered, apparently, with a royal seal of approval—to operate as a self-sufficient region, state, duchy, principality, call it what you will...for over eight hundred years? Elect our own parliament, set our own taxes, pass our own laws..."

"Pay our own bills, fund our own public services, build our own road, rail, sea and air links, feed ourselves, organise import and export links..." John Midler finished. "Yes, that's about right.

Unless I've omitted anything important? It's never quite as simple as people think, is it?"

"If I've understood what the professor is saying," JRK cut in with the merest suggestion of a raised eyebrow at Roger Allyn and an even less obvious blink of approval. "If we were granted this right 'in perpetuity', as the text says, eight hundred years ago, then Merseyside has, in effect, been governed by an illegal regime all that time. In effect, we have been denied certain fundamental human rights."

It took all Roger's professional aplomb to keep some sort of control over the fierce debate that this remark set in motion. Outside the studio, the telephone lines went into meltdown.

Dominic caught Paul's eye across the room and hefted his mobile, indicating an incoming message.

Gov't agrees £30m from EDF to support refurb of Liverpool Waterfront, the text read. Scrolling the page revealed more details. The Environmental Development Fund had agreed to donate the sum towards the estimated £300m cost of dredging the river and building a state-of-the-art container port, which would make it possible for even the biggest container ships to dock on both sides of the Mersey.

"You're the number-cruncher, Dom. What d'you think?"

"Not impressed, Paul. What bothers me is what's *not* being said. There has to be a catch. It's too much of a coincidence, coming out of the blue like this. It feels more like a bribe than a 'business investment'—and it wouldn't surprise me if somewhere further down the line, they come back to us with the argument that it was a loan, not a gift. If recent form is any guide, they'll try to enforce a repayment or demand a share in the profits."

"You sound confident we'll be able to turn a profit from the venture."

"Trust me, Paul. Numbers are *my* game, remember? Opening up the Mersey for any ship, anywhere in the world, to come and trade here is a licence to *print* money. Liverpool was once the biggest, busiest cargo terminal in Europe, if not the world. This is how we'll rebuild the city's reputation *and* her finances."

Paul looked up, suddenly aware that the general confused hubbub of several heated discussions had died away. Everyone except Roger and Professor Midler had stopped arguing and was now staring at them. Roger pointed to a green sign overhead, which confirmed that the studio mics were off and continued to interview John Midler one-to-one.

"Something new, Paul?"

"Dom's just shown me some breaking news. Good news, on the face of it, but there might be a problem further down the line..."

Paul relayed the gist of the newsflash to a close huddle as far away from the two live debaters as the confines of the studio would allow. Dominic's phone, displaying the text message, was passed to Roger, who mimed to John Midler that he should keep talking about the significance of the discoveries and give him the opportunity to scroll through the main points.

"Thank you, Professor Midler. I'll give you the chance to get your breath back now, and I'll bring in another of today's guests to discuss a breaking news story which will also influence the development of Liverpool in the immediate future. Paul Freeman is assistant to and manager for the first independent candidate to serve on Liverpool City Council, J. R. Kirwan. My producer has just informed me that you have some very interesting news for us, hot off the press, so to speak?"

"Thank you, Roger. I haven't got the details yet, this is something which has literally been announced only a few minutes ago, and it comes direct from Brussels. Essentially, EU funds have been allocated expressly to Merseyside as a recognised Objective One zone eligible for support to encourage investment from industry and the creation of employment opportunities."

"Is there a specific sum which has been mentioned or at least hinted at?"

"Considerably more than the £2 million bribe we've been offered by the Coalition Government—which would almost certainly have strings attached, anyway. In the region of £20 million and with further investment available if we can show positive results within a period of three years."

"And how do you propose to go about that? Considering how long Liverpool's fortunes have been in decline, three years isn't a particularly generous amount of time to stop the rot, let alone reverse it, build upon it."

"Roger, in one sense, we've already taken the most difficult step—the first step along the way—when we took on everyone who applied for the navigator gangs who built the Tramlink. They showed us that it was possible to complete such a massive project ahead of schedule *and* keep costs below the budgeted price.

"This simply means that we've got more work on offer and funds to finance it. And did you know, we were over-subscribed for the Tramlink? In fact," Paul said, as he leant towards the studio mic, "we had a couple of thousand on a waiting list, and we're going to be needing every one of them, even if every single member of the current team of navvies signs up for another contract."

"You mention funds and financing for the new project, refurbishing docks on both banks of the river..."

It was clear Roger was about to play devil's advocate and toss in a loaded question.

"...I understand that everyone who worked on the Tramlink *and* every one of your suppliers was paid promptly and in full, with no delays. Very commendable, and well done! But I have to ask you, where did the original funding come from to make this possible? Because I can't believe for one minute that the sort of funding we're talking about could have originated from any private funding initiative. And you saying the Government's £2 million offer of support is a derisory amount, so I assume your financial backing lies elsewhere?"

Shit! That came a bit sooner than I'd hoped for, Paul thought. However, he'd known that he'd be asked for some sort of explanation sooner or later and was as prepared as he could ever be. Conscious of JRK watching him from the other side of the live studio window, he glanced at the notepad in his hands to cover the couple of seconds' delay in responding.

"Roger, I'm not at liberty to reveal the identity of our financial backers—not yet, anyway—but I can assure you, there was no money lost on the Tramlink Project. The funding already promised from the EU will simply make the Docklands Project easier to finance."

JRK re-entered the studio, carrying a note he'd received from Dominic Ion.

"Roger, I'd like to add a little more to what Paul's just explained if I may? This is from our chief number-cruncher, Dominic Ion."

He smoothed out the note.

"As Paul has already stated, we are *not* prepared to accept what amounts to small change and beer money from the UK National Coalition Government towards the Docklands Project because we suspect that the offer comes with far too many codicils, clauses and strings attached, leaving us under an obligation to repay the money at some future date when it will somehow have become a loan as opposed to a grant.

"We are confident that the Docklands Project will bring many benefits to the local economy, both in the tourist trade and by the increase in commercial traffic passing through the port.

"One of the economic models we're looking at would be to float the Docklands on the Stock Exchange and pay our employees a mixture of cash and stock options. In effect, they would all become shareholders with a personal interest in the success of their labours. We would do this by offering the shares directly on the European market in Brussels, Bonn or Paris, bypassing London altogether. This is the logical solution to our intention to secede from the United Kingdom as an independent, self-regulating region with our own currency as well as an autonomous, effective Regional Government."

Predictably the radio station's switchboard went into near-meltdown yet again, this time almost before JRK had finished making his statement. In the not-too-distant future, this radio interview would be pinpointed as the defining moment when the radical regionalist campaign for an independent Project of Merseyside officially began.

CHAPTER EIGHTEEN

"YOU CAUGHT EVERYONE napping with that one, JRK."

It was early evening. By leaving separately and at staggered intervals, the original Gang of Four had managed to meet again in an inconspicuous corner of the Pogue Mahone. It was less than five minutes from Radio Merseyside's studios, but ensuring nobody had been followed had added an extra half hour to the change of venue.

JRK grinned. "It's called prestidigitation, Paul. The conjurer's sleight of hand, misdirection. You *think* it's magic, but only because he's made you look at what *he* wants you to see."

Dominic arrived with the first round of drinks just in time to catch the end of this.

"Well, it certainly confused me, and I'm still none the wiser," Nuala commented with just the suggestion of a half-serious pout forming on her lips.

JRK took a deep draught from his pint glass before replying.

"I'm pretty sure that Roger was about to ask about our financial assets, and that's a subject I'd rather avoid for the moment. It's all very well for Steve to say that our legal right to this treasure trove is all above board and so on, but until we've established that in writing, I felt it best to distract his attention..."

"You certainly managed that, mate!" Paul nodded in approval and lifted his glass.

"We need to make a decision about that, too, and pretty soon," Dominic insisted as he settled into the corner. "As the nearest we've got to a treasurer, I'm hogging the chair for a few minutes."

He sounded confident but glanced automatically at JRK to check his reaction.

"Carry on, Dom."

"Thanks. Right, this is how I see things developing. I'm going to assume that Steve's assurances about the provenance of the treasures we've discovered are well-founded. I'm not a legal expert. That's his speciality. He ought to know what he's talking about.

"Basically, whatever the market value of this hoard of treasure may be, if we're going to be able to *use* these funds, we have to find a buyer, or buyers, and sell them—legitimately, with receipts, and everything above board. It's not going to happen overnight, and we still haven't talked about how and when we're going to announce to the world that we're actually sitting on a fortune.

"As works of art, they're going to be worth a damned sight more than the market price of the precious metals they're made from. Think of the cost price of the wood and strings used to make a Stradivarius and you'll see what I mean. Nowhere near the millions it would cost to buy the genuine article at an auction."

"Thanks, Dom. Point taken." JRK looked around the table with the light of battle in his eyes. "Right at this moment, we need some cash on the table to fund the campaign. We've been handed the golden opportunity to do this painlessly on the open market, and I propose we go ahead. It's a big step to take, and I'm sure we've all got our own opinions. I suggest we all go home and think about it—for *and* against—and be ready for a formal vote when we meet tomorrow morning—say, breakfast at eight o'clock?"

***

"That was a damn sight better than breakfast at one o' the fast-food places."

Paul had called in a favour from a friend who ran a city-centre pub. There wasn't a private room available, but they'd been served breakfast in a discreet corner, and the early bird regulars had been directed to other tables.

"Never thought about it until now, but that has to be a plus side to the change in pub licensing hours," JRK remarked as he refilled his coffee cup. "Now, down to business. Dominic, you're our finance guru. What can you tell us?"

"Steven and I spent most of the night reading through the laws concerning treasure trove." Dominic had a ring file in front of him, but it remained closed: he spoke confidently and apparently from memory.

"There's a significant amount of coinage, which I'm sure will be easy enough to sell. As far as I can tell, it's all cast in high-quality precious metals—mostly gold, as you'd expect in what was intended to be a King's Ransom. The stock market's still governed by the gold standard, and the price of gold is one thing which is always going to be a reliable marker in the market, all over the world."

"The age and historical significance of the coins themselves can only enhance their value," Steven added. "And that can only work in our favour. We can expect to get *more* than the market price of gold from any dealer. Some are beautiful works of art in themselves, and a collector is always going to offer more for them than a precious-metals dealer."

"I'm inclined to go for the...expediency of swift action. We don't want to start a bidding war and risk delays," JRK countered. "As Dominic said, the coins are likely to be the easiest asset to realise. I'd be happy to take the first offer, as long as it's reasonably close to today's market price so we've a healthy balance in the campaign account. We can always come back to an assessment of the market price of the art treasures later."

"Gold's touching eight hundred and thirty-five pounds an ounce—Troy ounce, that is," Nuala interrupted, scanning a FTSE page on her laptop, "so I'd guess each coin is worth a grand—some of the really big ones, considerably more than that."

"And we don't want to flood the market," Dominic warned the group as a whole. "Remember what I said last night. That will only cause a drop in the market price, and that's the last thing we want."

"Okay, are we agreed on this?" JRK looked around the table. "I think it's important we *all* have a say in this. I'm going to call for a formal vote in a minute, but I'd much prefer it to be unanimous, so if anyone has any reservations, this is the time to air them..."

No voices were raised in protest. A simple show of hands confirmed the united support of the tight circle of friends. Nuala began dialling market traders, JRK strolled over to settle the breakfast bill, and everyone else began the short walk along Church Street and Castle Street, heading for the original excavation site opposite the *Echo* offices.

Billy Lynch stood in the trench, leaning on his shovel, sipping from a mug of tea.

"Found anything else, Billy?"

"There are a few more boxes, Paul, but they look a bit iffy t'me. I didn't want whatever's in them to get damaged, so we decided to wait for youse."

"Fair enough. Nuala, will you ring the prof or his sidekick, pass on the message? Thanks! Billy, have you got a couple of spare hard hats? Some of my colleagues haven't had the chance to see what you've been doing down under..."

Thirteen plain wooden cases, each about the size of a typical tea chest, had been carefully stacked in the main chamber. Yozzer wriggled backwards out of the narrow passage on the uphill northern flank, pulling something with him.

"Found summat else, Gaff. Norra box this time, but it's heavy! Must be eight, nine foot long, an' it's wrapped in loads o' sackcloth or something. Gizza hand t' pull it out."

As Yozzer had said, the latest find was too long to be stored in a wooden box or crate, and surprisingly heavy. Despite the copious amounts of cloth wound around it, it was slim.

"Try to keep it off the ground until we know what it is," Billy warned. "We don't want to risk damaging it by dragging it across the floor."

Yozzer heaved the package a few steps further and passed the end to JRK before retreating, cradling both hands under the object, easing it forward, feeling for the balance point. Dominic received the end from JRK and passed it to Paul. Once Yozzer had guided it out of the tunnel, he scrambled back into the chamber and automatically brushed himself down as the three bearers carried it to a vacant table and laid it carefully in the centre. It was heavy enough to cause a chirrup of protest from the table's folding metal legs, but they held firm and settled without buckling. Right on cue, the slamming of a car door followed by running footsteps heralded the arrival of Professor Midler and Maureen.

"Now perhaps we'll find out what Yozzer's found to add to the menu." JRK beamed.

A hard hat, jammed tight onto John Midler's thick grey thatch, appeared at the door: the rest of his long, thin frame flowed behind it. He waved a tacit greeting to all present but had eyes only for the latest discovery, spotlighted under the beams of three powerful torches.

"Ah, something new—and totally different to anything we've examined to date. What do we have here, I wonder. Yozzer, was it you who found it? Did you notice anything else?"

"Far 's I c'n tell, this is the very last item in the tunnel, or the last of any size. The tunnel looks to me 's if we've got all we're likely to find, other than small stuff which might be hidden in the dust 'n' rubble."

"Good work. If you think there's nowhere left to look, that's good enough for me—at least, for the moment."

He had his mobile in his hand and immediately began taking a seemingly endless series of still shots from every conceivable angle.

He placed the phone/camera into one of the pouches on his belt and opened up a different one, a deep pocket filled with disposable surgical gloves.

"Someone else will have to take over recording the next stage. I'll need both hands to remove the covering—more likely several layers of covering. I'd like three lots of video footage, taken from each side, but I only want one soundtrack. Two of you can mute your phones and I'll add a running commentary while I work..."

John laid out the tools of his trade on a side table. They resembled a surgeon's array of scalpels, clamps and other tools, most of which seemed to have at least one razor-sharp cutting edge. Maureen appeared at his elbow, ready to pass a tool or help change a damaged glove. The commentary describing what he was doing was delivered confidently and with authority.

"I can see a definite edge, which I have to assume is the end of the last piece of cloth used as a protective covering. It's at the narrower end, and I've decided to begin my dissection there. I'll try to keep as much as possible of the cloth in a continuous strip, but if glues have been used—and they probably have—this may not prove practical or even possible."

Using one of the tiniest blades available, he teased at the edge only he could see until it lifted just a fraction. Immediately, he stopped and peered closely at the result. Maureen passed him a powerful magnification lens.

"Some sort of open-weave material, probably an early example of cotton. To have survived until today, it has almost certainly been treated with a preservative. Removing in a continuous strip will be difficult, if not impossible."

Silently, he gave Dominic the 'throat cut' signal to stop the audio track. All three cameramen paused their recordings. Clearly, John had something on his mind, something he wasn't prepared to share with the rest of the world just yet.

"I'm open to any ideas about how to remove this covering without destroying it."

"How about sponging warm water on it?" Maureen blurted out. She reddened as the thought of her boldness hit home, but continued defiantly, "We're talking about cheap, serviceable materials that are several hundred years old anyway and probably nowhere near as strong or robust as they were when they were new. Perhaps the simplest answer will prove to be the best?"

John Midler nodded immediate approval.

"Maureen, I think you're right. Why look for a more complicated solution when we've got a simple one? And using water with no chemicals or other additives in it means we're not likely to damage the cloth or devalue any significant historical clues it might give us."

"And we can test it on a small section of cloth first, to be on the safe side," Maureen felt confident enough to add. She was enormously relieved when her mentor nodded once more with an encouraging grin.

"Let's keep it simple, then. Billy, any chance you've got some hot water handy from the last time your crew had a brew-up?"

***

Maureen found herself conscripted as sponge-bearer to John's scalpel-wielding.

"Your fingers are slimmer than mine, and the cloth mustn't get *too* damp," John grunted. "It's so old it could easily dissolve completely, and we don't want that."

The contents of John's satchel reminded Maureen of a hospital surgeon's collection of scalpels and other items: there was also plenty of sponge foam used to separate and protect the tools.

Whether it was the age of the cloth or the passage of time, the glue—if that was what it actually was—reacted favourably to Maureen's ministrations, and John was able to ease the bindings free from the leading edge without difficulty. He managed to release almost two feet of tape about two inches wide before the first break. He held it up and inspected it carefully.

"I don't think it tore. This looks more like a short strip, which would make sense if it was the last piece of cloth used to seal off the job."

This seemed to be the case as the layers of cloth were stripped away. Some came away in longer strips, but the width remained fairly constant. There were no marks or inscriptions to be seen, and each coarsely woven strip was hung to dry on strings at one end of the cavern. The second layer was a heavier cloth, and wider, but peeled away just as easily. When the object itself was uncovered, the needle-sharp tip identified it immediately.

"A spear!" said Billy, clearly impressed.

"Close, but no cigar!" John corrected him gently with a smile. "If you look at the other end, you'll see it has a guard where you'd expect to hold it. I'd say it's actually a lance, as used by knights on horseback. That's why it's a couple of foot from the end, to make the weapon easier to balance."

"An' it's also too 'eavy t' chuck," Yozzer added, remembering how awkward it had been to drag it single-handed to the end of the tunnel before it could be manhandled into the chamber.

"Would this be someone's personal property?" JRK asked. "Any chance there's an inscription, a name somewhere near the handgrip...hilt...guard? Is there a correct term, John?"

"Give me a moment. I know this one, I think... Yes! It's called a vamplate—not to protect the hand, though. It was actually to prevent your hand sliding up the lance when you hit your target—usually another knight.

"But it's not likely to have a name anywhere. Generally, a knight could only use the lance once—in the first attack—and then use a sword, or a mace or a flail for close-quarter infighting. The lance would remain where it fell and maybe collected by the victors after the battle for re-use, assuming it hadn't been too badly damaged."

"So why was *this* lance packed away so carefully and included in a shipment of gold, silver, jewels and other valuables?" Billy asked. "There has to be a reason."

"You have a good point there, Billy. Perhaps it *did* belong to someone well known at the time, quite possibly someone whose name has been remembered in history.

"Let's hope we can find some documents which will give us a clue," Maureen said. "Surely, there has to be a record of everything in this hoard of valuables. Something this size, being moved in secrecy, has to be payment for something significant, perhaps a King's Ransom—and I mean that literally!"

"You could well be right, Maureen, but as you say, we have to hope we come across a manifest, an inventory of some sort. That would make our task easier—"

"'Scuse me, Prof, but this chamber isn't exactly the most secure location to be leavin' valuables overnight..." Billy interrupted. "An' we should really be gettin' on wi' shiftin' the stuff somewhere safer."

"True, Billy. I hadn't forgotten the security angle, and I wouldn't expect anyone to stand guard through the night. It's too cold and draughty for that, anyway. If we get this out into the trench, do you think it'll all fit on one van-load?"

"It's not the size o' th' load, Prof, it's the weight. I reckon two, maybe three trips will do it. We're only taking it as far's the uni, aren't we?"

CHAPTER NINETEEN

"I DON'T WISH TO be a killjoy, Professor, and I'm not trying to be a smartass..."

"I can hear, the next word is 'but'—right, Dominic? Go ahead. Your opinions are as valid as anyone else's."

The lance had become an immediate focus of attention as soon as it was taken to the central lecture hall, which had been commandeered as a repository for the treasures unearthed so far.

Dom nodded his thanks.

"You said yourself, Professor..."

"John, please! I'm no more an expert than you in this period of history."

"Okay. You told us, lances were generally a single-use weapon, and I understand the reason for that. But somewhere, I read that—for this very reason—the vast majority of lances were of wood. Yet this one is not only forged of metal but was also clearly wrapped up to protect it from damage. There isn't a mark on it anywhere, not a speck of rust or the least little blemish to hint it's been used in battle, nothing."

"Excellent point, Dom. The whole shaft is, as you say, unblemished. It's possible that it was never used in battle but became a...talisman or rally point for troops, in the same way, filmmakers would have us believe our US cousins will defend their flag to the death.

"I can't say more until I've had a chance to run some tests, try to determine the age of the weapon. However, if it were to prove old enough to be from, let's say, the Court of King Arthur, property of Lancelot or Gawain, I could understand why knights—or kings—of a later era might consider it a good-luck charm as well as being an object of no little beauty."

Nuala had been sitting at a side table, which was almost completely covered in notebooks without appearing untidy or chaotic. A selection of mobile phones filled the few square inches of table surface still available. Suddenly she pushed back her chair and stood to get everyone's attention.

"Someone's just found a lengthy document that is almost certainly a list of the major items. Should they bring it—"

"No!" the professor interrupted. "Far safer if I go to them. Let's not run the risk of it being damaged in transit.

"Maureen, I'll need you. Dom, are you a historian? Paul? JRK?"

"Science is my field," JRK conceded, "and Dom's our number-cruncher, but I know he reads a lot of historicals. Paul, you majored in English, so this is possibly more your field than mine if you fancy... ?"

Paul and Dom were on their feet, clearing their respective workspaces before he'd finished speaking.

"It's almost certainly in Latin, which is fine by me," Paul commented, "but you have to promise me we can share Maureen's talents. She was a big help with the Magna Carta document, and especially Clause Sixty-Four."

Two or three minutes of slightly chaotic Musical Chairs ensued. JRK was left to supervise the activity in the treasure room while John Midler led the away team to study the document.

A length of age-darkened material awaited them, running the full length of two tables pushed end to end. The top and bottom edges dangled in mid-air, not touching the floor, and there was a slight but definite curl, which had to be the result of the document being rolled for who knew how many years, undisturbed in the sealed underground grotto.

The handwritten text was as clear and distinct as if it had only just been penned. It was also self-evident from a number of slight but distinctive variations in writing style that more than one person—in all probability more than a couple of dozen—had been involved in its compilation, but each scribe had an eerily similar, immaculate and careful script. Maureen was struck by this: she was accustomed to seeing a wide disparity in the personal styles of individual handwriting.

"It's quite possible the document was put together by a group of monks who all learned their letters at the same abbey from the same tutor or tutors," John said. "It would certainly have been written in a single sitting, even if that meant a concentrated effort over two, three or however many days it took to complete the exercise. Let's have a closer look..."

Holding a magnifying lens that had appeared from nowhere, he bent close to the first line of writing.

"Very neat and tidy," he said approvingly. "You'll notice that each line begins with a number, and the scribes have taken the trouble to align them. Right to left. That should make it easier for us to read, with the units underneath each other..."

Once the numbers had been identified, reading and translating the descriptions of each item became relatively easy. *Aurum* and *argenta*—gold and silver—were constantly used and soon became familiar even to those with little to no understanding of ancient languages. Jewels and precious stones, especially when they weren't mounted on rings or set as bracelets and necklaces, were almost invariably described by their colour rather than named as, for example, a ruby or an emerald. This worked reasonably well most of the time, but reference to a 'pink' stone raised a few eyebrows until one of the students opened a chest and pulled out a diamond which had a pink tinge entrapped within it, the result of some mineral that had settled in the heart of the stone when it was being formed by the pressures around it during countless millennia past. A careful check confirmed that the chest contained seventy-two stones of various sizes. Each was an uncut diamond, and every one carried the same beautiful, soft-pink tinge reflected evenly on every facet of its surface.

There was a microsecond in which everyone in the room gulped an involuntary half-lungful of air in amazement at the magnificence and purity of the warm, rosy glow filling the chamber with living colour, sparkling in the artificial light of the torches directed on the stones. The myriad of complicated facets and irregular planes of the uncut stones seemed to magnify the light, which throbbed in the heart of each stone. The least shake or unavoidable tremor in every hand holding a torch made the glow pulse and dance as if it possessed a true life of its own rather than just a reflection from a beautiful but inanimate object. For several interminable seconds, there was a total silence. Nobody dared to breathe.

Dominic Ion broke the silent tableau: as he stirred and held out his hand to the student who had found the first of the stones, the rustle of his sleeve was as loud as the simultaneous ripping of several copies of *Yellow Pages* by a team of circus strongmen.

He studied it closely under a powerful flashlight, using a magnifying glass he'd appropriated from somewhere or other.

"I defy anyone to put a price on these stones, even in their uncut, unpolished form. I'm not going to attempt guessing the weight, but even famous rocks like the Koh-i-Noor diamond don't even come close to the size of this one.

"Then there's the colour. From time to time, I've read about *pink* diamonds in pulp fiction, action stories and the like. I'm not an expert, but these look like the genuine article to me, and if they truly *are* diamonds, they're simply unique and, as such, literally priceless."

Paul knew Dominic best and found it hard to imagine the staid, conservative accountant reading anything other than a bank ledger or an economics graph, but he let the remark go unchallenged.

"I take it that these stones—because of their nature and colour—are so rare—"

"Unique," Dominic corrected.

Paul hesitated, nodded and continued. "Okay, point taken! Unique. So you mean they're 'priceless' in a positive sense, not 'valueless', I hope?"

"Market forces. They're worth whatever price the buyer is willing to pay in order to acquire them. But yes, in short, that's *exactly* what I mean."

JRK glanced around the room, making a swift head count.

"At the moment, we're a total of twelve people who know of the existence of this...what shall we call it? An unexpected bonus for the party finances? Our in-house legal eagle has already decided it comes within the definition of 'treasure trove' and belongs to us as the finders.

"I trust you all—you wouldn't have been considered for this work party if I didn't—but it's vital not a word of this creeps out before we're ready to announce it publicly. Nuala, I'll ask you to prepare a document we can all sign, agreeing to keep schtum on this until further notice. For now, I'll ask for a show of hands. We can leave the signing formalities until tomorrow when we've had a good night's sleep. Thanks, everyone! Go home and rest. You all look as shattered as I feel."

CHAPTER TWENTY

"Bottom line, Dom. How much?"

Dominic Ion was still wearing the same clothes he'd had on the previous day. To Paul, he looked as though he'd opted to work through the night: it wouldn't have been the first time. Still, he seemed reasonably alert and ready to carry on. He raised both hands above his head in a gesture of surrender.

"I told you last night, it's all down to how badly somebody *wants* such a stone as this, and how much he or she is prepared to offer. I can tell you this, though," he added as he punched keys on his iPad, "last week, a diamond called the Pink Lady set a new record for a single jewel, $83 million—that's about £60 million, by the way—and the cut, finished diamond weighs coppers short of sixty carats. Look at the size of it!"

Mounted on a ring, it was considerably broader than the strong, muscular, male finger it adorned, concealing it completely from knuckle to the first joint.

"It started life as a rough diamond weighing about one hundred and thirty-five carats, which I suppose would be about the size of a golf ball," Dominic continued, "and you can be sure, a market will be found for everything, down to the least little scrap and shaving peeled off in the process of cutting and polishing it."

"Okay," Paul said, "I'm guessing this is a rough diamond, which we can expect to weigh somewhere in the region of half its present weight by the time it's been cut and polished. Is that right?"

"Fair rule of thumb, Paul."

"But you also said yesterday—or whenever it was you warned us about selling even a few of the coins and other treasures we found—flooding the market will bring the price tumbling down, and we've got *seventy-two* of these rocks! How do we go about it?"

"Very carefully," JRK commented. He sounded calm, and something in the way he sat casually at the table hinted that he'd given the problem some thought overnight. He carried on.

"Dominic's right, of course. However we release the news, whenever the world learns of the existence of these diamonds, the market price of diamonds in general—and every other precious stone for all I know—is going to be affected immediately. Whether they go up or down's a different matter, but I'd expect them to show a significant fall once the market settles, though I doubt they'd nosedive or become totally worthless."

"I should be earning my keep, I guess," Paul said. "This sounds like a good time for Nuala and me to cobble together some sort of press release. It has to be released today, though, or people are going to question why we chose to sit on this info a second longer than absolutely necessary."

Nuala was gathering her paraphernalia, pads, pens and papers together even as he spoke. They commandeered a side room with a door that could be closed, and JRK took charge of the main workspace, issuing orders with the efficiency of a sergeant major. The room emptied rapidly, leaving JRK alone with Rik Hines.

"Come on then, John. Gizza job!" Rik said, deliberately mimicking the tagline from an eighties hard-hitting TV drama set in a strife-torn Liverpool. JRK grinned almost sheepishly: for once, he seemed unsure of himself.

"I'm not trying to exclude you from anything, Rik, but you're a successful businessman in your own right, and you've got where you are today entirely by your own efforts. You're The Man, as they say. I wouldn't feel right giving orders, if you know what I mean?"

"That's bollocks, John. You know that as well as I do. We all gotta start somewhere, and as far as I'm concerned, this is *your* show, and that makes *you* The Man. I've been lucky enough to press flesh with some high-profile, powerful people over the years, and if there's nothing else you need me to take care of, I could always sit by a phone and call in a few favours from one or two of them. I'm talking about influential people, and none of 'em is short of a few bob. It looks as if we've got a certain amount of finance we weren't expecting, but you have to admit, political campaigns don't come cheap, and you can't have too much cash backing you."

Rik folded his lanky frame around the improbable geometric ergonomics of the nearest computer chair. Without hesitation or reference to an address book, his fingers flew over the numerals on an outside line.

"Beny? Rik here. ... Yeah, thanks, the party was great fun! My shout next time, okay? Listen, I read about your latest raid on Sotheby's. ... Wouldn't insult you by trying to buy it from you, mate! You'd beggar me anyway if I so much as tried, and I've nobody particular to wear it even if I did acquire it! It looks oversized even on your fingers, and to be honest, I can't see it as a woman's piece of jewellery, ever. It's just too big!

"No, just a question, really. Would you be in the market for a companion stone if I were to find one? ... No, much smaller. ... I haven't had it assessed yet. All I can say is, the rough diamond I'm looking at right now seems to be about the same size as your finished stone. ... Yeah, that's what I thought. Perhaps half that size by the time it's cut and polished. Maybe thirty carats, tops.

"That was the other reason I rang you. You're the insider where jewels and gems are concerned. I know nothing about them. You must have used someone from the trade to assess the Pink Lady, though, and I wondered if you could let whoever know I've got a job for them? ... No, I'm not poaching, and I won't even consider offering anyone else the stone before you've had a chance to look at it—giving you first dibs, as we used to call it.

"No, I can't tell you where I am, other than I'm not at home. You can get back to me on my mobile. ... Cell phone, it's the same thing. You know us Brits are fond of calling something by a different name! Email's probably more secure, though. ... Yes, use my private addy. I can pick that up through any PC wherever I happen to be working— ... No, I'm afraid I can't say how long I'll be here, but it won't be any less than the next three days. I'll probably have to go out and do the old meet-and-greet routine, kiss frogs, hope they turn into princesses. ... Great! Look forward to it, Beny—and remember, you promised to come to *my* place next time! Shalom, my friend!"

Rik ended the call and glanced across the table, grinning at the expression on JRK's face.

"What? Okay, so I stayed on his yacht a few weeks ago, but I'd no idea he was even thinking about bidding on that particular gem. In fact, it wouldn't surprise me if it was a spur-of-the-moment instinct bid."

"Nice to have the cash to be able to make such an impulse buy, all the same," JRK remarked.

"John, in all honesty, he's probably going to recoup that much and more before the end of the year. Why d'you think I dripped the idea of acquiring a few more perfect stones from our collection? If we're going to finance your campaign with capital raised from this treasure trove, we need to make it clear to those who can afford to buy our goods just how much they're going to have to bid to be in with a chance of purchasing what they want! Beny's a shrewd businessman, and the idea of having a couple more pink diamonds to complement the one he already has is something he won't be able to resist."

JRK shook his head, dazed by this totally unexpected turn of events.

"I knew you hobnobbed with a pretty impressive crowd of movers and shakers, Rik—at least, that's how it seems from reading the glossy mags and Sunday supplements—but I never realised..." He faltered, for once at a loss for words.

Rik grinned. This time, there was a definite suggestion of daredevil glint in his eye, suggesting he was privately enjoying the filthiest joke nobody would ever dare tell in public.

He reached for the phone, using the other hand to extract a slim address book from the inner pocket of his jacket.

"You ain't seen nutt'n yet," he croaked with a heavily camped melodramatic stage leer. "Still, I need to make sure I get all my phone numbers right. There's a limit to how many I can recall without looking them up, and there are people in my little black book who'd most likely send the boys round to break *both* my legs if I don't invite them to bid in the auction..." He said this with a nod in the direction of the small mountain of pink stones in the centre of the table.

"How many people do you actually know with enough cash behind them to enter a bidding war for rare and precious jewels?"

Rik shrugged. "Not as many as I'd *like* to know, but enough to make for an interesting day at the races."

He stopped mid-dial and replaced the handset, overcome briefly with helpless but genuine, childlike laughter. Once he'd regained control, he wiped his face dry of the floods of tears he'd shed and took a long pull at a bottle of water.

"Between you and me, some of the names in my little black book don't always play by the rules. One or two of them might not be as squeaky clean as they'd like you to think, but their hearts are in the right places."

He reached for the phone, making no attempt to conceal the wicked gleam in his eye.

"Watch and learn. I'm about to set a cat among the pigeons! There's no reason I should let Beny wriggle out of this too cheaply. A bit of competitive bidding will give him a kick in the proverbial!"

CHAPTER TWENTY-ONE

"THERE ARE ALMOST thirty guests on the list, and most of them could comfortably fund the economy of a moderate-sized country. Every single one is on the Forbes list, and they're *all* paranoid about security."

"Thanks, Nuala. I had a feeling this would be important, and I've called in a *big* favour." JRK grinned. Nobody could have guessed that he hadn't slept for almost three days.

"They might all be gazillionaires, each with an army of bodyguards, but I've persuaded them to meet up in the VIP lounge at John Lennon Airport early tomorrow morning.

"From there, they'll transfer to City Centre on a private run on the Tramlink direct to the Pier Head. Their army of security and bodyguards can supplement the staff we'll provide at that point but will *not* accompany their employers at the auction.

"We've supplied appropriate catering and leisure facilities for them, naturally. They'll be wined and dined in a private wing of the new hotel in the ferry terminal."

He laid aside the clipboard he'd been pretending to consult: his grin, if possible, became still wider.

"The auction itself will take place on board a river-cruise ferry, which will steam up and down the Mersey for as long as proves necessary to dispose of all the items on offer. Our opulent guests have all agreed that a ship in mid-river is a secure location where such a large number of the world's richest businessmen can safely meet."

"Business*men*?"

"Yes, Nuala, I know there are two female names on the list, but 'businesspersons' just doesn't have the same zing to it. Likewise, 'businesspeople'—doing business is hard enough in today's financial climate, without the eagle eye of the PC brigade," JRK conceded, but there was no malice in his words.

"The fact is," he continued, "all these people are prepared to drop everything and come to the private auction, and they're all prepared to pay serious money for what we have on offer, largely on the say-so of Rik Hines. The auction lots have already been transferred to the vessel and will be under heavy guard until the auction takes place. I think that covers all the bases."

Alex Cummins placed another cup of coffee in John's hand and linked her arm around his. She'd seen even less of JRK in the past week than she'd come to accept as par for the course, but she had no intention of allowing him to run himself into the ground.

"Do you remember what a *bed* looks like?" she reprimanded lightly. "There's a large slug of Jameson's in that cup, and you're going to lie down and let it take effect. There's nothing more you can do until it's time to do some meeting and greeting when the *playboys* arrive with their minders, and you won't be actively involved in the auction itself. Not unless you've got a few billion salted away somewhere so secret even I don't know about it."

JRK's nose had already identified the active extra ingredient in his mug, and he allowed Alex to have her way without protest. His body reacted immediately: he began to unwind and relax before Alex had guided him the length of the room to a wide, comfortable leather sofa. Opening his seemingly galvanised throat, he drained the coffee as he reached his intended destination. His eyes closed as his knees sagged, and he was asleep before his head hit the scatter cushions stacked across the arm of the settee.

***

When *Merseytram 1* had served the last scheduled flight into JLA, the crew returned it to the depot as usual just after nine-thirty.

"Ey up, George. There's twice as many cleaning crew here tonight! What's going on?"

"Nobody said anything at the meeting this morning. Maybe there's some VIP trip been scheduled for tomorrow?"

"If there is, it can only be a last-minute booking—and whoever it is must have a load o' cash t' splash! Just my luck to 'ave the day off. Bet there'll be some decent tips handed out."

"I'm not on until midday, myself, Pat. Who's down to drive, I wonder..."

The VIP guess was accurate, but the regular crew's disappointment about missing the opportunity to earn tips was wide of the mark. Pat's staffing enquiry was politely deflected, but they were both told that they would receive a suitable bonus in their next pay cheque as compensation, which was enough to mollify both drivers.

There was considerably more than twice the usual complement of cleaners on duty, and they were scrubbing furiously almost before the tram had ceased moving.

"They'll be done in record time if they keep that up," was George's comment as they swiped their time cards and headed for their usual swift one at the Baltic Fleet pub.

"I could almost b'lieve they're getting her ready for another trip tonight," Pat remarked.

He was right: they were. *Merseytram 1* was restored to her pristine state of perfection and eased away from the shunt yard just before eleven p.m.

CHAPTER TWENTY-TWO

BEFORE HE SHRUGGED into a driver's uniform jacket and donned a cap, which nestled somewhat precariously on his uncontrollable hair, Rik Hines had personally shaken hands with every member of the cleaning crew and handed out discreet brown envelopes that were sufficiently well-padded to suggest they contained a decent-sized bonus. In return, he expected—and was given—a promise of silence about the overtime arrangement.

"I'm licensed to drive trams, remember?" He laughed when he saw the expression on Paul Freeman's face. "The fewer people who know about this 'private hire', the better! And apart from that, there's no way I'm going to allow someone else to have *all* the fun!"

Paul and Nuala Ion were the other members of the welcome committee working the Arrivals lounge at JLA. JRK, Alex Campbell and Nuala's brother Dominic were waiting to receive the visiting guests at the Pier Head end of the track.

A number of small private planes had arrived without undue ceremony earlier in the evening. By the time Rik had piloted *Merseytram 1* to the airport and across the private spur that terminated a couple of hundred metres inside the perimeter fence, the last two Lear jets had landed and were taxiing to a standstill as close as was safely practical to the VIP suite.

Rik's features were as well-known to the *glitterati* of society as most rock icons, and he was greeted with genuine, open smiles and applause as soon as he entered. By the time he'd circled the room once and shaken every hand, the last two guests had made it through landing formalities and joined the select club. Without appearing to chivvy anyone or call for unseemly haste, Rik allowed sufficient time for them to rehydrate their throats after their flights before hinting with a raised eyebrow that it was time to move on.

Ever the showman, he paused before pressing the button on the handset which would open the doors.

"Ladies and gentlemen! She may not be the crystal carriage favoured by Cinderella, but I know you won't be disappointed! Welcome aboard *Merseytram 1*—and I promise, she *won't* suddenly turn into a pumpkin at the stroke of midnight."

As the doors opened with an almost-inaudible *hiss*, Paul caught himself with a smile on his lips at the random memory of a surreal scene involving a pair of doors in *The Hitchhiker's Guide to the Galaxy* whose sole purpose in life was to please by opening and closing satisfactorily. Having opened, and after ensuring that all were present and accounted for, the happy doors sighed just as contentedly in closing, and the visitors were whisked smoothly to meet the host who had invited them, and their chequebooks, to the special unique auction offering an astonishing range of jewellery, the likes of which had never been assembled under one roof anywhere in the world.

As they slid silently past the Albert Dock and Rik's hand hovered above the throttle, ready to slow as they approached their destination at the Pier Head, the radio crackled into life.

"Walking pace, Rik. There's a security cordon around the docks."

"Now, why doesn't that surprise me? Is there anyone in Liverpool who *doesn't* owe you a favour, John?"

"The chief constable insisted, Rik, and as soon as he sensed there was something blowing in the wind, Brigadier Groth wanted the army involved as well."

"I thought security on this was watertight, John! Is there a leak somewhere? If there is, it'll spook our honoured guests. They're nervous enough to start with."

"Nervous? Try paranoid!" Paul muttered. Rik ignored him. For the moment, the passengers remained in blissful ignorance. The driver's cab was efficiently soundproofed, and the brief interchange of radio messages remained private.

"I'll stake my life there's been no leak," Dominic's voice cut in, authoritative and full of confidence. "I wouldn't put it past the chief constable to contact his oppo in the army, but I'm certain he'd have done it through secure channels."

By now, the tram had slowed to the requested walking pace, and the cordon was less than fifty metres ahead. Three ranks—about a dozen bodies—moved a few paces left or right to leave the track clear. Two bullseye lanterns provided a begrudged minimum of light to ensure the safety of the men themselves. Those were extinguished as soon as *Merseytram 1* had passed, and the outward-facing line reformed immediately.

JRK was waiting for them, wreathed in smiles. He greeted each guest as Rik introduced them. After the final flurry of handshakes, Rik looked up.

"Ladies and Gentlemen, on behalf of the city of Liverpool, I thank you for coming here at such short notice. I'm sure you won't be disappointed by the range and quality of the individual items offered for sale, and I promise you can absolutely depend on the integrity and professionalism of the auctioneer who has agreed to take charge of the sale. Jeremy Reed has agreed to waive the commission he would normally accept and is donating it to the funds which this auction is intended to raise for the city's coffers.

"I'm also aware that for most of you, time is money. As you'll see from the catalogue, there are over three hundred lots available, and they have already been taken aboard the ferry under the strictest security. Mid-river is one of the safest places I can imagine for a high-security meeting, so let's get this party started!"

Nobody else would have dreamed of addressing some of the richest men and women in the world in such an informal, casual manner, but coming from Rik Hines, it sounded warm, encouraging, almost inevitable. He turned and sauntered across the short boarding bridge, thoughtfully cushioned by a deep-pile red carpet, as if he simply assumed everyone else would follow his lead—which, of course, they did.

***

"Ladies and gentlemen, before we begin this closed auction..."

Jeremy Reed, joint owner of one of Liverpool's oldest and most respected auction houses, clearly felt that a word of caution was appropriate.

"The is a private sale. Contrary to the usual conditions, there will be *no* telephone bids.

"Also, under normal circumstances, letters of provenance and similar documents confirming authenticity would follow with each lot. However, considering the antiquity of the items offered for sale, and the fact that the last *legal* owner or owners are long deceased, this will not be possible. A number of random samples have been assayed. The purity of the gold and the quality of some of the jewels has been confirmed. We can safely accept that every item will be of similar vintage to the tested items in this treasure trove, but I am bound by the regulations which govern auction sales to issue a formal *caveat emptor.* Every item is bought as seen. Establishing ownership—for insurance purposes and other practical matters—is up to the individual buyer."

"So, I have before me Lot One."

A photograph appeared on a giant monitor to give everyone present a good look at the item, twelve almost identical gold rings.

"Although there is a slight variation in their individual weights—and therefore the precise amount of gold in each ring—they are all twenty-four carat, one hundred fine, and without inscriptions, engraving or other adornment. There is no way of telling who the original owners were, so it was decided to sell them as a single lot. Who will start the bidding at one thousand pounds? Thank you. Do I hear two?"

Seven thousand pounds was probably somewhat more than the stock market value of the gold itself, but it was a loosener and a fair price considering the antiquity and potential historical value of the jewellery.

As other small but valuable pieces of jewellery were presented and bid upon, the calls came more swiftly and decisively. The excitement and tension in the river cruiser's spacious dining area grew more intense with each bid: several bidding wars broke out as the lots presented became larger and heavier and began to resemble true works of art as opposed to ostentatious ornaments.

"…and so we come to Lot Thirty-Seven, an ornamental dirk with filigree silver chasings on the handle and a corresponding decorated sheath. You'll notice that the sheath has the letters '*R R*' engraved just below the rim, but there is no further indication as to who commissioned the work or who it was intended for. Close inspection reveals no sign of use as a potential weapon. It is almost certain this was commissioned for use as an ornament. The hilt includes a two-carat diamond of exceptional clarity, surrounded by matched pairs of ruby and emerald—"

"Five thousand."

"Seven."

"Ten!"

The bidding suddenly escalated from brisk to distinctly aggressive and was eventually secured by one of the female bidders for £28,000. Paul thought this a fair result. He knew very little about jewellery or antiques, but he thought the piece looked as if it had been designed to appeal to a feminine disposition.

An experienced auctioneer, Jeremy Reed had managed, with very little to guide him other than his own sense of value, to rank the lots in some rough approximation of what he personally expected them to fetch. His business acumen hadn't failed him and had the added effect of increasing the tension of the bidding wars as each final bid was higher—sometimes by a significant margin—than its predecessor. Considering its innate beauty, it seemed only right that another ornamental dagger offered in the catalogue simply as 'Lot 42' was the first item to realise over £1 million sterling. By the time Lot 50 was held up for approval—a gold cincture beset with a dazzling array of gems in what seemed like every colour of the rainbow—any memories of the first seven-figure sale were rapidly fading on a distant horizon.

"Ladies and gentlemen, we come to the final item in this sale, one which I have no doubt is of great interest to all present.

"Dawn is just beginning to break, and I have a suggestion for you."

He turned to JRK and Rik Hines, who stood at his side.

"Every diamond I have handled has shown itself to best advantage in the natural light of the sun. I propose we all adjourn to the foredeck for a few minutes, and someone takes the stone up to the bridge to catch the light from the rising sun. I've heard tell of the dazzling light show caused by exposing a pink diamond to brilliant sunshine, but I have never had the good fortune to witness it myself. Can I ask our hosts if this is both possible and safe?"

JRK glanced first at Paul, then nodded and fished a small object from his pocket. It resembled a mobile phone, but the short antenna was a giveaway: this was a generation-old shortwave R/T, which JRK used to speak to the captain of the vessel standing at the helm. He spoke a few brief words, then listened intently to the reply.

"Our captain says there is no appreciable swell, and we have almost a quarter of an hour before sunrise proper, so there's plenty of time to go out on deck without rushing or taking chances. Rik, I'd like you to join me on the bridge. Without your support, I don't believe we'd have managed to contact any of our honoured guests nor even *think* about making this unique gemstone available."

A request was relayed to the engine room, and the engine throttled back to a speed barely enough to maintain way in the weak midriver current that bore the vessel downstream.

The buyers reconvened on deck: there was ample room for all. JRK nodded to Rik and led the way to the catwalk around the enclosed bridge. Rik noticed the helm jigging a few degrees left and right, responding to the minute adjustments being made by the captain below decks at the tiller as he navigated blind, dependent on radar and sonar readings.

With their upper bodies clear of the vessel's bodywork, JRK and Rik were in a perfect position to catch the first rays of the new dawn's sunrise low on the horizon. JRK unwrapped the stone and turned to Rik, who shook his head.

"This is your show, John. It's only right you do the honours."

JRK glanced over the stern of the launch as the sun cleared the distant treeline. Reverently, like a priest lifting a host in a bejewelled monstrance, he held the diamond high, using the very tips of his fingers.

The multi-faceted stone flared immediately. The soft damask rose light flooded over the silent spectators on the foredeck, colouring their upturned faces with an impossible hue of perfect health, perpetual youth, peace and serenity. Although logic insisted that there was no question of the stone becoming too hot for JRK to hold, Rik almost expected the intensity of the light exploding from its depths to startle his colleague into losing his grip, searing deep, painful burn marks into his tender flesh.

JRK stood secure, reassuringly solid and unmoving. He held the stone high above his head, bowing in reverence, possibly submission, or an acknowledgement of the sheer beauty of the silent pyrotechnics. The glow of light seemed to spread an extra lustre of health and vitality, washing JRK slowly, lovingly, in pulsating waves from his head to his feet.

Even the fibreglass and timber used in the vessel's decking, hull and fittings seemed briefly to be imbued with a spark of sentient life. Every square inch of surface glowed, called into existence for the first time in that special, unprecedented moment.

JRK stirred fractionally and exhaled: Rik was as certain as he could be that his friend hadn't taken a breath in all the time he'd held the precious stone above his head. Without conscious thought, Rik offered the soft cloth in which the diamond had been wrapped. JRK accepted it with a nod of thanks and swathed it carefully around the stone. Even through the half-dozen layers of material wrapped around it, the pulsing heartbeat that had been awakened in the perfect roseate crystal could still be seen clearly.

"Ladies and gentlemen. We have been privileged, I think, to witness something truly remarkable this morning. I propose a few minutes for reflection, refreshment and private thought before we proceed to the auction of this final lot. However, I would like to remind you of the security precautions we agreed upon before the auction began. I ask you to refrain from contacting friends and business colleagues either by phone or by internet until the sale has been agreed."

***

A sober, contemplative mood settled on the conference room as the prospective buyers returned from the foredeck. Most chose to serve themselves a stiffener from the bar, and the coffee percolator also took a moderately severe hiding.

JRK carefully handed the precious gem in its protective swaddling to Jeremy Reed. The auctioneer's expressionless professional demeanour wavered momentarily when he saw and felt the steady, rhythmic throb of the living light pulsing from the stone. Even through the layers of folded cloth, the pink glow could be seen: his sensitive fingertips registered a slight but definite increase in the temperature of what he was holding.

It was definitely above body temperature now, a comforting warmth that spread ease, loosened tensed, knotted muscles and left him with a sensation of wholeness and unbounded health.

JRK bowed automatically, unsure if he were honouring the man or the object he held, then backed away rather than turn his back. Somehow, that would have felt an inappropriate act, verging on discourtesy. As the auctioneer began to peel away the protective shroud, JRK sat at a table at the rear of the elevated platform stage with the rest of his group.

"What's the score, John?" Paul demanded. "How did you engineer...?"

JRK shook his head.

"Haven't a clue! It was nothing I did. It was just like all that was needed was a touch of the sun! I swear, that diamond or whatever it is has a life of its own. One thing's for sure. By the time I wrapped it up and handed it over, I could *feel* a regular pulse—if that's the right word—a heartbeat, maybe? And it had definitely warmed as well, not exactly hot but a degree or so above body temperature, that much is certain."

"I wonder what it's likely to fetch?" Nuala murmured softly. She had a curious, faraway look on her face and seemed unaware she'd spoken. Dominic broke the momentary tableau, flipping open one of his notebooks.

"I think I've recorded everything up to now. Here's a running total..." He let the pad circulate and continued, "I'm not going to question anyone's ability to pay for what they've already bought, but they've all had their hands in their pockets many times already tonight. All the same, I won't be at all surprised if this final item raises more than everything else put together."

There were an impressive number of zeroes on the notepad already. It circulated the table to the accompaniment of muted whistles and gasps of astonishment and returned to the group's unofficial treasurer.

In centre stage on the podium, Jeremy Reed had completed his preparations. Lot 301 sat snugly in the mouth of a champagne flute, which the auctioneer had concealed under a mantle of spotless white satin. Its inner fire still pulsed firmly, regularly.

Paul had never felt in better health. He had to ask himself: if being reasonably close to the source of such rude health for quite a short time could have such a positive effect, what might it do for whoever would succeed in the bidding war that was about to begin? He glanced to his left, where Nuala was sketching the jewel on its display stand.

"If she only knew how I—"

Nuala dropped her pencil. Her hand flew to the back of her skull as if she'd been stung.

"Ow!!"

She'd been concentrating on her sketch; she couldn't possibly have known he wanted to speak to her! Yet the short phrase echoing in his ear *before* she dropped the pencil was without question 'spoken', for want of a better description, in Nuala's voice.

Sitting next to her gave Paul the only excuse he needed to reach out, hold her, console her.

"What's the matter?"

"Nothing...at least, I don't think it was anything, and it's gone now! It was odd, though. I had this sudden flash-and-it's-gone pain in the back of my head, and so intense! It really *hurt*! Still, it's gone now...mmm, that's nice! Don't stop!"

Paul discovered he was still massaging Nuala's neck, though he had no memory of consciously deciding to begin the therapy. He hesitated for a fraction of a second, then carried on.

As they sat back at the table, Jeremy Reed completed his final preparations. A single discreet glance around the room was sufficient to silence all casual conversation amongst the prospective purchasers of the final, unique lot in the night's auction.

"Ladies and gentlemen, the final item in this auction is an extremely rare pink diamond. It has been assessed at just over eighty carats in its present uncut, unpolished form.

"The Pink Lady sold recently in a cut and polished form. It had a weight of sixty-two carats and sold for £60 million sterling.

"Before I suggest an appropriate reserve price or opening bid, I must remind you all that the circumstances surrounding the discovery of this jewel were such that it has not been possible to supply any documents relating to the provenance and previous history of the stone itself. I can assure you that it has been examined closely and confirmed as a genuine diamond with an exceptional clarity, and as we have all seen, infused with a remarkable, even pink flush. Because it will inevitably be a smaller cut stone than the Pink Lady, I'm asking for an opening bid of...forty million pounds sterling."

Paul's fingers froze in mid-air. If they'd been in contact with Nuala's neck, he might have caused her serious injury. There followed a brief moment of total silence, but the auctioneer's calm words provoked no gasps of outrage or astonishment. A nod and a wave from one corner of the auditorium was noted and accepted, overcalled immediately from the opposite side of the room, and the bidding began in earnest.

Sixty, then sixty-five million were soon left in the slipstream of overtrumped calls: the fact that the stone was smaller than the recent top-priced Pink Lady seemed immaterial to the invited representatives of the world's current Rich List. It occurred to Paul—and without a doubt to the other non-combatants—that one of those present would inevitably be much poorer—at least temporarily—by the time the bidding was over.

"One hundred."

Beny lost patience and broke ranks, raising the ante by five million rather than one. He seemed determined to acquire the perfect companion for his Pink Lady, whatever it cost him.

Paul was suddenly aware of holding his breath just as tightly as Nuala's hand. Would there be another bid? The seconds dragged on: the silence was becoming unbearable.

"Going once."

Jeremy Reed eased the gavel a fraction of an inch off the table.

"Twice.

"For the third and final time, at £100 million sterling…"

The gavel fell, and echoes ricocheted like gunfire around the room.

"Sold to Mr. Samuel Beny. That concludes this auction, ladies and gentlemen. Please leave your details with one of the tellers and make individual arrangements for the delivery of the items you have purchased."

***

"I'm shell-shocked."

JRK slumped into the nearest chair, giving voice to the thought that was, in one form or another, running through the minds of everyone else in the room.

He looked across the table and added, "Dom, can you give us some sort of approximate total? I rather think we've raised far more than we dreamed possible."

Dom didn't even bother glancing at his notebook.

"As far as approximate is concerned, I think this is the first time I've been able to say 'to the nearest million' and call it an estimate! Even the auctioneer's commission fees don't make a significant difference. You can count on something very close to £200 million—possibly more."

"That won't put us in the same league as the G8," said Paul, "but it's certainly more than the annual budget of any number of smaller countries."

"It means that we can invoke the legislation of Clause Sixty-Four as it appears in the document we dug up and suspend payment of *all* taxes—that's personal, corporation, VAT and anything else we can withhold—pending negotiation and blah-blah…" JRK appeared to be thinking on his feet.

"I suggest we make an offer of the traditional tithe. That would mean setting the local rate of taxation at ten per cent, which is a guaranteed vote winner with everyone living within the boundaries of the proposed Independent Merseyside."

Nuala frowned. "That sounds more than a little clumsy. Surely, we can do better than that, especially if we want to sell the idea as a finished package to our…"

She hesitated.

"Come on! Help me out, here, residents, citizens, voters, electorate…?"

A spirited discussion began. Rik Hines wanted 'something short, snappy, easy off the tongue' as a name for the party representing the region.

"We all know there's naff all difference between the main parties these days. Labour, Tory, left, right, centre…"

"Up, down, in, out, shake it all about…"

"Very funny, Paul! But you understand the point I'm making, I trust?"

"Sure, Rik! People have been saying that for years now."

Alex wondered if something that included a back-to-basics philosophy might work.

"Maybe something like 'Grassroots something-or-other'," she suggested.

Jim shook his head. "Anything with 'grass' in it has too many negative vibes in this part of the world! It might be slang, but you know what people associate with *that* term."

"Tell you what," JRK said thoughtfully, "If we ponce it up a bit—I'm thinking of the 'roots' element…"

Paul's PR instincts kicked into gear. He could see where the leader was going with this line of reasoning.

"In Latin, a root would be *'radix'*. How about including 'radical' in the party name? Does that sound bolshy enough to appeal to yer av'rige Scouser?"

"I think we're on the same page, Paul," JRK answered. "We could also underline or reinforce it with, oh, I don't know—something that rhymes?"

"Can't think of a rhyme for 'radical'," Nuala chipped in. "Maybe another word beginning with 'r' would do the trick? Region, perhaps?"

She looked around the table.

"It's not *just* what's currently Liverpool on the map. It's bigger than Merseyside, too! There are five local authorities involved—six, if you include Halton. We don't want anyone to feel they're being left out. How about 'Radical Regionalist'? Would that fit the bill?"

"Sounds good to me!" JRK nodded. "Do we have any other suggestions, or should we take a vote on it?"

By a simple and unanimous show of hands, the motion was carried, and Nuala made a note of the time and date when the Radical Regionalist Party was officially formed.

CHAPTER TWENTY-THREE

"WHERE ARE WE going to deposit the funds from the auction, Dom?"

"Good question, Paul. At close of business last night, funds have been transferred to our personal accounts. Yourself, JRK, Nuala and me. But we can't leave them there, obviously. They were never intended for us as individuals. The money raised from the sale was always going to provide the financial stability of the whole Merseyside region."

"And Beny's transferred his payment into my account." Rik entered the room in time to catch the end of Dom's reply and add a further update.

"That wasn't meant to happen, either," Dom muttered.

"Maybe not, but he said it was quicker and easier for him to transfer funds to me. He's bought…other items from me in the past and had the account details to hand."

"Hmm. Okay, I won't ask you what the other 'sale items' were, Rik…"

"Glad you see it like that, Dom, because I wouldn't tell you or anyone else what private transactions Beny and I have had in the past. If I did, I'd have to kill you straight away!"

"Thanks for nothing, Rik! Still, as Beny is our biggest single customer—and by a *wide* margin—I'd be wise to stay in your good books."

"Are there still any payments outstanding?"

"Not a lot. One or two have asked for a little leeway, but everyone's paid a minimum of fifty per cent up front, and the balance will arrive in a month, two max."

"Fair enough. We *are* discussing the transfer of funds that total more than the annual budget of any one of a number of countries. We can afford to be patient," Rik said as casually as an offhand remark about the weather. "But regarding the eventual destination of this working capital...

"As a matter of fact, that's precisely what I wanted to talk to you about. I guess this falls into the category of government business, so I'm going to ask if Nuala will take the minutes of what's said and done. On the other hand, you're all elected officials, and I'm not. Does that cause any constitutional problems? Because all I want to discuss is our funding, and the only people whose personal bank accounts are currently awash with public funds are the five people in this room. Should we call Steve in for a legal opinion?"

JRK glanced around the room before replying.

"Gut feeling. I think we can trust each other, and as you said, the funds we need to find a home for are secure, and nobody else has access to them. Rik, not being an elected official is something we can attend to if you're ready to put your shoulder to the wheel. I, for one, would be glad to have you on board as a member of my cabinet..."

"Synod," Paul said. "I don't want to sound pedantic, but we did agree to use the term, so this is as good a time as any to get into the habit."

"Happy to stand corrected. Rik, are you happy to be the first appointment I make to the Radical Regionalist Synod?"

"Listen, folks, if that's all it takes, that's fine by me. But shouldn't there be a vote or something? And what role d'you want me to play?"

"Play? Not what I'd call it, Rik," JRK replied. "How does Minister for Employment sound? That should be right up your street, given your track record."

"Sounds fine—if there are no objections?"

"Duly minuted," Nuala said as her pen flew across the notepad where she was keeping a full and accurate verbatim record of everything said so far. "And I'm happy to go on record as seconder to JRK's proposal. Show of hands?"

Rik Hines became the fifth Synod member of the nascent RR party on a simple 4-0 vote. A quick phone call also brought Steve Dunning to the university office that had become the central admin office for the new Regional Government.

"I've had a few days to plan and set some practical things in motion," Rik said as the growing group—now six, with Steve—settled around the table.

"I told you last week I was planning to establish a Jomfru brand cash handler. Not a bank, not a building society, something closer to a credit union where the customers feel they have a direct say in day-to-day operations and some influence on policies. Paul, I think it was you who mentioned an empty property here in City Centre which might be suitable premises?"

Paul nodded to confirm it.

"Thought so. I've made an offer on the lease of the building and agreed terms. I'm waiting for the paperwork to catch up with me, but as far as I'm concerned, we can pick up the keys right now and move in tomorrow."

"Pretty quick!" JRK was impressed.

"I'm not one to let the grass grow under my feet, and the sooner we get ourselves established, the sooner we can move on. In fact, I was only waiting for a positive PR opportunity to make the launch day of Jomfru Cash a day people will remember for a long time—and for all the *right* reasons."

"What d'you want, Rik?" Paul asked with a smirk. "Circus performers and balloons? Marching bands playing all up and down Church Street on opening day? Free biros for everyone who opens an account?"

"Nothing quite that tacky, Paul! Still, the free biros are a good idea…never mind. The usual freebies will no doubt do some good, but I'm trying to look at the bigger picture. You see, if we can tell everyone they should look at the funds that are already *at the bank's disposal…*"

"In other words, already in the coffers, or vaults, or part of the bank's assets in general," Dominic cut in with a sudden grin of understanding. "Rik, that's brilliant! What better way to prove a bank's dependability and track record?"

"Even if it's just getting out of the blocks and hasn't actually *got* a track record," Nuala said.

"Exactly! This is an opportunity for us to show the people who matter—the ones we want to vote for us and hopefully switch their bank accounts to us—just what they can expect the Synod to do for them, and for the region as a whole. They should know that the region's economy is in good hands and that we can promise to do the same for their personal finances.

"We're agreed, then, on the basics. We can work out the finer details as we go along. Now, Nuala, do you *really* have a problem with the idea of marching bands in the street?"

***

"The band marching up and down Church Street this morning shouldn't have been too big a surprise for the traders and customers, considering what we've come to know about the flamboyant Rik Hines over the years. Today was the day he chose to open the latest franchise operating under the distinctive Jomfru logo. Rik, why have you opted for Liverpool rather than your own backyard to launch a new bank? Every other financial institute is fighting to establish themselves in the City of London."

"It's a bit too late to change anything about where I was born, Kevin, but I hope to come back as a Scouser in the next life!"

Rik was on song, even larger than in real life, if that was possible, despite the early morning chill.

"It's really a no-brainer. Without going into details, what I've paid for the premises here in Liverpool might—with a bit of hard bargaining—get me a year's rental on a site big enough for a phone box anywhere in the centre of London. Any responsible banker is going to consider the cost-effectiveness of the bank's premises as part of the unavoidable overheads, and I decided to invest in Liverpool."

"You say 'invest' in Liverpool. I believe there's a further special reason for your decision?"

"Yes, there certainly is!" Rik's height and his instantly recognisable features had already attracted a crowd of early morning commuters around the plinth JRK had ordered outside the new bank's premises.

"It's vital for any financial institution to be able to assure their customers that their money is safe and the bank's aims and business practices are beyond reproach. Regrettably, we've seen a couple of high-profile cases in recent years where this hasn't been the case.

"You also have to show that you have the funds and the backing to survive the lean years as well as the years of plenty, and I'm pleased to announce that one of the first and most-valued customers at Jomfru Cash will be Liverpool itself. Or, to be more precise, Jomfru Cash will administer the finances of the Regional Government of the Independent Synod of Greater Merseyside.

"All trade and commerce with other regions of the UK will be funnelled through our Liverpool branch. This will also apply to all direct import/export business worldwide. There will be an amnesty period from today until the first of next month—fourteen days—to allow for a smooth transition to take place.

"In future, the tax year will run from the first of July—the anniversary of the month in which Liverpool's Charter was originally signed. Liverpool will set a tithe—in effect, income tax—of ten per cent. This is the sum Greater Merseyside will pay per head of population to the Central Government of the United Kingdom."

"What sort of financial security are we talking about?"

"You have to respect a client's right to privacy. The person you need to ask about the financial background is the Synod's Chancellor of the Exchequer. He's here with me, financial advisor Dominic Ion."

"Thank you, Rik."

Dominic took the microphone: the outside-broadcast camera refocused on him.

"For far too long, a succession of government administrations of various political persuasions has denied Liverpool and the North West of England the opportunity to grow and develop as a region. Every regional development plan, every tranche of government spending, has favoured the South of England in general and the Home Counties in particular. For the last six financial years, we have collected and sent more tax revenues south—often propping up failing businesses—than we have been allocated to carry out regional development in the North West. The people of Liverpool have had enough.

"As you know, we have recently seen the first fruits of a very special job-creation scheme by re-laying the tracks of a moth-balled railway spur, upgrading it to a state-of-the-art, modern tram service, which provides a fast, efficient link from our expanding airport directly to the city centre.

"The second Mersey crossing—the Gateway bridge—had already been started and is expected to be completed on time and under budget. The men who worked on the Tramlink Project have all been retained to build the bridge, and more men have applied to become navigators, as they prefer to be called. Unemployment in the six boroughs that make up the region of

Greater Merseyside is almost non-existent, and there are several plans in hand that promise continued work for many years still to come.

"Mr. Hines' decision to launch Jomfru Cash here, rather than in London, was only partially due to the far more realistic prices of property in this region."

Dom was beginning to enjoy himself and appeared far more relaxed as he spoke.

"During some routine renovation work in the oldest part of Liverpool, close to the docks, a long-lost historical site was discovered. The most significant find was a document pre-dating Magna Carta, in which King John granted Liverpool a charter and the right to form its own council, enact its own laws, collect taxes and provide for its own citizens. In simple legal terms, Merseyside has been mistreated for nine hundred years by what has, in effect, been an illegal regime.

"At the same time and in the same location, a significant number of valuable objects were discovered. These were taken out, catalogued and assessed. Legal opinion declared them Treasure Trove and unquestionably the property of the Crown.

"The documents prove conclusively that the Crown, in this instance, is the city and people of Liverpool. I am therefore pleased to announce that on this day, when we welcome Mr. Rik Hines and his new venture, Jomfru Cash, we can also confirm that his first and currently most affluent customer will be the City and Synod of Liverpool, with an opening balance in excess of £250 million sterling. We believe this will provide the stability and security we need to run our own businesses, provide health, education and essential services and function efficiently as an autonomous, self-governing, independent, radical region within the UK."

CHAPTER TWENTY-FOUR

"DOM, IT'S GETTING close to the first of July. Any chance you can prepare a detailed financial statement of where we stand when we start our new tax year?"

"Already got that in hand, JRK. I'll bring it with me to the *Fyraften* tomorrow."

The nickname for the informal afternoon planning meetings held in a number of local pubs and restaurants had been adopted from the European tradition of ending the working week a few hours early on Fridays, giving employees the option of socialising with other staff before going home or using the couple of hours on offer to do some shopping or for other practical purposes.

In the first couple of months since this loose understanding had been introduced, there had been no significant dip in productivity or sales targets, and the vast majority of firms had reported an improvement in staff morale and a distinct drop in the number of people ringing in sick. Many firms had improved or expanded existing canteen facilities on site. Others that had never offered this to employees had opted to install them, and most workers seized this opportunity to socialise at the end of the working week.

"We're booked at the Lion this week," Paul said, flicking through his diary. The pub was ideally located for anyone working in City Centre and offered a range of lunch options as well as a constantly changing variety of CAMRA-approved beers. He glanced sideways at Nuala, head down and writing furiously on her notepad. She didn't look up but raised her free hand as if sensing he wanted to tell her something. After a few seconds, she straightened up from her cramped position and, without comment or glance in Paul's direction, pushed the notepad towards him. His eyes were drawn straight to the last couple of lines she'd written on the page:

> You want to make anmt at F. meet abt L/pool W in talks w/ EM jobs CL + others emps:
>
> STOP THINKING SO LOUD!!!

Nuala's abbreviations were easy enough to interpret, but Paul knew for a fact he hadn't told her about his grand announcement yet. He'd come straight to this conference following several long, private phone conversations and hadn't had the opportunity to speak to her or anyone else. How could she possibly know? As he re-read the capitalised final line on the page, he felt the frozen feet of a thousand fire ants marching up his spine. There was simply *no way* she or anyone else could have known this.

This wasn't the first incident hinting at some form of precog, or at very least a form of rapport, between himself and Nuala. There had been several, and they'd been more frequent and more intense over the last few weeks. Taken in isolation, none of them had been significant or world-shattering, but the sum of the parts, as the saying went, was without question more than the total of the individual pieces.

One thing he did know: the very first incident of this nature had been the precise moment towards the end of the mid-river auction when he'd been about to tell Nuala something and seen her clasp her hand to the back of her neck as if stung by an invisible insect. He hated the thought that he was, in some inexplicable manner, responsible for something that caused someone else discomfort. Not just *any* someone, he reminded himself bitterly, but someone he'd *like* to think of as special, someone who might even have similar feelings towards him.

Oh, yeah? And how's she going to know about that if you don't tell *her?* his sly, cynical alter ego mocked. Savagely, abruptly, he banished the thought before it could extend a poisonous tentacle, attacking Nuala's vulnerable state of mind. He hadn't the slightest doubt: if that were to happen, he'd lose the opportunity to persuade her to think of him as someone closer, more intimate—in every sense of the word—than a casual work colleague.

He placed his hand on the notepad to prevent anyone else present from reading the private message intended for his eyes alone. A second later, he felt the feather-light contact of her hand laid on the back of his. The mental rapport was stronger than ever. He felt her terrors scattering in several directions at once, like frightened rabbits fleeing a hungry fox. He didn't understand what was happening, but he didn't really care. All that mattered was he had to act immediately, positively, to protect and safeguard Nuala from whatever real or imagined threat she was experiencing. He concentrated every ounce of power he could summon to send every calming thought he could muster and felt her flinch—in shock or surprise?—as the muscles in her hand tensed momentarily on his, then relaxed, accepting the healing flow of his support. In that special moment, time became meaningless for both parties, eddying around an unseen object in it its path before resuming. He felt her unquestioning gratitude, though neither of them understood why or how they could possibly feel the powerful emotional rapport they were experiencing.

"...okay, Paul?"

The inflection was his only clue to indicate he'd been asked a question. He just had to hope he wasn't making a total prat of himself as he temporised rather than offer an answer that didn't follow directly as the sensible answer to the query.

"Sorry, John, I think it's fatigue catching up on me. What was the question?"

"I noticed both you and Nuala seemed a bit distant for a moment. Are you okay? That applies to both of you."

Nuala nodded—possibly a little quicker than might have been expected—but she didn't speak. Paul glanced at her, at the same time tossing a mental bolt, which he had the satisfaction of somehow knowing she'd caught and held. He took a short breath and answered on her behalf as well as his own.

"Just tired, and I know Nuala never stops working! Nothing a few hours shuteye won't cure. But I wanted to say, I've got some positive news, which I want to make public knowledge at tomorrow's session at the Lion."

He suddenly saw the 'Get out of Jail' card he needed and picked up Nuala's notepad.

"I'd asked Nuala to ensure I get a slot at tomorrow's meeting to make it official.

"I've got two separate pieces of *very* good news to announce, both employment-related, but if I tell you now, we've got to be certain the security surrounding this is absolute. No excuses, no exceptions. Agreed?"

"We don't know what we're agreeing to yet," Dom pointed out, "but I don't have a problem judging your assessment of whatever you've managed to set in motion. If you say security's involved, even *vital*, I'll take your word for it."

"Okay, thanks for that. Believe me, it's not an exaggeration to say the timing of when and how this news is released is vital.

"We've made some big strides already in reducing unemployment in this region to almost nothing. But you know as well as I do, so far, it's been noticeable mostly on *this* side of the river. What I want to announce tomorrow is going to have the same effect on the Wirral peninsula—literally everywhere, from New Brighton to Runcorn, Warrington and beyond."

CHAPTER TWENTY-FIVE

THE VENUE FOR the *Fyraften* meeting that week wasn't as spacious as some of the others. This gave Paul some misgivings.

"The whole idea of these meetings was to keep them informal and also open to anyone who fancied dropping in," he groused as the last available seat he could see was claimed ten minutes before the usual two-o'clock start time.

"Yeah, a bigger room would have been a good thing," JRK admitted, "but it could also have meant that certain things we might want to keep private would be heard by—"

"By the world and his wife or any nosy bugger passing through with a pint in his hand, I know!" Paul sighed. "At least we managed to get the back room, so the Lion's regular lunchtime crowd can stay in the main bar. Can you call 'em to order, John? I've got a lot on my agenda today, and I don't know if anybody else has anything to say. I'm happy to wait until everything else has been discussed before I wade in."

***

"Thanks, Dominic, for a financial statement that you managed to make sound interesting *and* possible for us ordinary mortals to understand! It's good to know our finances are secure and backed by tangible, inflation-proofed assets.

"Over the past few months—no, let's be honest and say years, shall we?—one national government after another has clearly shown a preference for Manchester over Liverpool every time they remember to look further north than the Watford Gap.

This is just *one* of many things we can now put right, thanks to the independence our newfound wealth has made possible.

"First: We will continue to maintain and pay for the upkeep of all our transport links with the rest of the country by road, rail, sea and air. Repairs and maintenance of the links beyond our borders will no longer be subsidised, as is currently the case, by the local taxpayer.

"Point Two: Following on from this, we will be responsible for the provision and performance of all public transport, our buses and trains, our motorways and all the necessary infrastructure. Manchester, as we all know, was given £450 million to develop their transport system. We can do better, and with less.

"Three: Taxes will be reset at the traditional measure of a tithe—ten per cent of the sum every working man and woman earns. Extra hidden taxes such as purchase tax or VAT will cease to exist. The displayed price will become de facto the agreed selling price. Cheating on tax will be rendered a pointless, obsolete tactic.

"Four: Education. We were recently awarded £500 million to improve our schools and skills-training budget. This came from European sources, *not* the suits in their comfy London offices, so it's ours to spend as we see fit on educational matters.

"Training and life-skills education will be given the highest of priorities, with jobs—*real* jobs—available for everyone who completes a Modern Apprenticeship in any of the skills required to make sure the local economy functions and grows.

"Five: Policing, hospitals and other public services. Concentrating all our resources to deal with these matters within our own region will make it far easier to keep a check on what these services cost. Working within a much-reduced geographical area will make it easier to control what is being spent.

"Six: The construction and use of fixed access points to the region—effectively, the building and staffing of passport control, plus customs and excise facilities at appropriate road and rail sites and the expansion of existing facilities at John Lennon Airport—

will pay for itself in a very short period of time. This will also supply a steady income for the local economy in years to come. Every registered resident will be issued with a SmarTag allowing free and unlimited border passage as a driver or passenger in a private vehicle or a significantly discounted price on public-transport tickets."

Paul gave up all pretence at reading from the notes he held in one hand, most of which he'd long ago committed to memory anyway. He looked slowly around the silent room before continuing:

"Almost everything I've touched on today is perfectly possible provided we can get *as an absolute minimum* the same terms and conditions Central Government has already gifted Manchester, and let's not forget, we already *have* a decent tranche of cash from Europe, which London can't touch or control.

"But I've saved the best 'til last," he added. The growing murmur of inevitable questions that had been threatening to intrude on Paul's final words rumbled to an untidy stop, replaced by an expectant silence.

"Late last night—after I'd tidied up all my notes and checked all my figures one final time—a very interesting email landed in my inbox.

"Core Holdings—the main investor behind JLA, the new cruise terminal and several other Merseyside projects—has agreed to make a further £250 million available for the refurbishment of Birkenhead docks, the south bank of the river, and a significant youth training/apprenticeship scheme."

The cheering and applause lasted several minutes: bar staff and regular customers in the main bar couldn't be held back and were soon congratulating random people they'd never met for achieving something they couldn't fully understand but realised was—probably—a good thing for the town of their birth. For them, that was enough, especially if, as suggested, someone had found a way to strike at the hated Mancs.

CHAPTER TWENTY-SIX

"LOOKS LIKE WE got visitors, Sarge."

"Copy that. Do you have range and numbers?"

"Estimated quarter mile. Five, six maybe. On foot, no vehicles, no lights."

"Remain in place, observation only. Sounds like civilians, one for the Rangers."

"Understood. Obs Four out."

The squaddie manning Observation Point 4 on the flat roof of the former Copy Lane police station returned his attention to his night glasses. This time he was certain: he counted six shadows, now apparently moving more quickly and with the confidence of over-optimistic amateurs who think—mistakenly—they've avoided the final trap awaiting them at a border crossing. They'd circled around the harsh, shadowless glare of the lighting that illuminated the courtyard and parking area outside Switch Island Passport Control. By attempting to bypass the official checkpoint, they were already advertising themselves as illegals: the sentry on duty at Obs Four was under no illusions regarding their likely treatment at the hands of the Rangers.

He hadn't heard anything about resisting arrest or cases of an unexpected death in custody since border control had been established on the major routes into and out of the newly created Greater Merseyside, but from the rumours he'd heard, you didn't mess with the Rangers.

He decided he could allow himself a smoke, as long as he followed the soldier's habit of cupping it in his palm to conceal the telltale glow of the ember. As a professional soldier, he'd seen action in several of the world's trouble spots, but he'd had no hesitation in switching his allegiance from the Union Flag to Merseyside's banner when the choice had to be made. His pay was still secure, and the new lower rate of income tax meant his money definitely stretched further. As he smoked, he had time to think about what he knew of the Rangers without losing his concentration on his night-watch duties.

The Rangers weren't combat trained. They didn't carry weapons: they *were* weapons, a civilian force whose sole raison d'être was to assist the regular army in preventing illegal immigrants from entering the land of opportunity which Greater Merseyside had become in the six months since the Synod had formally seceded from the not-so-United Kingdom and opted to organise its own affairs under the leadership of John R. Kirwan and the Radical Regionalist Party.

The Rangers weren't an organised body. Mostly, they seemed to operate in ones and twos. Rumour had it that they could live off the land almost indefinitely, construct a bothy—and dismantle one—in minutes without leaving a trace, disappear into thin air when it suited their purpose: for all he knew, they could walk on water, fly without wings...

A discreet *burr!* on his radio signalled a message from HQ.

"Obs Four, confirmed interception of six WBs. Excellent intel, remain vigilant."

"Acknowledged, HQ. Obs Four out."

Six WBs—wannabes—taken by the Rangers, he thought. Even if there were no more incidents this night, he felt he'd already earned his keep. And who knew? One or two of them might possess some sort of skill that would make them useful to the community they were so anxious to join.

***

"It's happened again, Brian."

Brian Stanners nodded to indicate he'd heard and completed what looked like a delicate and extremely complicated manoeuvre deep within the entrails of a laptop before he emerged with the suspicion of a satisfied smirk on his face.

"What's happened again? A crash on Wall Street? Or have the Frogs buggered up the Bourse again?"

"Ha-bloody-ha, Stan! No, it's much closer to home. Every time we sink the footings to another span on the Gateway bridge, another bunch of WBs decide to try and swim across from somewhere upstream."

"Wish I could write a programme which'd keep 'em out, Jim, but I'm fresh out of ideas this time, I'm afraid."

"I'm not expecting miracles, Brian! You just happen to be the only person here at this god-forsaken hour o' the night, so there's nobody else I can moan to."

Brian's eyes glazed over. His thoughts were clearly elsewhere as his fingers rapidly reassembled the repaired laptop. The last four screws were so small Jim could barely see them, but Brian wasn't even looking. His hands completed the task as if on autopilot.

"As the teams continue building, and the gap between the two ends narrows, we're likely to see more and more trying to get across," Brian murmured. "And all the security and surveillance programmes in the world aren't going to stop people making the attempt, especially when they're desperate."

"I appreciate that, Brian, and I'm not asking you to provide a solution! I'm just concerned about the safety issues. Until now—as far as we know—there haven't been any fatalities, but there's no way we can patrol the river, provide security, save lives."

"Just a thought, Jim. Is this something the Rangers might be able to cover?"

"Hmm. Well, since they don't officially *exist*, we couldn't make any official approach or request, but I suppose it's one possibility—*if* I can get a message delivered, of course."

***

"Your cargo manifest, please? Thank you...non-perishable goods? Furniture components to be assembled on-site for retail sale. Zero-rated for tax purposes. Now, if I can just have a look at your load, you can be on your way..."

Throughout the night, as on most nights of the week, there was constant heavy goods and commercial traffic in both directions along the A580 East Lancs Road. Just outside St. Helens, the old Carr Mill Dam junction had been modified and completely rebuilt to accommodate both passport control and a state-of-the-art customs-and-excise facility. Local residents and businesses registered as local, based on Merseyside, had all been issued with an electronic SmarTag, which meant they could pass unchallenged at any time, using a fast-track lane governed by the tag on the windshield. The SmarTag could also be swiped to get free tickets on all public transport in the region.

"How long since your last fuel stop? Did you fill the tanks yourself or supervise the whole time the refuelling was taking place?

"Did you notice anyone acting suspiciously while you refuelled? Nobody approached or spoke to you? I'll need a dipstick test to get an idea how much fuel you have arriving on Merseyside, and a spot check for unregistered aliens attempting to enter illegally. Peter, bring the mirrors and check the chassis is clean."

***

"This train is for Liverpool. The next station is Stafford." There was a split-second hesitation before the next town on the route was named, due to the updated data being fed onto the master tape and broadcast on the train's PA system.

"Change at Stafford for Blackpool and the North. Passengers for Runcorn and Liverpool, please have your passports—and, for non-residents, your visas—ready for inspection between Stafford and Crewe. Change at Crewe for North Wales. This is the ten thirty-six

through train for Liverpool Lime Street. This service is currently on time, due to arrive at twelve hundred hours."

"Yes, sir, I appreciate it's a genuine oversight, but it's not 'just like paying an excess fare' ticket! I don't have the facility or the authority to issue you a temporary visa—even if such a thing existed, which it doesn't.

"Yes, of course you can use your mobile to ring your London office, but I'm afraid you'll have to leave the train at Crewe and wait until your secretary can fax you the visa you need before you can travel onwards to Greater Merseyside..."

Just after midday, Rik Hines thanked the driver of the *Jomfru* train from London for a smooth, comfortable and fast journey up from the capital. Despite protests about broken promises from an outraged admin in Manchester, the latest high-speed link had been made via Liverpool, with more than one-and-a-bit eyes on the potential tourist trade along the coast of Lancashire and into Cumbria.

"The Mancs can sulk all they like! Fact o' the matter is, they ain't got nuttin' t' show culture-wise nor any other-wise, compared wi' us!" Paul snorted dismissively, and he had a point.

Manchester had the arena, largely gifted by a fawning, obsequious Tory Government seeking to curry favour, and they also had the ballet, but stratospheric ticket prices for both attractions were a constant problem when it came to continued viability. Liverpool, on the other hand, had a smaller arena with more accessible ticketing policies and a wealth of local talent, which Manchester could never emulate. It wasn't long before all the big world names looking to play gigs in the UK were looking at Liverpool in preference to Manchester and even London.

"Good trip, Rik?"

"Yes, thanks, John. I managed to ruffle a few feathers, I think! Still, I had a word with a friend who owes me..."

"Is there anyone left in London who *doesn't* owe you a favour, Rik?"

Rik grinned.

"D'you mean, anyone *important*? As it happens, I haven't got any leverage in government circles..."

"I take it you mean *London* government circles! You've certainly made yourself indispensable on Merseyside. What sort of deal have you made this time?"

"I got an idea from the shopping list Paul came up with at the Friday session we had at the Lion. He said—amongst other things—that Core Holdings was ready to fund the redevelopment of the docks, both sides of the river."

"Yes, and work on the cruise terminal is already well underway."

"So I thought, maybe we should have a closer look at clawing back some of the freight trade that made Liverpool's fortune. We're going to be dredging the river to make it possible for large modern liners to use the terminal. We can develop berths on both sides of the river to handle cargo. With the advances we've made in cargo-handling machinery and containerisation, plus the state-of-the-art technology we have available, it's no longer so labour-intensive. And have you seen the cost of transporting goods by road or even by rail nowadays? I'm thinking we ought to take a serious look at any alternatives."

"Taking heavy goods off the roads would also be popular with the Greens and all the other ecological pressure groups," JRK said, "and we could maybe even look at resurrecting the Leeds and Liverpool Canal for cross-country freight."

"How does the guy who owes you a favour fit into all this, Rik?" Paul wanted to know.

Rik stiffened, and suddenly found the dregs at the bottom of his coffee cup extremely fascinating.

"I had to make an on-the-spot decision, guys," he admitted, "and although I don't think it's likely to come back and bite me, I should probably have spoken to you—or more likely a full meeting of the Synod—first.

"Alfie Evans runs a fleet of ships. Nothing fancy, nothing big, but powerful little tugs he's used for years, under contract to keep the shipping lanes in and out of the Port of London navigable.

"He's done the job for nigh on thirty years. Now he wants to retire and hand the business over to his son, who's been working with him since we both left school.

"I put it to him that, if he was prepared to relocate to Merseyside and do exactly what he's doing now in London, we'd find a way to make it worth his while. Nothing underhand or devious, no offshore accounts or anything of that nature. Maybe a grace period, some sort of tax-free agreement for a couple of months while he settles in? Perhaps fast-tracking his registration as a resident, liable to a lower rate of tax? I haven't exactly promised him the sun and the moon, but I certainly glammed up the potential benefits he could expect, and I really *should* have spoken to you first."

"In the circumstances, Rik, I don't think anyone'll hold it against you," JRK assured him with a swift glance sideways to check with Paul. "After all, the skills and the vessels involved are special talents, which have to be learned on the job over a period of years. I take it he'll be bringing his employees with him—qualified and experienced workers?"

"As many as want to, I'm sure—and from casual chat, that's likely to be most of them. You've no idea how much chatter there is in London about Merseyside. Everyone I spoke to seems green with envy at the way our economy's improving! Of course, we'd have to offer them similar Ts and Cs in processing residential registration, tax breaks and probably relocation costs, but I'm sure we can find a way around that."

"John, you made PR part of my remit," Paul said. There was a thoughtful look in his eyes. JRK nodded for him to continue.

"I've been thinking about some sort of grand gesture to make something special and memorable to mark our first Liverpool Day—the fifteenth of June, the date on the Charter," he added, though nobody present needed reminding of that.

"Anyway," he continued, "I've already been in contact with the Cunard shipping line, and if we can bring this friend of yours on board and have the river properly dredged, it might be possible to have the three biggest and best-known passenger liners in the *world* pay us a state visit to mark the occasion. Can you imagine it? We could see the *Queen Mary 2*, *Queen Victoria* and *Queen Elizabeth* docked here, side by side, in the shadow of the Cunard Buildings to celebrate the company's anniversary—their one-hundred-and-seventy-fifth and, technically, Liverpool's nine-hundredth!"

Rik was on his feet in an instant.

"You kept that one under your hat," he crowed. "I thought I was the one who's supposed to make the audacious gestures that grab the headlines and the news media publicity, but I never even dreamed of anything on that scale! How far have you got, Paul? Is it even close to a done deal?"

"Cunard is keen. They're looking for PR to mark their own anniversary, and we've got the best part of six months to get everything ready. That should be plenty of time, especially if we're getting the river channels dredged regularly."

JRK was on his feet immediately.

"Rik, with your connections and Paul's magic touch when it comes to good PR work, this all sounds very promising! I suggest we leave it for you to get together on this. Any objections? Do we need a formal vote? No? In that case, I think we can say the business part of this meeting's closed and grab some lunch."

Rik glanced at his watch and shook his head. "I promised to look in at the East Lancs border base today. If I leave now, I can be back in time for the *Fyraften* meet. If I'm delayed, start without me, I'll be there before you finish."

***

The clock behind the bar at the Lion ticked past three-fifteen and was approaching the half hour. There was still no sign of

Rik, and JRK decided he wasn't waiting any longer. People had homes to go to, and these meetings were deliberately kept low-key and outside paid work hours. He tapped on his glass and the meeting settled down to a mixture of serious drinking and casual chat in small groups around individual tables, mostly speculation about how Liverpool's immediate future might evolve. Suddenly the door flew open, and Les Harrison, one of the younger RR volunteers, burst onto the scene with a curious gleam in his eyes. He scanned the room and bulled his way across the snug to the 'top table'.

"Paul! Thank God I made it before the meeting finished."

"Calm down, Les. We've only just begun ploughing through this week's agenda! Catch your breath first—someone get him a drink—and tell us. What's the problem?"

A pint appeared from somewhere or other. Les took a quick sup to recover his breath—he'd clearly been running—and nodded his thanks.

"I borrowed our Frank's mo-bike t' get here quick as I could. I was out on patrol wi' a few o' the Rangers, up the East Lancs..."

He looked around the room again, and the wild gleam in his eyes dissolved into body-shaking mirth as he spluttered, "D'ya know, I've always wanted an excuse to say this..."

He paused. The grin on his face became impossibly wide. He struck a theatrical stance and announced in a burlesque music-hall parody of a 'reet broooaad' Lancs accent, "Eeeh oop, Boss, thuurrs trubble at t' mill. Intruders trying t' break in near the new Carr Mill Dam. One of un's took a potshot at Rik. He was there on a visit. He'll be okay, it's only a flesh wound near his shoulder. He's been took t' Billinge Hospital—that was closest—and we'll hear from them soonest. A couple of your guys rode shotgun wi' th' ambulance."

CHAPTER TWENTY-SEVEN

"WE DECIDED TO loop round north of the 580."

Les sat at the nearest table and nodded his thanks for the beer, which immediately appeared. He traced the details on an OS map, which opened out, showing the relevant area between St. Helens and Wigan.

"Who else was on duty?" JRK asked. "Anyone I'd know?"

"Our Frank and two other local lads. Like I said, I persuaded him to lend me his motorbike, an' he wasn't too chuffed about it, but he's bigger'n me, an' we needed some muscle on the scene. I'm pretty sure you won't know the other guys. They only came to join the Rangers a few days ago. This was their first taste o' the action."

"Fair enough. I appreciate that the Rangers have really proved themselves useful already, and I understand that a lot of them have all sorts of reasons for keeping out of the limelight, preserving their anonymity. The names aren't important. There were four of youse, all told, yeah? And you met up with…?"

"Six adults, four kids. Up at the top end of Carr Mill Dam. They came across some open farm land. We caught them as they tried to cross the old stone bridge, bypassing the customs post on the East Lancs."

"Did they give you any resistance? Were they armed?"

"No, they were just a couple of families, probably related. I didn't want to waste time giving them the third degree. I thought it best to get here with the info as quickly as possible. We took them to passport control and gave them some hot drinks. They were giving Frank chapter an' verse. It all seemed smooth and casual, like.

"We were just standin' by the open cabin door—it's a Portakabin, really, an' too small f'r the whole group. That's when it happened—the shot, I mean! There must've been someone else hiding in the bushes. The adults said there was nobody else with them."

"Could be an individual thought he'd have a better chance as part of a group?" Paul suggested, raising an eyebrow as he looked around the others.

Les continued, "The family group—cos that's what they looked like t' me, they were clearly travelling together—all said there was nobody else. They were just as s'prised as us when the shot come an' I work on a farm. I can tell yiz 'twas no high-power rifle. It sounded like a BB popgun, the sort kids use f'r target practice, knockin' empty cans off a wall."

"Is that why you decided to leave some muscle at the checkpoint?"

"We've had a few small groups chancing their luck around that particular border point every night for a week, maybe more, an' some of them...get a bit upset when we ask them *politely* where they're goin' or if they've any ID documents.

"Just a question of the numbers game, Paul. Yes, this group seemed pretty harmless, but there were ten of them, including the kids—plus another, presumably armed and still unaccounted for. It wouldn't have been on t' leave them with the security guards at the checkpoint. They've got enough on their plates watching the traffic coming up from Manchester and all points east. In fact, if you can get a team out there ASAP, we still have time to get back out tonight and patrol at least part of the perimeter. There are lots of open fields north of the 580—it's an area where we have to rely on foot patrols."

"Your Ranger team have already done one good job tonight, Les," JRK said approvingly.

"It's true, we have to look after our own, first and foremost, but we don't want to start building watchtowers with armed sentries and minefields. We should be making folk welcome. We don't want to be a divided city like Berlin, with a bloody great wall running through it. As Dominic said only tonight, tourism is likely to become one of our main sources of income, so we should be encouraging people to come and settle here."

"That's all very well, but we need time to tidy up, sweep the carpet, slap a lick o' paint on the front door and put the kettle on before we start inviting visitors," Paul said. "Which, by the way, is something I think we should pencil in for discussion in the near future. But for the moment, we have a live situation that needs sorting out tonight."

Nuala was still scribbling notes but laid her pencil aside as Paul paused, looking first at the half-full glass in his hand before glancing around the room.

"I've only had soft drinks all night. I can drive if someone's got a decent-sized vehicle we can use. Nuala, how did you…?"

"D'you really have to ask?"

Paul realised the time had come when he should no longer be surprised by the moments of intimate clarity between himself and Nuala. He tried to 'message' a hint of his personal feelings along with his grateful acceptance as he nodded, acknowledging her offer. This time, there could be no question of doubt. He felt an instant response and sensed that Nuala had made a conscious decision to send back a subliminal, silent signal. Paul caught his breath. Was she testing him or the reality—or otherwise—of their link, which seemed to be establishing itself with or without their direct intervention?

"Good question, Paul. Haven't got a clue. What do you think?"

Paul emptied his glass to win a few valuable seconds and glanced in Nuala's direction as she slid her notes into a shoulder bag and looked around, clearly hoping for the necessary car keys.

"We need to talk. I mean, *really* talk."

"Agreed."

A set of keys were relayed across the room and proved to be ideal for the purpose: Robin Stuart's pride and joy, a Land Rover Evoque with little more than factory mileage on the odometer.

"It's going to be a long night, Robin," Nuala informed him. "I'll have to ferry at least four people home—five if Frank Harrison can't take Les back on his pillion. I'll drop it off tomorrow morning, shall we say about ten o'clock? Fine! Yes, I'll take good care of it. I've heard every joke that's ever been told about women drivers, and I'll take any of yiz on, any day of the week!"

"*And you'll be my last drop,*" she concluded privately, for Paul's ear alone.

I could most definitely get used to this, he thought as he shrugged into his jacket. He tensed and whipped out a handkerchief to cover his cheeks as he felt the faint, telltale blush of embarrassment threaten to break out, betray the existence his unique and unfathomable ability to communicate with the gorgeous flame-haired secretary-cum-chauffeur shimmying across the crowded room and somehow managing to arrive at the street door without having to dance the usual *'scuse-me* steps or skitter to one side avoiding the Roman hands and Russian fingers of the Lion pub's half-tipsy regular Friday-night patrons.

The meeting broke up at an orderly but leisurely pace. JRK and Paul stood at the door and wished everyone a good weekend. By the time Paul had shepherded the last of the group outside, Nuala was waiting at the kerb with the engine purring. Compared with a normal Friday-night pub timetable, it was still early. However, being in Liverpool meant that the *relativity of time* was an unknown variable: one which was frequently scrutinised and found to be at the very least malleable, often impossible to measure accurately or with any degree of certainty.

The sun was still above the yardarm, the streets crowded with pedestrian traffic flowing with the draught beers from one pub to another, but this was the quiet time for vehicles. Most people had already arrived where they planned to spend most of the evening—and their wage packets—and it was far too early for the taxi-home element of the local economy to be in operation. Heading east, away from City Centre, they had the road more or less to themselves, and within twenty minutes, Nuala was pulling into the car park reserved for staff members at the recently completed Passport Control straddling the A580 East Lancs Road to define the official eastern boundary of Greater Merseyside.

***

"I never even thought to ask. Who ran Robin home from the meeting last night? I don't even know where he lives."

It had been a long night. So much had happened—and so rapidly—that Paul hadn't had the time to deal with all the organisational details he would normally have held himself responsible for as JRK's right hand and PR guru. The brief summer night was beginning to pale towards dawn, and he was Nuala's last drop-off as she pulled away from Jim's neat semi in Old Swan and turned south onto the Ring Road, heading towards Childwall and Speke.

"Robin takes his job seriously. His house is practically at the end of the main runway. He told me he got it cheap. Nobody else'd buy it, with planes taking off and landing all hours day and night."

"Ha! I very much doubt that!" Paul snorted. "But I have to admit, he strikes me as a good businessman, so I can imagine him haggling over the price."

They were approaching a complex double-roundabout: the conversation lapsed for a few seconds as Nuala concentrated on getting into the correct lane. Paul cast about for a way of leading up to the personal topic neither of them had touched upon as yet but had agreed had to be discussed.

"Nuala, don't take me straight home. If you pull into the car park at Calderstones, we can take a stroll in the park while we..."

"*Voice* our thoughts for once?" Nuala suggested when he hesitated. Paul felt his neck prickle with warmth. He was relieved the uncertain pre-dawn light and the random clutter in the SUV cast just enough shadows to disguise his blushes.

"I rather think that was one of the main reasons you offered to chauffeur us out to this evening's Ranger incident."

"Let's be honest," said Nuala, shifting to a lower gear, "it's not something we can ignore or pretend it's not happening, and as the...connection—or whatever you want to call what's developing between us—is clearly happening more and more frequently..."

"*And* getting stronger—at least, that's how it feels to me?" The hint of a question in Paul's voice betrayed his uncertainty, his concern that Nuala might not appreciate the unsought and inexplicable mental rapport.

Although the road behind was empty, Nuala signalled automatically as she turned into the public car park. Acting purely on instinct, Paul slipped his seat belt and was out of the car before the engine died, opening Nuala's door to help her out.

She rose gracefully from the seat, smiling as she laid her hand lightly on Paul's palm.

"You do realise, this is the first time you've actually held my hand?"

"Maybe that's true, but not because I didn't want to..." Paul murmured as he caught her free hand in his. Inevitably, they turned to face each other squarely. Prompted by the lightest possible pressure from his fingertip, no more than the flap of a butterfly's wing against the dead calm of a still, sun-drenched summer afternoon, the kiss that followed had been a long time coming, and neither felt disposed to end it prematurely. In slow-slow-slow-motion, the butterfly condescended to flap its wing a second time, and Paul was certain he could literally feel the earth move beneath his feet.

"You felt it too."

Their lips were still locked together, and Paul's hands were buried deep in Nuala's luxuriant, fiery tresses. There was neither fear nor surprise in the statement, which sounded calm, approving. It resonated deep within Paul's inmost being, uttered without question in Nuala's inimitable, honeyed contralto voice.

The day's first skylark rising to greet the sun's rays trilled a paean of joy across Paul's conscious mind. Nuala must have heard it, too: they eased apart and filled their oxygen-starved lungs with deep, satisfying gulps of the dew-moist, primrose-scented park air as they listened to the morning concerto tuning up. An unseen Canada goose honked a petulant bass, answered by the comical, slightly flatulent *parp!* of one of the resident ducks. By tacit consent, they strolled over to a park bench on the banks of the lake and sat to listen as the orchestra grew in numbers and in volume.

"It's so peaceful here," Nuala murmured, resting her head on Paul's shoulder.

"Agreed. The school I went to isn't far from here," he responded, "and although it wasn't the shortest way for me to get home, I often took a few minutes to detour this way before getting the bus home, clear my head, you know?"

"Have you had any thoughts about our *private* conversations yet?"

"It's the elephant in the room we agreed we'd have to acknowledge, Nuala, and we have to find a way of coping with it, but it's way outside anything I've ever had to deal with before! I've heard tales of twins—identical twins—who were supposed to be able to sense each other's thoughts and even actions, but it doesn't involve anyone I know personally..."

"Me neither," Nuala agreed. "But like you, I've heard stories. I wish there was some way we could *test* the...the link, or whatever we decide to call it."

"You mean, try to find out if we can *control* it in some way? Perhaps even find a way to *use* it for...something practical?" Paul finished. Even as he spoke the words, he felt the idea sounded lame and highly unlikely.

"What has it got in its pockets?" Nuala suddenly hissed with a grotesque stage-leer. Paul recognised the source of her feed line and responded with an equally camp theatrical grimace.

"Handses or nothing," he squeaked, pretending an admix of surprise and terror: for a moment, they were Gollum and Bilbo Baggins pitting their riddling wits over ownership of One Ring destined to Rule Them All. They sparred for a few minutes, each drawing deeply on their knowledge of the classic Tolkien novel, enjoying a child's wonder in discovering a friend with the same taste in literature.

"Seriously, though, you'll have to drop the bus off pretty soon," said Paul with a glance at his watch. "And we haven't found any obvious solution."

"And there's no mileage in discussing it with anyone. Nobody who hasn't experienced it themselves could possibly understand or appreciate the problem... if it *is* a problem?"

"I can live with it, Nuala. After all, it's brought us closer together, and for that, I'm very grateful."

"Me too," she agreed, sealing the agreement with another kiss.

"We just have to be careful not to cause undue comment," Paul cautioned when they surfaced once more as the park continued to come to life around them. "We've the chance to use it as a handy time-saver, assuming we can learn to control it. As far as I can see, there's no harm in us each knowing the other's inner thoughts—at least, *some* of them—as long as we also respect each other's privacy, and I think we're adult enough to know where to draw the line."

"I think that's about as far as we can take it for the moment," Nuala nodded as she stood, stretched and looked at her watch. "Come on, then! I'll drop you off and carry on to Robin's house. He'll be wanting to leave for work, but he'll have to drive me home. I'm not going to stand around for the cattle-truck back to Aigburth."

CHAPTER TWENTY-EIGHT

When Rob Stuart walked into his office at eight o'clock, half a dozen secretaries were already working flat out to deal with incoming calls, and the switchboard was backed up with a lengthy queue on hold.

His PA greeted him in Reception. She carried a clipboard with several sheets attached, and he could see that the top sheet was completely covered with notes in her compact, neat handwriting.

"It's been crazy here for over an hour already. Scandinavia started the ball rolling—they're an hour ahead of the UK. Most of them are cargo transport firms wanting more details about handling facilities, and we're getting enquiries from Germany too. I ordered coffee when I saw you pull into the car park. You've got a visitor. Les Harrison says he has a verbal report on Rik Hines' hospital admission and treatment. There's nothing in writing from the hospital, apparently. He said he was happy to wait outside your office."

"Thanks, Sue, you've obviously got everything under control. I don't know what I'd do without you! I expected news about Rik, but not this early. I know for a fact the incident happened quite late yesterday afternoon."

Robin avoided direct reference to the fact that he'd also worked late. Sue didn't need telling: she knew him well enough.

"Good to see you, Les," he greeted, gesturing for Les to follow him into his office. "How do things stand?"

"Straight to the point, Rob. Rik said I was to remind you that time is money. I thought it might save some time if you care to listen in when I interview Alfie Evans on Rik's behalf about relocating his dredgers up here. His son Alan will be sitting in, too. Alfie wants the handover to be seamless—and sooner, rather than later. He says he's done more than his fair share, and he wants to find a warm beach and a bar full of cold beers while he can still enjoy them."

Rob glanced at the pulsating red light on his desktop. Even with a robust and rigorous filter group of secretaries, it seemed there were still some incoming calls that had passed through the needle's eye and were deemed important enough to land on his personal line. With a resigned shrug and a roll of his eyes, he avoided the phone and called for his PA via a discreet intercom button beneath his desk.

"Sue, if he's fit enough, I want to set up a Zoom meeting with Rik Hines later today—yes, I *know* why he isn't in his office, but I also know he's a tough old goat, and I won't be surprised if he *buys* Billinge Hospital if that's what he has to do to get a doctor to sign a discharge note! Just... see what you can manage, okay?"

He paused for the briefest of moments to give the secretary time to catch up on her notepad, then added, "This Zoom meeting might be a long one. I'll need you to take notes, but first, I want you to contact everyone currently on hold and promise I'll return their call *personally* ASAP. It's not fair to expect them to sit listening to Muzak for hours on end."

"Ever the gentleman, Rob! Why am I not surprised to hear that from you?" Les accepted a refill coffee as Robin lined up two comfortable chairs in front of a TV monitor almost as big as a cinema screen.

"The cost of a few phone calls is a small price to pay if everyone who wants to contact me knows they can get on with their daily business while they're waiting for me to get back to them. Now, if Rik's given you Alfie Evans' contact details, we're ready to go."

***

"You know what, Alf, I'm thinking it might be a good idea if you hang on to your mooring and the yard in the Port of London," Rik said thoughtfully. The audio on the Zoom call was excellent. The fixed-focus camera showed him sitting bright-eyed and bushy-tailed in what was clearly a hospital bed, with a neat bandage wrapped around his left shoulder. "You needn't get yourself tangled up in a buying-and-selling chain that could drag on for months."

"Why keep paying rent and rates on a scrap o' land I'm not using?" Alfie retorted. "You know as well as I do what property prices are like here in London, and along the riverside's got to be the most overpriced slum area in the UK."

Alfie seemed genuinely confused, and his son Alan clearly wasn't following too closely. Robin raised one eyebrow, but Rik raised a reassuring hand.

"Let me run with this. I think I've got it covered."

He turned back to the TV monitor to address the Evans, father and son.

"I hadn't thought about property prices, but that could work to your advantage if you can find someone prepared to sublet it from you. However, you'd have to write in a clause stating that you reserve the right to use it on occasion yourself for a few days at a time.

"If we're going to try and move significant volumes of heavy-goods traffic *off* the road network in the name of reducing pollution, moving bulky non-perishable loads by *sea* could be an extra option instead of expanding the rail network. I'll grant you, it's likely to take longer to get there, and it won't work for anywhere that's too far from the coast, but we can at least explore the possibilities."

"It's worth thinking about, Dad," Alan offered. So far, he'd been a silent observer, and Robin was relieved to see him taking an active part in the discussion.

"Tell you what," he continued, "Dad, you can hop on a train and keep working out the details. I can load up with some of the cranes and other gear we'd need to operate out of our new base. That will give us a rough idea of how long the journey is likely to take, any hazards to be aware of, that sort of thing."

"Aye, we can give it a go," Alfie said, "but I'm not one for fancy hotels…"

Robin reached for his mobile. "I know someone who'll be only too happy to help out… Hello, Kathy? Robin here. Listen, I've an old salt coming to the 'Pool, and he's not 'comfortable' on land. Could you find him a berth on your tugboat for a couple of days?"

He finalised the arrangements with Kathy and ended the call.

"All sorted," he informed Alfie. "And Tugboat Kathy really *does* live on a boat. Not a tug, though. It's a canal longboat. It's not just moored, either. It's a working vessel. She runs trips and adventure holidays for kids and older teenagers, but she's no bookings for this week, so you're welcome to bunk down there.

"Her berth is close to the dock gates, Birkenhead side of the Mersey, so you'll be right in the middle of where the current development work is getting started, and Alan will have a guaranteed berth where he can offload whatever cargo he decides to bring with him."

***

"So once I got through the Channel and started heading north, it was pretty straightforward. The Channel's always crowded, of course, and every bugger's heading straight across y'bows 'twix Britain an' Europe, but I'm sure we can work something out. It's only a question of timing, after all."

"And looking at your cargo manifest, you carried pretty much a full load with you," Alf said as he studied his son's bill of lading. "Did that cause you any handling problems? Are we likely to have problems with currents or in bad weather? Neither of us have worked these waters before, son."

"Nothing we can't handle, Dad. Yes, I was pretty low in the water, but that just made us a bit more stable. We'd have to limit the load when really bad weather's likely, but that won't be a problem, and once we're settled in, most of our remit will be keeping the shipping lanes of the Mersey navigable. We won't be sailing south very often in the foreseeable future, and you seem to have brought all the useful lifting and handling gear on this first trip, so I don't see any problems there."

Without a word passing between them or any evidence of collusion, father and son closed their notebooks, pushed back their chairs and stood with the rehearsed split-second timing of a theatrical double act: neither seemed conscious of the incongruity of their actions.

Without thinking, the home team discovered they were also on their feet, prompted by basic business courtesy to follow the lead of their guests.

"Alf, I'll drive the pair of you round to Tugboat Kathy's berth and introduce you," Robin said. "We can detour past where you're moored and collect whatever personal gear you want to take with you. We need to get things moving, and you're going to be busy. It's just been confirmed that Cunard's three biggest cruise liners will all be visiting Liverpool at the same time to mark the anniversary in June, so the navigation channels on the river will have to be kept at optimum depth..."

CHAPTER TWENTY-NINE

Within a fortnight, Alf had found four experienced seamen to supplement the team he'd brought with him from London. They were chosen primarily for their in-depth knowledge of local conditions, and they were assigned two to each vessel, day and night shift. Alfie and Alan worked twelve-about, with Alan—officially—taking the night shift. Before the first week was out, and without fuss, formal arrangement or furious heated argument, Alan had managed to trim his father's hours back to no more than ten a day by adopting the very simple tactic of arriving early for his own shifts and lingering late afterwards.

The funds secured for the new river crossing came onstream, and construction speeds at the new Runcorn Bridge took several leaps forward. Further Euro funds meant that the refurbishment of Cammell Laird docklands and other projects—covered by Mersey Waters, sponsored by Core Holdings—was also progressing swiftly.

Alan arrived over four hours early one evening, at just turned six o'clock.

"Blimey, what's happened?" Alfie demanded. "Is the king dead, or are we at war?"

Alan grinned and held two identical manila envelopes high above his head.

"Registered post, Dad! One for you, the other for me. It's all right, though. I signed for both of 'em. They look like they got the same letter inside, so I thought we should open them together."

Rik Hines drifted into the cramped wheelhouse with a faint smile on his lips, like a cat who'd just polished off a litre of stolen cream. Alf raised one eyebrow suspiciously.

"I thought someone ought to be around to...to witness this moment," Rik murmured. "If I'm right—and I'm pretty certain I am—there's going to be a number of registered letters delivered around Liverpool over the next few days, but to the best of my knowledge, you two are the very first."

Both had by now slit open their envelopes and were reading the contents in silence.

"As I said, I believe it's my privilege to welcome aboard the next two honorary citizens of Greater Merseyside. Congratulations, both of you. From now onwards, you'll enjoy the same rights and benefits as everyone who's lived here all their lives, including the right to vote in elections and pay a much lower rate of income tax than you've been paying until now! Also, *most* of the tax you'll be paying will remain here, where it will be put to far better use than it was when we were obliged to forward it to the Central Exchequer in London."

Alan whistled through his teeth.

"I know we were told our citizen status was going to be fast-tracked, but I never dreamed it could be sorted out in...what? Less than two weeks?"

"You can thank JRK for that." Rik grinned. "He's the one with the powerful allies, political connections and other friends at court! I daren't begin to guess how many people owe him favours at the moment, but I've no doubt he'll be leaning on all of them heavily in the coming months.

"Alf, Alan came out to relieve you early at my request," Rik said, switching in an instant to become the practical businessman. "There are a few things I need to ask you about if you can spare an hour or so before you curl up in your hammock."

***

"Alf reckons they've broken the back of the dredging needed to accommodate the Three Queens visit. Barring totally out-of-season violent storms, he's certain the Mersey now has more-than-adequate draught for any vessel afloat."

"How well d'you know him, Rik? Do you trust his judgement?"

"No worries, John! When Alf speaks on matters nautical, you can be sure he's worked out all the pros and cons beforehand. Anyone who doesn't listen's a fool!"

"Fair enough. You've always shown good judgement in the past. Just let him know he can contact me any time. In the meantime, I need you in the office. We may have a problem elsewhere..."

CHAPTER THIRTY

JRK HAILED RIK across the crowded room and waved him to the last vacant seat around the table.

"Good you got here so fast. Grab a coffee and we can get started.

"There's one person in the room whom most of you haven't met before—I'll let them launch today's meeting. Liam Radcliffe is a spokesman for the Rangers, and this is the *only* subject on today's agenda! Liam, over to you..."

Liam's dress code was casual but neat, practical with a hint of outdoors, rather than boardroom collar-and-tie. He glanced around the table and grinned.

"I just want to say before we start, I think Rik Hines needs his head examining for being back at work barely a week after getting shot! And I'm saying it in public because I reckon this way, he's not going to beat me senseless in front of witnesses for saying it.

"I'm not one for delivering speeches. I'll remain seated, if that's okay? Can everybody hear me? Fine."

He took a deep breath and paused a moment, collecting his thoughts. He didn't refer to any written notes but spoke freely with confidence and authority and began with a swift glance at JRK.

"I'm assuming everyone here at least knows about the existence of the Rangers and hopefully has some idea of what we do? That will save time."

All nodded, some reacting more quickly than others. Liam continued.

"I'm speaking on behalf of the group as a whole, but we're an informal, not very organised group, and I'm not sure of current numbers, but I can tell you there are more of us every day.

"We're not military or even paramil. We're not a hit squad, and we aren't interested in becoming one. We're available—if that's the right word—to do the mop-up jobs that need doing, mostly outdoors because that's our comfort zone—but that doesn't mean we're environmental idealists or tree-hugging geeks.

"We've been beating the bounds since the day Merseyside decided to opt out of control from London and settle our affairs locally. We began by helping out at all the major entry points of Greater Merseyside. The tunnels, the Runcorn Bridge, and the building sites on both sides of the river for the new bridge, plus the East Lancs Road and, of course, Switch Island."

"Define 'helping out'?"

"Mostly directing traffic, Brian—showing drivers where to park and wait for documents to be checked at busy times of day, that sort of thing. Generally, most people have taken it fairly calmly, though I won't deny we've had the odd spat with one or two people who seemed to think they could just breeze through C and E—"

"Customs and excise?" Nuala sounded puzzled.

"Or 'clear and enter', but it comes to the same thing," Liam replied, "And the incident that led to Rik's injury is still the only one I'm aware of that resulted in a trip to the hospital. As it stands, we've no guidelines regarding possible tariffs on goods being imported, but establishing a log to identify non-Merseysiders entering the region was simple enough. We prefer to see a passport or other photo ID, but national insurance cards, driving licences and other forms of ID are all valid.

"The only problem is, there are other access points all round the perimeter of the region, which anyone who—for whatever reason—wants to *avoid* the official checkpoints. Most of them involve crossing open fields or even rivers rather than on any road you'll find on a map.

"Apart from Rik's injury, there was no further comeback on that occasion. The family group were genuine refugees, prepared to accept our principles of making our own decisions, and the Scouse modus vivendi. They also had a range of skills they were prepared to use to make a positive impact, contribution, or whatever you decide to call it. In short, they were just the sort of immigrants we want to welcome to the community."

"How about the shooter?" Paul asked. "Did anyone manage to find him?"

Liam hesitated and glanced at Les, standing in the corner.

Les shrugged. "Soft Lad still won't tell us his name," he grunted. "Probably means he's afraid of someone further up the pecking order. He's only himself to blame, though. He'd climbed up a tree to get a better shot, but my dogs Rocky and Rebel had him trapped before he could get down."

"They're loud, but they'd probably lick him to death," Liam muttered, getting a general grin from the room.

"What makes you think there's some sort of organised...what? Illegal immigration? People trafficking?" Rik asked.

"The A580 heads t'wards Manc-land," Les answered. "Seems they've decided Liverpool's the place to be for a decent future. We've had a steady flow of wannabe travellers every day this past week, and the numbers are steadily growing."

"But that might not always be the case," Liam picked up. "In fact, most of those who try to enter the region by unofficial back doors are almost certainly doing it because they *know* they've something to hide. A criminal record or some other skeleton in the cupboard, who knows? But if we don't take some reasonable precautions to guard against this, we could have some serious problems."

"Employment and housing, for starters," JRK commented with a nod of thanks to the speaker. Liam sat back, grateful for the chance to relax.

"We're as close as makes no difference to full employment at the moment," Dominic commented, "and once we've finished the Mersey Gateway and the customs facilities at Switch Island and on the East Lancs, we'll be looking for more construction work. Housing should be a top priority. We certainly have enough well-qualified builders to tackle the project."

"And let's not forget, there are far too many empty properties around town which need refurbishing," Paul interjected. "Surely, that would be quicker and easier if we need accommodation to be made available ASAP?"

This sparked a spirited discussion that involved everyone in the room. There were no objections or votes against either idea, but it soon became obvious that they needed some expert advice on the costs and relative merits of refurbishment versus newbuild.

"Nuala, see if you can get hold of Billy Lynch, will you? I rang him last night to invite him to this meeting. He said the new bridge is at a crucial stage and felt he had to be there to supervise it..."

***

At first, Billy sounded just a tad reluctant to offer an opinion, particularly over the phone and without comforting columns of solid figures marching across the pages of a company ledger.

"If that's what you need, Billy, you'll have to come down to my office to see them. You push yourself too hard, you know! There must be *someone* on the site you can trust to crack the whip for a couple of hours while you give us the benefit of your wisdom?"

Perhaps it was a coincidence or something as simple as being amplified through a speakerphone, but when Billy replied, his voice sounded different.

"I can be there in... maybe half an hour? But I need to get back this afternoon."

"Deal, Billy! We'll take an early lunch break. I'll make sure they keep a plate for you."

***

"We're well ahead of schedule on the bridge, Mr. K, and if I can find a few more navigators for each shift, we could even improve on that. They don't need to be qualified builders. I can use anyone prepared to carry a hod or use a spade."

JRK looked to his left, but Dominic Ion was a step ahead of the game: he had the South Liverpool Job Centre on speed dial within seconds. He was immediately connected with a live response and excused himself from the table for a short, rapid conversation. When he returned, he had a smug grin on his face.

"It helps to have a direct line. There's a limit to how many times I can listen to the first eight bars of Vivaldi's 'Winter' while I'm on hold waiting for a response. Anyway, my contact says he can maybe rustle up a dozen or so for immediate start, perhaps a similar number by next Monday. Will that do for starters, Billy?"

"I'll take on anyone willing to do the humping and heaving. If they're on site by eight o'clock and can be trusted to follow instructions, they'll be paid."

Dominic lifted his pen.

"Billy, what's the financial situation as far as our expenses are concerned? You must have a considerable wage bill already."

"Thanks for asking, Mr. Treasurer. We're comfortably covered by the Objective One funding we got from Europe and well within budget as far as our supplies and materials are concerned. We can have the bridge completed within two weeks, I think—

three at the outside. We'll be looking for a new project to keep the crew gainfully employed."

"Which brings up back to my main reason for asking you for some input, Billy," JRK cut in. "D'you think we'd be better going for new-build houses on brownfield sites or renovating older vacant properties, mostly dotted around the inner city?"

"I'd have to look at them, the locations, and just how much work needs doing on the individual properties but gut feeling? It *ought* to be much quicker to refurbish houses as long as the foundations are sound. If we want to have accommodation available in short order for families coming to live in the region, that would be my choice."

"Which parts of town are we talking about?" Paul wanted to know.

"Lots of vacants in Anfield, Everton Valley, Toxteth," Steve answered. "Not City Centre, but not far from it. We have to persuade people that these areas can be revitalised, made more attractive places to live and work. We do a lot of conveyancing work, so I know a fair bit about where properties have stood unoccupied for any significant length of time."

Dom leaned forward once more.

"Listen, this might sound crazy, but...what if we could offer some sort of incentive scheme? Like a kibbutz, for example. Instead of renting the houses, which a tenant would never *own*, we could offer to sell a basic empty shell for a nominal sum—it could be as little as a pound, or a fiver, tops—to anyone who's prepared to sign a contract to carry out whatever work needs doing themselves. We can even offer them—within reason—the materials they need at a not-for-profit cost price. They move in immediately, and our wage bills will be considerably less if they're doing the majority of the work themselves."

"*Seem-ples!*" said Paul, making a double-click sound with his tongue. Everyone grinned as they recognised a certain irritating TV advert involving meerkats. At once, the atmosphere lightened. Nobody had noticed the insistent increase in tension during the past few minutes of discussion, but they were all aware of its sudden absence.

JRK glanced at his watch.

"Right, unless anyone has something really life-threateningly urgent under Any Other Business—"

"Can I butt in with a query from a colleague?"

John Midler was an occasional—usually silent—guest at the Friday-afternoon sessions. Since accepting responsibility for the safekeeping of the new Magna Carta and the accurate translation of the hand-lettered text it contained, he had immersed himself in the task with the same love, devotion and zeal as the original scribes. He had insinuated himself into the room unremarked at some point during the discussions, sitting patiently in a corner waiting for a lull in the proceedings.

"Apologies, Professor! We don't see you as often as we'd like to. How's the translation work going?"

"As usual, set two experts to study the same document and they'll come up with at least three different opinions. I've got a team of six—it's like trying to herd cats!"

He shrugged resignedly as spontaneous laughter rippled around the room.

"It's going as well as can be expected. Nobody's actually threatened to cut anyone's throat yet, but we've had a few close run-ins.

"However. I'm here today with a request from another faculty at the university. Barry Newman, Head of Engineering, can't be here himself, but he's given me a whole stack of blueprints and details, and he explained the project to me in simple, non-techie terms. If I can understand it, I'm pretty sure I can give you the basic principles."

"No need to be so modest, John," Rik chided. "We all have our own special fields, but I'm sure you can give us the nitty-gritty."

John Midler passed around the cardboard tubes and manila files he'd brought along. These were unrolled and opened, swiftly covering every table in the room.

The professor stood back for a few moments and allowed the rest of the group to study the blueprints, designs and explanatory notes before moving to the end of the table, waiting for the murmur of comments and questions to subside.

"We have three extremely talented postgrad students who have submitted the designs for a new way to harness energy from natural resources instead of burning our finite fossil fuels.

"They propose raising a tidal barrage across the Mersey. We already know the time and the height of every tide, and they've supplied figures that indicate we could comfortably supply power to the whole of our region. We would also be able to export surplus electricity to other parts of the UK via the National Grid."

"How realistic are these figures, though?" Billy Lynch wanted to know. "They seem pretty impressive, but have they been checked, confirmed by someone totally independent and uninvolved?"

"The Team—as they call themselves—has no financial interest in this. They have nothing to gain, nothing to lose—other than their reputations as engineers looking for the next job of work," John Midler assured him. "You can be certain they're the last people who'd want to blind anyone with science or gild the lily in any way."

"There's something of this nature on the Thames, which has always fallen short of expectations," Alfie commented. "Why should we believe this will be any better?"

"Technology's moved on a couple of generations since then, Dad," Alan reminded him. "The materials we'd be using are stronger, more flexible, more adaptable than anything available when *that* was built. Same goes for the other one on the Severn. Plus, this one's based on Scouse nous, local pride, and the muscle needed to back it up and make it work."

"Cor bloy-mey, Guv'na. The geeza's gorn na'-ive!" Rik Hines declaimed, hamming the scene for all the humour he could possibly bleed out of it. Alfie and Alan were too accustomed to the badgering and banter of the East End and pubs along the banks of the Thames to take offence and laughed twice as hard as everyone else.

"Did your colleague...?"

"Barry. Barry Newman."

"Thanks, John. Did he give you some idea of how much we're generating from the wind farms we've been installing in recent years? I'm sure we've all seen those which have been built along the coast, but I seem to recall reading that there is a significant number out in Liverpool Bay, where nobody can moan about them spoiling the view or interfering with the breeding habits of the Lesser-Spotted Endangered Species Floozum Bird."

"The wind farms were mentioned in despatches, JRK, but only in passing, as it were. Essentially, each installation is capable of generating sufficient energy to pay for the cost of building it and bringing it online within six to eight months of operation—dependent on weather conditions, of course.

"If we continue to roll out this programme as well as building the river barrage, we'll cease to be dependent on the National Grid for our electricity needs that much sooner—possibly five years from now. Best-case scenario, we could be *exporting* power generated from renewable sources to the rest of the UK in about three years' time."

Brian and Dominic were engaged in a silent, no-surrender, head-to-head battle of laptop supremacy at the end of the table. Each hit the 'enter' key for the final time in a dead heat that would have taken an endless number of slow-motion video replays to judge. Their respective monitor screens displayed two completely different sets of data.

"I'd say the figures quoted for the production of clean, free electricity from the barrage alone are realistic. They might even be just a touch on the cautious side," Brian said with what was, for him, a rare show of excitement.

It was like Centre Court at Wimbledon on Finals Day: every eye in the room immediately switched to Dominic.

"I can't promise anything, guys. Not without knowing what's going to happen to the UK's inflation figures over the next few years or whether Iraq intends to irradiate the whole of the Middle East just for the hell of it or Uncle Sam decides to nuke the bejaysus out of what was once Syria...

"But my best guesstimate suggests that the profit-and-loss columns, based on stock-market mean figures and averaged out over the last three months look pretty reliable. I can factor in a certain amount of leeway, feed in two to three percentage points either way, but the figures are still comfortably within the parameters I'd expect. That's as much as I can say right now."

"Sounds good to me, Dom! Any further questions? No? Good! We've set our next target. Let's make sure we can see it through! Nuala, have you got everything you need to write up your usual detailed minutes? Thanks to one and all. Let's get this job done!"

CHAPTER THIRTY-ONE

IN THE IMMORTAL words of the song, the smile was definitely returning to the faces of everyone living on Merseyside in the next few months as the big bad bogeyman, the spectre of unemployment, was banished from the realm.

"Seems to me the only people who've lost out on things are the tossers who sat so smug behind their desks at the Job Centre all those years. I never knew anyone 'oo gorra proper long-term job from them, not ever."

It was Friday night, and Billy Lynch held court at a town centre pub with his regular crew.

"Mmm, I knew one or two who pulled their finger out once or twice, but by an' large, you're right, Billy!" Norm said. "I heard some o' the smarter ones saw what was comin' an' put in their notice before it all went pear-shaped. One of 'em lives near me—he gorra transfer to the bins, last I 'eard."

"Sounds like he found his real 'job for life' if that's true," Billy opined. He was adept at keeping a straight face, and sometimes it was impossible to decide if he was serious or telling a joke. He glanced around the bar, spotted a vacant table and indicated with a tacit nod that he wanted a word with his team. With a signal to the bar for a fresh round of drinks, he led the way to the relatively quiet corner and waited for the order to be delivered.

"Okay, lads, I've got something in mind—something I've been thinkin' about for a while. In fact, something you might want to be thinkin' about yourselves."

He took a pull at his fresh pint and paused while his friends automatically followed suit.

"Yiz musta noticed, same as me, y'r cash is goin' further than it useter. 'S a fact, innit?" He barely waited for the inevitable nods of agreement and carried on.

"Constant full-time work's a great thing t' have, an' I'm lovin' it after all the tough times we've 'ad in the 'Pool—and so's my bank manager," he added, getting a general laugh.

"So I'm thinking, why not go for this homes-for-a-quid scheme? Because if ever I knew a bunch o' guys I'd pick and trust to help me rebuild and refurb a house, it'd be youse four. An' if it all goes well—why wouldn't it?—we could do it all over again until we've all got bran'-new 'ouses we've built *exakly* to our own specs at a fraction o' the market price."

"Hang on, though, Billy! If we're all workin' full-time on refurbing a property, what do we live on? I've got kids, a family."

"Fair question, Yozzer. I haven't looked into the details yet. I wanted to float the idea wit' youse first. But there must be a way we can include some sorta living wage for ourselves in the overall costs of doin' all the work ourselves. Otherwise, there's no point in settin' up the scheme in the first place."

"And from what the TV an' the papers are sayin', there's loads o' people applyin' to get onto the scheme. Gut feeling. I say go for it, Billy, and I'll be the first t' join in."

Andy had been with Billy since their days in primary school. He stuck out a meaty paw, within which Billy's outstretched hand all but disappeared.

Peter, the sparks of the team and generally the quietest, beat Yozzer by a microsecond to add his hand to the five-way shake of agreement.

"We need to book some time with whoever's organising the finances," was his practical contribution to the group discussion, which was quickly agreed as they settled down to discuss a far more important subject: the success or failure of the Reds and the Blues in the weekend's football fixtures.

***

"You can relax, Billy! I'm a businessman, first and foremost. Always have been! I'm offering you exactly the same deal I'd offer anyone else wanting to take up a refurb house. The fact that I *know* from personal experience you're a hard worker who gets results is simply the icing on the cake."

Once he'd seen Billy Lynch's name in the appointments diary, Rik Hines had insisted on conducting the interview himself.

"I've had Dominic run the ruler over the figures you submitted and tweak them into shape, but the difference between your proposed figures and his is largely cosmetic. I like the idea of you all working together on five properties. That way, I can have you all back together working on other projects much more quickly! You've already proved yourselves one of the best navigator teams I've known, and I *need* you to make yourselves available ASAP. Allowing yourselves—what did you call it?—yes, a *living wage* for the duration is a sensible way of ensuring your families don't suffer financially while you're building them new homes."

"And we reckon we can be finished with all five properties in five to six months if we can just get our heads and go for it—maybe less, depending on the state of the buildings we're working on," Billy said confidently.

"I haven't asked any of yiz if y' fancy bein' neighbours," Yozzer interjected, "but if we were to choose properties in the same area—not necessarily the same street, but close by, we might be able to refurb more than one property at a time. That could also be a cost-saver!"

"It's certainly worth looking at," Billy agreed. "Come on, Rik. Show us something we can get our teeth into! Me, I wouldn't mind Dingle or Toxteth, maybe with a nice view o' the river, but

Anfield or Walton an' a short walk to either o' th' footie grounds wouldn't be bad, neither! It'd be a good deal for Jomfru Money as well as rewarding a hard-working group of friends who, by the way, have already made a significant impact on a lot of the construction work that's been completed."

***

"I've done it strictly by the book, Dom," Rik justified. "I'd have liked to show them my appreciation by cutting them some slack, perhaps shave a few percentage points of interest charges, but they're smart enough to know what the going rate for the job's likely to be, and I wouldn't want to risk offending them, offering them charity or some sort of special deal. One thing I learned quickly about Scousers is they've got their pride and don't take kindly to being patronised in any way."

"True, so true," Dom commented. "And looking at the number of applications to join the Housing Project we've had already, it reminds me of what my da used to call the 'Woolworths principle'—stack 'em high and sell 'em cheap! All these people have got money—*real* money—some of them for the first time in their lives, and the bank lending them the cash they need to invest in their own futures isn't in any real danger of losing out on the deal."

"Dom, I think that's the first time I've heard it called a 'principle' of any sort, but it's exactly what I was taught by my old man when I started up as a barrow boy in the East End! Give 'em what they want, they'll come back for more—always."

***

Both the Scouse da and the Cockney old man were proved to be right in the weeks and months which followed. The initial applications list grew and was close to being over-subscribed several times before the balance of available properties and the extended groups of families and friends wanting to take possession of Housing Project stock settled to a comfortable balance, and further areas of the city with houses in need of a careful makeover were added to the Project directory.

Slowly at first, then with increasing speed and confidence, Liverpool was regaining her place as the UK's Second City. This title had been lost about the same time as the dissolution of the Commonwealth and the disappearance of most of the 'pink bits' on school atlases. Fuelled by Rik's slash-and-burn street-trader attitude to cut-price barter and wheeler-dealing, the self-proclaimed Independent Republic of Greater Merseyside was soon able to offer considerably lower tariffs and charges for import and export of a vast array of goods and materials, ruthlessly undercutting the exorbitant rates levied by the monopolistic cartels operating out of ports in London, Southampton and elsewhere in the country.

There were even grumbles and hints of the old familiar lies about Liverpool basing its former trading glory on the profits made by the atrocities of the transatlantic slave trade. The unstated but heavily insinuated implication was that the city was prepared to go to any lengths and ignore all moral codes to make a fast buck.

Alfie Evans hadn't been idle in his appointed task of clearing the shipping channels and keeping them navigable for the largest container vessels to berth and unload bigger and more profitable cargoes from every point of the compass. The former lucrative trade in sugar cane from the Caribbean was re-established, bringing the spinoff of more employment in the related processing at the refinery and a number of jamming and conservation plants around the city, which had been in the doldrums for at least a full generation. Car parts and components flowed freely to and from China and other non-European venues, feeding two major manufacturers, one on each bank of the river.

The order books were once again full to capacity at Cammell Laird shipbuilders. There were also advanced plans to rebuild the dockland areas flattened by the Blitz of 1941, including a new state-of-the-art football stadium to replace a ground which had been around since the earliest days of organised football. Almost overnight, the north docks became an attractive homebase for smaller fishing vessels.

Alfie and his son Alan had—with some regret for all concerned—moved out of their billets on Tugboat Kathy's barge and settled in a Housing Project cottage nestling close to the riverbank. Neither had any real skills or experience of landlubber construction processes but contributed to the building with brawn and enthusiasm, willingly assisted by navigators—of the earthbound variety—guided in their direction by Rik, Paul and other members of the RR team. Somehow, they still managed to work the full twelve-hour about-shifts they'd established since their arrival but had taken on more hired help to ease the burden.

"The visit of the Three Queens couldn't have come at a better time," Paul stated with evident satisfaction at a Friday-afternoon *Fyraften* meeting late in July. "It really put us in the spotlight, and the port's never been busier, at least not in my lifetime! Everyone I speak to is reporting full order books and jobs a-plenty, which they're struggling to fill."

"All the same, we *do* have one problem we need to take a serious look at, and in a way, it's related to the economic success of the region," Dom cautioned.

JRK, acting as the nearest thing to a formal chairman of the meeting, nodded for the treasurer to continue.

"Everyone at this table knows about our Rangers, even if a fair number of them seem to prefer to be known by either their first name or a nickname. Almost all of them are volunteers and don't appear on any payroll, but one or two of the head honchos are a bit more forthcoming with their personal details and are actually paid a modest...let's call it a retainer and not trouble the taxman with our petty-cash records, okay?

"Les Harrison's the most active organiser amongst them and one of the few who gets a regular wage, though it's guaranteed far less than he's been worth to us over the past six months or more! Les, the floor's yours. You can explain this far better than I can."

Les took a thoughtful sip at his glass and leaned back in his chair.

"I don't need to explain for any of you the how or the why of the Rangers' role in and around Merseyside," he began, "and many of them probably wouldn't be too keen on being identified or thanked for their...contribution to society."

"As we all know, the entry and exit points on the main routes were easily dealt with—the bridges, the tunnels, and the motorways have all been redeveloped as customs and visa control centres, and the distribution of SmarTag discs to every resident and local business has been a great success."

"That's true, Les. I could almost believe I've seen smug, self-satisfied grins on the faces of people using the SmarTag fast lanes during the morning and evening commutes while non-residents have to have their documents checked, then pay to get through the tollbooths," JRK commented. "That was definitely one of Paul's best PR stunts. The revenue it generates is almost a side issue."

Les continued, "The problem we're seeing isn't on the roads or the river. Every night, there are incidents on open fields and woodlands, even on some of our beaches along the shore, where Rangers are discovering individuals and small groups of friends and family trying to enter the region without going through the immigration channels at passport control. I've got some figures here—" he flourished a small notebook "—which are almost certainly out of date, but they'll give you the general picture of how many times a group of Rangers have come across illegal immigrants trying to enter the region over the past few weeks."

"Can you give us an idea of how many Rangers you can call on, or an area that's particularly difficult to patrol—I assume a lot of this happens at night?"

"No names, no pack drill, Paul! But I can get a team together with a single phone call, and each team leader rings round his contacts. It's important for a lot of them to keep out of the limelight, and so far, it seems to be working. Any piece of open land off the main highways is likely to need a watchful eye.

"Our main problem is it's not easy to get to and from such places without transport, and foot patrols means boots on the ground—obviously—so the most urgent need is actual numbers, people prepared to work unsocial hours at short notice."

"Sounds a bit like our former Fearless Leader and his zero-hour contracts if you ask me!" JRK grunted, provoking a ripple of gallows humour from the group.

"Nuala, don't make this an official minute to the meeting, but we need to make it a top priority to pass the word, get as many volunteers as we can to make themselves known—is it okay to give your mobile as a contact number? Thanks! Keep us posted, Les, and let us know if you need more bods."

CHAPTER THIRTY-TWO

"WE GOT INCOMING."

"Roger that. Location?"

Unlike earlier generations of ex-army stock, the wireless R/T handsets used by the Rangers were a convenient size, had excellent reception and never betrayed the user's location with embarrassing bleeps and squawks at inopportune moments.

"Small craft approaching from the north. Hugging the coastline, so too close to be a commercial fishing boat. No lights, so not wanting to be seen. Over."

"Confirmed. Got him in sight now. Can you deploy your team on the beach? Will you need backup?"

"We can watch from behind the dunes, cover the northern sweep of the bay. If you can get a second team in place somewhere between Crossens and Southport central beach, it'd be useful, but we can cover that too."

"Understood, Team Eight. Remember, you're the official welcome committee for these people, so don't wade in mob-handed. We want to give a good impression, and we can always use people with genuine skills to offer."

"Copy that, Control. Will keep you informed. Out."

A tacit hand signal galvanised the remainder of the four-man patrol. They drifted from one shadow to the next between the sandhills and dunes, all but invisible as they moved as a unit north to a point which would leave them close to a point on the beach where the local tide and currents beached most of the small craft attempting to enter Greater Merseyside by sea.

"I can assure you, sir, we're not Customs and Excise or Passport Control! Nor are we interested in whatever you did or might have done *before* you decided to travel here. Everyone entering Merseyside starts with a clean sheet, so to speak, but we need to know a few basic details. Name, age, qualifications, the sort of things you'd tell someone at a job interview. That way, we can offer you any help you might need to get settled, make a fresh start…"

***

The crew of the vessel turned out to be four adults and two teenage sons, all related, traditional fishermen from Blackpool who had packed what they could fit into a variety of battered suitcases and backpacks and slipped their moorings forty miles or so from the nascent Promised Land of their southern neighbours.

"We weren't sure o' t' prospects o' fishin', but we reckoned us could do summat round't docks in Liverpool…" The 'v' sound almost disappeared in the slow, unhurried Lancashire burr of the old salt who was clearly speaking on behalf of the whole family.

"An' t' lads are well up in them new IT 'puters an' like. They've had a good schooling! Reckon we've a good bit t' offer, an' there's none of uz minds gettin' our 'ands dirty."

Despite the lengthening days, this was the coolest part of the short summer night, but the Morgan family declined the offer of a hotel room for the night.

"Too much trouble to shift all us suitcases an' such! We're berthed at t' quayside—easier to settle that sort o' thing in t' morning when we've all had a good night's sleep—or what's left o' t' night, anyway."

***

Les Harrison thumbed through his notepad.

"It was a typical Monday night, John," he said as he skimmed the details. "All told, reports from patrols operating either side of the East Lancs—mostly on the northern side, where there's more opportunities over open land away from the road network—and two incidents involving groups trying to swim the river upstream of the Runcorn crossing."

"Really? I'd have to be pretty desperate to even *think* about coming in that way! How many people were in the groups? Surely, they must realise they're putting their lives in danger."

"One group was a family of three. Father said they built a raft, but it sank just before they got across. They were all wearing life jackets, but their possessions were swept away, including all their ID papers, passports and such. They're being treated at Runcorn General—it was the nearest hospital. With no papers or possessions, there wasn't much else could be done at that time of night."

"What about the others?"

"Better organised. Six adults, athletic types. They said they'd been planning this for some time, even training for the swim. They had what they'd decided were the absolute minimum possessions they needed inside waterproof containers, which also doubled as float aids. I didn't get to interview them myself, but I'm told they're all well-qualified, at least degree level, and they cooperated in every way. They sound as if they're the sort of people we want to encourage, willing to contribute their talents and skills."

"Right, Les, I want this family given top priority. They were prepared to leave behind literally everything to join us, and they've lost the lot. The least we can do is provide them with whatever we can to help them make a start."

"And the ID problem?"

"I know there's a chance they could be spinning a yarn but put yourself in their position! They've got literally nothing. We *have* to give them something to help them get back on their feet.

"And it won't harm our PR rep to be *seen* to be offering a helping hand, either!" Paul Freeman had entered the conference room and caught most of the conversation.

"Fair enough, but that wasn't my reason for making the offer," JRK insisted. "We should always be ready to lend a hand if someone needs it. You never know when it might be your turn to ask for a bit of a leg-up."

***

By October, Les Harrison was able to report to the Synod that attempts at illegal entry to the region had been significantly reduced.

"It seems we've got the message across," JRK said. "People are going through the official channels, applying for visas and so on."

"And, more importantly," Paul took over, "most of them are actively *looking* for a job or have been told about job prospects by someone they know. Quite a lot of the families who tipped them off are even prepared to vouch for their friends, act like sponsors, help them find somewhere to live and other practical matters."

"Has anyone any idea of the region's current headcount—even a rough figure?" Dom asked. "And how's the supply of housing? Are there still properties available, or are we reaching a saturation point?"

Billy Lynch was first to respond.

"Don't know about the population figures, other than they're definitely up! But we've built on a lot of the brownfield sites on the outskirts of City Centre, which have been lying unused for decades. We're not going to find ourselves short of room to build more affordable social housing or do-it-yourself projects in the immediate future."

"All the same, an official census of some sort would be a good idea," Rik said. "For one thing, we should put together an up-to-date electoral roll in good time so we can organise a formal election by next July. If we're serious about being a democratic regional authority, we owe it to those we represent to let them have their say as soon as possible, and it's already been over twelve months since we told London we were doing our own thing."

"I haven't heard any grumbles or murmurs of discontent yet," Paul said, "but you're right, Rik. We have to organise an official election as soon as possible. At least we can reassure everyone their opinion matters, make sure they *know* they're valued in the community and that their vote *will* make a difference."

"Best make a start, then," JRK said. "Nuala, I want you and Paul to concoct one of your best press release docs and get it over to the *Echo,* both radio stations *and* the local TV studios over in Toxteth. This should get to all of them at the same time, or as close as possible. Les, any chance you can draft in some of your Rangers to help the full-time post deliverers with mailshots? And we'll need to print a run of voting slips as well as some guidelines regarding what format the vote will take."

"We can prepare a template, John, but we can't finalise it until we know the names of all the candidates."

Brian didn't often join in general chat, but when he did, it was always worth listening. For the moment, he appeared to be totally engrossed in evaluating and rejecting a succession of blank forms, any of which could be customised with the names of up to ten or twelve candidates.

"These two are probably the easiest to work with," he said. "One has space for six names and up to two lines of policy statement, so each candidate can leave a personal message beneath his or her name.

"The other can accommodate ten names, but there will be less room for policy statements—and a voting paper with more than ten names on it would be confusing and counterproductive."

"Sounds good, Brian," JRK approved. "We can get John Midler to organise a print run at the uni. They're used to high volumes of identical papers from all the years they've been setting exam papers. Plus, it leaves the *Echo* presses free and available for any urgent news or other developments."

The room emptied rapidly as the *Fyraften* group dispersed to chase up their own appointed tasks.

CHAPTER THIRTY-THREE

"I THINK THE STATS speak for themselves."

JRK leaned back from the table, stretching the cramped muscles in his back as he pushed an untidy pile of papers to one side.

"It would have been a difficult election to lose considering there was only one candidate to vote for in the majority of wards," Paul pointed out.

"Yes, and let's not forget," Nuala added, "that in the other wards, it was generally a question of which candidate the voters decided would be the better choice since they were both campaigning for the same thing. Proper devolution of power along the lines which the Radical Regionalist Party has always followed."

"Yes, I know, but that's not my point," JRK said. "Two things impressed me in the stats. One, we managed to print off and distribute slips for every voting station, and none of them ran out before the polls closed. Two—and more importantly—we had a turnout of almost ninety-three per cent, with coppers short of four hundred thousand people eligible to vote! Ninety-three per cent! Even the Jocks didn't get anywhere near that when they had their say on Scottish independence."

"And they didn't get a ninety per cent 'yes' vote on that question, either," Paul reminded him. "They obviously don't have someone with your charisma to lead 'em! Excuse me one moment." Pulling his phone from his pocket, Paul left the meeting.

"Brian, can you confirm the figures are accurate?" JRK asked the quiet, self-effacing IT guru. His fingers blurred as they danced over his keyboard, and without hesitation, he nodded a couple of heartbeats later.

"Nice to know," JRK breathed. "And while we're at it, Brian, I want to thank you for keeping the whole structure of the campaign together—especially the voting slips you created. They were really simple to use. Well done!

"Billy, I'll bring you in here. We must have passed the half-million figure as far as total population goes. How's the housing situation? Are we coping with demand?"

Billy Lynch looked like a cat with a belly full of double cream.

"We've managed to repair and refurbish almost all the derelicts that have been pimples on the city's ars…sorry, landscape," he corrected himself.

"The original navigator teams that put together Tramlink and Mersey Gateway say Toxteth is unrecognisable. It's become a 'des res' part of town once more. Liverpool and Everton FCs both have room to flex their muscles in their respective new grounds. There are still several brownfield sites we can convert to residential use, as long as they aren't on contaminated land, so we're ahead of the game as far as housing provision's concerned."

"It's also keeping our employment figures considerably better than anywhere else in the country," Brian chipped in, "which in turn is persuading more people to enquire about coming to live and work in Liverpool."

"Don't forget, the river has *two* banks," Rik added. "Liverpool2 is making Birkenhead and Wallasey just as big a draw as Liverpool. Cammell Laird have full order books and a waiting list for apprenticeships—traditional ones, not those cockamamie shams the Whitehall shower have been boasting about! There's still cash flowing *to* the region from EU sources, but we're no longer classified as an Objective One charity case. This is genuine inward investment from someone who shares our belief in ourselves."

"Fine, as long as they don't come expecting a divvy on our profits as soon as we're up and running as a profitable concern," Dominic growled, taking a few people by surprise. The group's number-cruncher generally kept his opinions to himself, rarely displaying any emotions.

Nuala laid a comforting hand on her brother's wrist.

"Cheer us all up, Dom! How's our general finances at the moment?" She knew from lifelong experience how to smooth her younger brother's ruffled feathers.

He was instantly transformed, exactly as Nuala had anticipated. He assumed a more formal position in his chair, seeming to gain several significant inches: a puffed-up Toad of Toad Hall without the character's overweening sense of self-importance.

"It's true what they say, and I've said it myself many times. Money makes money," he declared with a self-satisfied smile.

"Essentially, the proceeds from our assets auction last year gave us good, solid foundation capital. Then, when Rik set up Jomfru Money, based in Liverpool, we suddenly had a credit rating that attracted some serious investors. Obviously, we had to dip into the pot a few times to get some things going, but since then, the inward investment from Europe has more than compensated for that. In round figures, our end-of-year accounts are going to show a net profit—we'll have more money in the kitty than we started with."

Paul slid back to his usual seat between JRK and Nuala.

"I just had a very interesting phone call," he said. "No less a personage than the UK's current Fearless Leader congratulates Liverpool on the—and I quote—'commendable and impressive voting figures'—end quote—in what he refers to as our recent *local election*."

"Cheeky bugger!" Rik snorted. "He only got himself elected last time because nearly half the country couldn't be bothered turning out."

"Hang on, Rik. I said it was an interesting call, but that's not the juicy bit. That's just political BS from someone who's been in the game for years! No, listen to this!"

He docked his mobile into a laptop and turned on the speakers. The easily identified cut-glass Eton and Oxbridge voice of the prime minister of the (dis)United Kingdom—now comprising England, Wales and Northern Ireland—filled the room.

"There's a matter I'd like you to place before Mr. Kirwan, something which I imagine will have to be put before your... cabinet."

The fractional hesitation before the last word of the sentence didn't go unnoticed.

"Synod! He *knows* that," Brian muttered.

The recorded phone conversation continued.

"As you're no doubt aware, the buildings used to house the Mother of all Parliaments date from the early 1800s and had to have major structural repairs after being a frequent target of the Luftwaffe *during World War Two.*

"Further repairs are now needed, and architects estimate they could take a minimum of six months to complete, costing over a billion pounds."

Paul's voice cut in.

"Prime Minister, I sincerely hope you're not going to ask for a sub! With respect, your track record regarding funding for any regions of the country other than the Home Counties is, frankly—"

"Mr. Freeman, hear me out! I assure you, I'm not *going to ask for financial assistance! There is funding set aside for such maintenance work, and it won't even become a direct cost to the taxpayer.*

"However, the estimate of one billion pounds is a 'low end of the spectrum' figure, contingent on a number of factors, and this is why I chose to contact Liverpool.

"The architects have advised me that the work can be completed swiftly and at the price quoted if *both Houses can sit elsewhere for the duration.*

"I'm sure you know your history, Mr. Freeman. The War Cabinet met in Liverpool, so there's a precedent established. If we don't find a suitable alternative location, this essential repair work will take far longer and could easily cost up to £8 billion."

"I'll relay your request to JRK and the Synod immediately, Prime Minister, and contact you as soon as possible. Hopefully, we can find a solution that will be acceptable to all concerned."

The recording ended with a soft click, which nonetheless seemed to echo forever around a room stunned into silence. Collective breaths were drawn, and for a moment, there was pandemonium as everyone tried simultaneously to express their instinctive reactions.

JRK eventually managed to restore some sort of order, mostly by shouting loudest while bludgeoning the table with his coffee mug.

"Let's say the message from Mr. Fearless Leader has been relayed, as promised, and heard by at least the main players on the Synod. We can't make an official decision without a full Synod meeting, of course, but I'm open to whatever anyone has to say right here and now."

Rik was first to his feet.

"The man's an idiot. He'd not last a day as an East End barra boy! He's only gone and given us not just the rock-bottom minimum price they've been quoted for the job, but also the max figure it *could* cost if it all goes to hell in a handcart!

"Westminster's been screwing this city for decades. I'm a Londoner, and even I'll admit that! Now's the time to turn the tables, get your own back. Tell 'em you're prepared to lend a hand—and tell 'em it's going to cost another billion to rent St. George's Hall for the duration. Point out they'd still be saving five or six billion compared with the cost of rebuilding both Houses around them.

"They can also get used to the idea of using their allowances to feed and water themselves. That's what the allowances were supposed to be used for, anyway! And you should also point out that being so close to the train station means they can reach their constituencies and make themselves available for the voters who elected them quickly and easily every weekend! Have I missed anything?"

The question was rhetorical: Rik Hines hadn't missed a trick since he left school and bought his first barrowload of tat to sell at a considerable profit.

General discussion ebbed and flowed, encouraged by a variety of cold drinks, mostly alcoholic.

"We can do this," Dominic enthused. "It would be such sweet justice after the way they've shafted us at every turn since I don't know when."

"Try since 1941 and the damage done to the docks during the Blitz," JRK suggested. He was only half-joking: even those born long after the war ended were only too aware of the desolate, abandoned and unkempt remnants of Liverpool's docklands, once the city's main source of profitable business.

"I say we call their bluff," Brian cut in. "One billion's a nice round figure. I say double it. Ask for two. Then we can allow ourselves some wiggle room and graciously agree to accept, say, one-and-three-quarters. We could even offer them a special deal with a favourable currency exchange rate—just this once."

"St. George's Hall, though." Nuala seemed worried. "It's always been a popular tourist attraction. Don't you think it would affect our tourist trade?"

"The Houses of Parliament are just as big a crowd-puller in London," Paul reassured her. "People pay good, hard cash to gape at the monkeys in Chester Zoo. What makes you think it would be any different ogling MPs in St. George's Hall?"

Paul's acerbic comment was as vivid as it was unexpected. Everyone laughed.

Nuala nodded and scribbled in her diary.

"I'll prepare some minutes and let you have a formal agenda you can present at a full Synod moot as soon as possible—hopefully tomorrow..."

***

It proved impractical to convene a moot of the full Synod so swiftly, but the following day, twelve delegates from each of the Six Boroughs arrived at St. George's Hall. Some of the delegates from the Borough of Halton were attending their first Synod: Halton had only recently been invited to become a part of Greater Merseyside.

JRK insisted that all seventy-two delegates gather in one of the side chambers in the town hall specifically reserved for private and confidential debates. Although they disliked this embargo, the news media had always accepted that some things were too sensitive to allow full public access.

"I'm not here to threaten with a big stick, but there's just one thing I want to make clear," he said as soon as a full head count had been made and the door secured.

"Today, we're in full view of the media, and not just th e local TV, radio and press, who are no threat. They're all without exception on our side.

"All the major national dailies, plus the BBC, ITV and a sprinkling of European and other international agencies are through that door in the council chamber. We're *not* going to look like the Yahoo Henrys we've all seen acting like juvey delinquents during PM's Questions, shouting abuse and tossing paper cups at each other! We're better than that, and I expect you to observe some basic manners and courtesy throughout.

"Yes, we'll debate everything on the agenda, and I'm not asking you to nod and vote 'yes' blindly on every point raised, especially if you feel strongly about something. It's vital we demonstrate that we take ourselves seriously, but we need to demonstrate that we can conduct open, honest, no-holds-barred debate without acting like little children. Most importantly, we need to show anyone who cares to listen that we are responsible adults, more than capable of administering our own affairs. Agreed? Good! Let's show 'em we mean business!"

***

"We're only just getting started, but we appreciate you have deadlines to meet if you're going to report back on our first full Synod in time for the main evening news slot."

JRK managed to sound understanding and sympathetic to the slightly frantic requests from the assembled media teams for a pause in the debate to allow them to condense the salient points into short soundbites for radio and TV coverage.

Six hours of lively, fast-moving and, at times, emotional debate had flown by while the Synod members had remained cheerful, polite and eager to contribute without once coming close to displaying the schoolboy antics JRK had specifically warned them about. The lead story on the national *BBC News at Six* was reflected in every other radio and TV channel's treatment of the story and in every newspaper that was not heavily influenced by extreme left- or right-wing political camps.

"The first full meeting of the Greater Merseyside Regional Council took place today," an anonymous off-screen reporter announced.

"The main topic under discussion was a proposal to offer the National Government the opportunity to take up a 'short-term

tenancy' in Liverpool while urgent and essential rebuilding work takes place in both Houses of Parliament."

The outdoor-broadcast shot of St. George's Hall dissolved and was replaced with a head-and-shoulders shot of Paul Freeman being interviewed in a studio.

"This isn't the first time Liverpool has provided temporary accommodation for the National Government," he told the interviewer. *"The Wartime Cabinet met in a bunker beneath one of our railway stations, and we were proud at the time to do our patriotic duty.*

"But this time, it's going to be different. Since 1945, the only thanks Liverpool has had from London has been a series of more and more intensive, even spiteful, measures designed to prevent growth, development and economic success in Liverpool and the North West in general.

"That is why we're looking at the present situation from a commercial point of view. The minimum costs for refurbishing Westminster are already public knowledge, and we're prepared to offer them the opportunity to keep their costs to a minimum. But we have to be realistic. It's only reasonable to expect some form of remuneration for the inconvenience, and we consider the rent we've set to be little more than a drop in the ocean, set against the economic investment Liverpool has been denied time and again over the past eight decades."

"How much are you asking?"

"That's a private matter under the Data Protection Act and the laws governing landlord and tenant. You really ought to know better than to ask," Paul warned the BBC interviewer. *"Now, unless someone has a question which* isn't *in equally bad taste... ?"*

The final exchange was scrupulously edited away from later news broadcasts, but the overall effect, ending with Paul's reference to the depredations Liverpool had suffered at the hands of every government since the end of WWII, was equally powerful. It came as no surprise that there were one or two muttered comments about 'whingeing Scousers' from 'Disgusted in Romford' and the Usual Suspects, almost all of them hiding behind a London postcode, but by and large, the reaction of the rest of the country was positive: a significant increase in the number of written immigration enquiries received in the next fortnight was all the evidence needed.

***

"Prime Minister, the terms and conditions of the tenancy agreement between Greater Merseyside and your government is identical in every respect with any other short-term contract between a landlord and a prospective tenant." Paul was negotiating the finer points via his iPad. "A deposit is *always* required—in most cases, a minimum of three months' rent. And you must admit, when we consider the manner in which this city has been starved of vital funding and regional development opportunities over the years, your credit rating in Liverpool is... not very good at all.

"Yes, I appreciate that £250 million *is* an exceptionally high figure, but that's the twenty-five per cent deposit on a £1 billion rental agreement. Any Year Five child in a Liverpool primary school can do the maths—and let's not forget, that's the *minimum* estimated cost of the repairs you need to set your own house in order. As you've already stated, attempting to soldier on in a building which is falling down around your ears while contractors work around you is out of the question. Apart from the inconvenience and the time it would take, the cost would be prohibitive."

"I can only say, sir, if you'd visited Liverpool more frequently, especially in the last few years, you wouldn't *have* to ask me about our excellent road, sea and air links. The rail link is immediately opposite St. George's Hall. You won't even have the cost of a cab fare to factor into your day-to-day expenses. I concede that the West Coast train service could be improved, but once again, we haven't had any incentives or financial backing to develop a rail connection which might be considered fit for service."

"Yes, I agree, it would be in Merseyside's best interest as well as yours if some significant investment in developing the West Coast service were to be made...and the person best suited to make it happen for you is sitting at my side and has heard everything we've been discussing. I'm sure he needs no introduction, but allow me to bring Liverpool's financial driving force, Mr. Rik Hines, into this conversation..."

Paul passed over his tablet: Rik was more than ready to continue the one-sided Skype discussion with a visibly punch-drunk PM, who seemed on the verge of agreeing to sign just about anything placed before him.

"Just a few details, sir. I'm sure we can provide all the skilled and experienced navigators that a rail upgrade along the West Coast will need—within our own boundaries, that is. But I'm sure they can be persuaded to lend their muscle and skills to the project as it spreads southwards." He added, "At a fair price, of course."

CHAPTER THIRTY-FOUR

"THERE'S NO QUESTION about it, JRK! Money really *does* attract more money. It's almost like some sort of financial magnetism."

Dominic scrolled rapidly through several screens on an array of laptops that showed the investments being made in Liverpool by major multinational firms. Every line contained an impressive number of zeroes, and the figures were constantly updating.

"For the record, I can tell you that the seed money we received from the river auction has been more than recouped..."

"Seriously, Dom?" Paul said. "That's amazing! That was barely twelve months ago."

"Actually, it's just short of fourteen months," Dom corrected him, "but that's not the point! What I'm saying is, this level of inward investment was inspired by the way we set out our stall from the outset, and it's attracted the attention of major firms throughout Europe. This year, we could well be one of the biggest foreign capital earners in the UK, and when you set that against the region's population figures, it's going to be a pretty healthy per capita return."

"Speaking of which," Brian interjected, "we might have to start vetting immigration applications before long. Our house-building programme is keeping up with demand, and we're as close to full employment as makes no difference. Applications to move into Merseyside are starting to level out, but we might have to consider some sort of waiting list before we run out of suitable housing development sites."

"Do we have a fairly accurate population census figure?" JRK asked.

"We passed one-and-a-half million last week," Paul said, "and we're processing applications as fast as we can. Most families have sponsors and confirmed jobs arranged, but there's a limit to how much land we can build on."

"And all my Rangers tell me the number of people trying to sneak in illegally has fallen to almost nothing," Les added. "The message seems to be getting through. It really is far easier to use the official channels. As long as the applicant has a definite job offer waiting for them, we've no reason to refuse entry."

"The navigators will be coming home soon. That will make a big difference to the Housing Project completion rate."

"How far south did they get, Billy? Last I heard, they were somewhere around Stafford?"

"We've smartened up the M6 as far as Stoke." Billy shrugged as if this was something of little or no consequence. "Then we decided we'd lend a hand on the West Coast rail link. I found a couple o' guys who showed a bit o' promise. I left them in charge of the M-way Project to make sure the handover to the Midlands gangers goes as smoothly as possible.

"The rail link is a different ball game altogether, of course! In a way, it was good we had the experience of building the Tramlink from JLA to City Centre. It was like a scaled-down version of a similar, much bigger job.

"As long as the rolling stock's available on time, we'll have the track for it to run on—both passenger and freight. But there's just one thing..."

The room went deathly quiet when Billy paused. He seemed unsure of something, which was almost unheard of.

"The track's going to be in constant use, twenty-four seven, yes? So there's going to be a lot of constant stresses and strains on the rails and on the land beneath the tracks.

"I don't have the maths in my head, but I'm pretty sure we're going to need a *lot* more ballast to make sure the line's secure and well bedded down! Especially if we're hoping to provide a variety of passenger and goods services all day, all night, we can't afford any 'rain stopped play' nonsense or the 'wrong sort of leaves' closing down huge sections of the rail network twice monthly."

Brian's fingers were blurring over his keyboard before Billy had finished speaking: the team's other number-cruncher, Iain, stood hunched over the PC wizard's shoulders, following each line of data as it appeared on the screen and offering an occasional comment or suggestion.

"If there isn't an app for that yet, I'll invent one," Brian muttered as he paused for a moment, reviewing the screen data before hitting 'enter'.

"That's as close as I've ever heard you come to cracking a joke," Paul said. "Brian, are you sure you're feeling okay?"

"Who said I was joking?" Brian retorted but had the grace to grin as he spoke. The monitor screen cleared briefly, then immediately repopulated with seemingly endless rows and columns of data, which meant nothing to anybody other than the two resident PC 'genii'.

"We need to break this down and interpret it, but it looks as if there's a solution there somewhere," Iain said. "So as long as it doesn't mean we'd have to blow up Mount Snowdon to provide enough ballast, I'd say it's possible. Let's go for it!"

***

The navigators came home in style, having completed an unheard-of mile-a-day average of top-quality high-speed rail laid between Stoke and Warrington without major service disruption, even through the busiest period of the summer holiday season. Mount Snowdon stood unscathed, visible on clear days, towering as always over the Welsh hills. Most of the required ballast had been found through a more environmentally friendly policy of recycling rubble and other inorganic materials that had become unsuitable for re-use in housebuilding projects.

They were met by the senior members of the Synod. The Welcome Committee included Professor John Midler and Maureen Lynch, reunited with her father, Billy, for the first time in what they both thought of as far too long. They met outside the now fully functional Passport and Immigration Office, which most of them had been involved in building, but few had had the opportunity to inspect their handiwork since then. They'd been too busy working away for almost two full years and had seen little of their respective families in the meantime.

Rik Hines wasn't prepared to stand on ceremony. In fact, he blatantly pulled rank and insisted on taking the helm of his Big Boy's Toy, the *Merseytram 1*, to meet them at Runcorn and give them a well-earned heroes' welcome.

The final leg of the journey was a leisurely meander with a contemptuous disregard for anything resembling a timetable. Three extra carriages had been tacked onto the standard six-car unit, and the whole tram had been transformed, beribboned and ballooned in keeping with a Rio Festival parade entry. Most of the seating had been removed and replaced with long buffet tables, filled to capacity with food and drink. The navigators, clean-scrubbed, many wearing for the first time in weeks a smart-casual dress code, didn't need Dame Shirley's musical invitation to help themselves and get the party started.

There hadn't been any official statement or PR release advertising the details of the homecoming, but the community bush telegraph was as effective as ever. The full route was lined with pedestrians, private cars and even coachloads of passengers from schoolchildren to pensioners' clubs, waving and cheering the conquering heroes with equal enthusiasm to the staunchest of royalists greeting Queen Elizabeth II a few years earlier on her diamond jubilee tour of the nation.

Silent, accusing glares were directed at Paul Freeman from a number of Synod members, including JRK, but he was adamant.

"I had nothing to do with this, guys. We weren't even sure what time they'd be arriving at Runcorn until this morning! And Elfin Safety would never have let me do it. They'd have had us tied up in pretty bows of red tape about crowd control, traffic regs, Portaloos and probably the Litter Act of Nineteen-Umpty-Ump! Not guilty, no way!"

And with that, his accusers had to be content.

CHAPTER THIRTY-FIVE

"WE GOT A good deal on our outsourcing of St. George's Hall, John."

There was just the hint of a satisfied cackle in Dominic Ion's voice as he tapped a final key and checked the totals. He stretched, catlike, and eased himself away from the computer screen.

"HM Gov. has paid the final instalment of rent as agreed. No hiccups, no late payments..."

"So no need to *send in da boyz* or threaten with bailiffs. I think I'm almost disappointed!" JRK pretended to sulk, but the grin on his face gave his words the lie.

Sitting at a different laptop, Paul Freeman was dealing with the morning's email. Suddenly, he stiffened and froze as if momentarily forgetting how to breathe. Only Nuala seemed to notice: he hadn't spoken or given any audible signal of whatever had taken him unawares, but she was immediately at his side.

"Is one of youse 'avin' a laugh?"

Paul's deep Scouse roots rarely showed nowadays, and only ever at moments of great stress or emotion.

An instant chorus of denials sounded from every corner of the room: it was easy to imagine large, multicoloured cartoon question marks bouncing off every solid surface like a child's Superball.

Clearly, Paul was unconvinced. He glared right back at the room full of his closest friends, mutely daring one of them to waver, drop their gaze, confess to taking part in an elaborate practical joke. One or two had started to approach, but everyone, without exception, turned statuesque in mid-step. None seemed anxious to encroach on his personal space while he was in such an uncharacteristically fey mood.

Several ageless seconds oozed by before Paul's eyes ceased to blister holes in the meeting room's wall hangings and furniture and returned to smoulder a degree less dangerously on the monitor screen.

"Even if this is genuine, does he *really* speak like that?"

Nuala was closest and scanned the screen over Paul's shoulder. Despite the shock that had briefly paralysed him, leaving his basic senses numb, he felt the light pressure of her hands on his shoulders, her breath in his ear, the caress of her hair on his cheek. He was acutely conscious that this was the first occasion the affection that had been growing steadily between them had been displayed in public. Mentally, he shrugged. There was nothing improper or clandestine about the relationship between them, but now it was almost certainly too late to pretend it didn't exist.

"I think I need a drink. Nuala, will you read it out, please? Word for word, as it stands on the screen. Because if this *isn't* someone's idea of a joke..."

Paul grabbed the first bottle of water offered to him and gulped at it greedily. Nuala read silently to the bottom of the screen without comment. Everyone else remained where they were, allowing Paul to recover his aplomb and Nuala all the time she felt she needed.

She paused and looked around before relaying the text of the email.

"Paul has asked me to read this verbatim, every word exactly as it stands on the screen. I'm pretty sure you'll all understand how come the cat's got his tongue on this!"

Without further comment or preamble, she read, with just the slightest tremor of—could it possibly be amusement?—in her voice:

To: J. R. Kirwan, Synod Leader, Merseyside

Our Government has informed Us of the honourable and professional manner in which you were able to provide them with temporary accommodation recently when they were in urgent need of assistance. For this, We offer our sincere thanks and appreciation.

Our own Principal Residence is also in need of major repair and refurbishment. We deem our properties in Scotland and Wales too remote to be practical locations for the duration of the necessary work, a period of up to eighteen months.

We are in discussions with our beloved cousin, Lord Sefton, whose family home lies within your administrative region. We would consider it a boon if We may proceed with the above arrangement, subject to a mutually agreed disbursement from the Privy Purse covering increased security costs and other essential expenses. This would be in addition to (and unconnected with) the short-term tenancy agreement We intend to establish with Our much-esteemed cousin.

Sincerely,

under my Hand and Seal
Charles III R

ABOUT THE AUTHOR

Paul was born in the Year of the Tiger, with an insatiable feline instinct to roam.

Most of his teaching career was as a supply teacher in towns and cities throughout North Europe (though oddly, he taught little English).

“You can take the boy out of Liverpool...” but sooner or later, he’ll be back. The reason? Grab a copy of *Home Rules,* pull up a comfy chair, pour a coffee, r e a d...

BY THE AUTHOR

For Children

Johnny Dupl'eau [sequel soon]

Rocking Horse Droppings [Springfield Park]
Hans & the Heinkel [Newsham Park]
Game Sett [Sefton Park]

More 'Park' stories on their way...

For Adults

The Chapel of Her Dreams (romance/mystery trilogy, vol. 1)
The Island of Her Dreams (vol. 2 available soon)
Plague Sally (historical thriller, sequel under way)
The Spear of Destiny (fictionalised WW2 sub hunt)
Taking the Heat (eco-thriller, climate change)

More tales complete, eagerly seeking publishers!

Printed in Great Britain
by Amazon

26627530R10173